UNRAVEL

A DEADLY SECRET. A DESPERATE FIGHT FOR SURVIVAL. TRUST IS A DANGEROUS GAME.

S. Q. ORPIN

BLACKBERRY PRESS

A NOTE FROM THE AUTHOR

As an esophageal cancer survivor, I wrote this story with deep respect for everyone navigating illness; patients, caregivers, and the loved ones who walk beside them. If you or someone you know is looking for resources or support, your local cancer center, online group, or the American Cancer Society can help connect you.

For the doctors, nurses, researchers, and staff whose expertise, compassion, and tireless commitment make healing possible. Your work changes lives every day.

*To **Dr. Randhawa**, thank you for seeing what others might have missed, insisting on answers, and setting the course that changed everything. You assembled an incredible medical team, watched over me at every step of the way, and never stopped checking in. Your care and determination saved my life, and I will carry that gratitude with me always.*

*A special and heartfelt thank-you to **Dr. Uchiyama**, whose skill, kindness, and steady guidance gave me a second chance at life. Your dedication and fierce advocacy will forever be part of the reason I am here to tell this story today.*

WELCOME TO BLACKBERRY FALLS

A deadly secret. A desperate fight for survival. Trust is a dangerous game.

Shelby Kincaid had it all, or so it seemed. A thriving career as the event manager at Blackberry Falls Resort. Loyal friends. A quiet life in the lakeside town she grew up in.

Then came the cancer diagnosis.

And everything changed.

Now her days are filled with doctor's visits and a creeping sense of isolation. The town that once felt like a sanctuary seems unfamiliar and quiet in all the wrong ways.

When a woman's body is discovered at the base of a popular lakeside walking trail, the police initially label it a tragic accident. But once the victim is identified, Shelby's name rises to the top of the suspect list.

Whispers spread. Trust erodes. The once–tight-knit coffee shop group fractures, and loyalty gives way to suspicion.

Determined to clear her name, Shelby digs into the victim's past and uncovers a tangle of lies, betrayals, and secrets someone is willing to kill to keep hidden. But in a town where everyone is protecting something, the truth comes at a price.

In Blackberry Falls, even the quietest trails lead to dangerous truths.

And the deadliest secrets... are the ones closest to home.

A gripping small-town mystery filled with atmosphere, emotional depth, and unforgettable characters.

1

THE EDGE OF SILENCE

Exhaustion clung to her like a threadbare sweater, coarse, familiar and unwelcome. Sleep had been a stranger for days, and it showed. Shadows pooled beneath her eyes; her shoulders sagged under the invisible weight of a responsibility she didn't remember choosing and wasn't sure she could carry much longer.

Up ahead, the coffee shop glowed warm and inviting, a welcoming place that promised comfort to most people. Inside, her coworkers would be gathered in their usual coffee circle, laughing, gossiping, happily oblivious to the damage they had done. On any other day, she might have ducked into a quieter venue, kept to herself, and spared her nerves. But skipping her routine would draw questions; small ones at first, the kind that had a way of snowballing.

Her expression stayed carefully neutral as she crossed from the parking lot to the winding path, though regret flickered in her golden-brown eyes for anyone perceptive enough to notice. Secrets had been stacking higher, pressing down until each breath felt shallow and forced.

She usually hovered on the outskirts, where no one asked

too many questions. Recently, she had tried to step outside her comfort zone and nearly succeeded. But the truth had been creeping in, like a winter draft slipping through a warped window, peeling back layers of deceit and exposing small indiscretions that were insignificant on their own but monumental when gathered.

The pea gravel crunched beneath her shoes, each step edging her closer to the confirmation she had been avoiding. The air was damp and heavy, faintly scented with rain and freshly cut grass, smells that tugged at memories she wished she could bury again. For some, the town inspired nostalgia. For her, regret and loneliness echoed in the shadows. She reached for the coffee shop's pine door, tracing the carved animals in the woodwork with her fingertip. Around here, even the art felt ominous and watchful.

The eclectic coffee shop at the lakeside resort buzzed with the usual early morning activity amid the heavenly scent of robust dark roast coffee. Locals of the picturesque hamlet of Blackberry Falls were eager to get to their jobs while the tourists consulted maps and travel guides, excited to engage in the attractions depicted in professionally framed photos artfully displayed on the walls and experience the tranquil landscape visible through the large windows with a panoramic view. The Blackberry Falls Resort was a gem on the west side of the lake, offering thoughtfully refurbished rooms in the historic building, a state-of-the-art spa, a high-end restaurant, and a bustling bakery coffee shop. Although not a world-class destination, it had developed into a popular location because of its proximity to Seattle and its expansive lake, scenic trails, waterfalls, and good fishing. The Pacific Northwest weather was predictable enough in the summer months to please the tourists and satisfy the locals.

With her red-rimmed eyes fixed on the polished hardwood floor, she nodded briskly to residents she would rather ignore, her smile never reaching past her chapped lips. She pushed through a cluster of tourists weighed down with hiking gear, swallowing her disdain, after all, their indulgent spending kept the business alive and half the town employed.

Out of habit, she scanned the pastry case. Her reflection flashed back at her in the mirrored surface of the espresso machine, and she recoiled at the bloated distortion. Tugging at a loose strand of hair, she registered the rough texture of her overly highlighted, chemically straightened style. She forced the craving for a brûlé donut back into the pit of her stomach and ordered a large, extra-hot, soy milk, half-caf macchiato, two pumps of sugar-free vanilla, no foam, a sprinkle of cinnamon, and a light drizzle of sugar-free caramel.

Her irritation deepened as the buxom owner barely glanced at the order, too engrossed in chatting with a gorgeous blonde across the counter to hear it properly. The barista continued pouring cheerful vanilla lattes, each crowned with a perfect heart. The blonde laughed. Her handsome husband leaned in to kiss her neck as he accepted his drink. The familiarity made her jaw tighten.

While she simmered, another man's broad shoulders blocked her view as he greeted his brother and sister-in-law. The coffee appeared in his hand, courtesy of the barista who happened to be the second wife of his three marriages.

The café felt plucked from a Hallmark movie, warm lights, rustic charm, townsfolk greeting one another like lifelong friends. She watched bright-eyed children weave between tables; blended families forged through soap opera worthy connections. She had grown up here and still felt like an observer, destined to orbit a life she would never belong to.

She sidestepped a man with bulging forearms maneuvering a hand truck through the crowd, singing along to music only he could hear through his headphones. He shot her a sly grin, and her stomach lurched, she wanted nothing to do with that overly tanned imbecile ever again. Cutting between the display case and a knot of chatty customers, she escaped through the exit before the woman with the pixie cut, warm despite her terrible cancer diagnosis, could trap her in conversation. The woman's slimmer figure sparked a twist of envy, earned at a terrible cost. Her too-tall husband eased her into a chair as townsfolk swooned and asked about her health. She turned away, bile rising with the untamed anger envy she refused to name.

She retreated to her older-model hatchback and locked the doors, distancing herself from the hum of the parking lot. The macchiato was still hot enough to sting her tongue, and the bitter aftertaste assaulted her senses. Through the windshield, the mid-March weather promised a break from a week of dreary rain as a speck of blue peeked through the mist clinging to the trees. She scanned the lot, making sure no one was aware of her actions, cocooning herself from watchful eyes eager to gossip. Her hand slipped into the cluttered console, pushing past gum wrappers, napkins, and a folded resort brochure. She found the small cylinder and adjusted the waistband of her leggings, careful to keep her movements hidden.

Cars continued to fill the lot, people from town and visitors alike, each one heading toward the coffee shop lost in the intricacies of their own lives, none of them interested in what she was doing. She twisted the cap, turned the dial, and pressed the needle to her skin. The familiar sting came and went in silence.

Near the back door of the kitchen, she spotted the head chef with a tidy chestnut ponytail, deep in conversation with the rusty-red-haired restaurant manager. From the way their hands accented the conversation, it wasn't about menu specials. Her feelings ranged from pity because of what she had recently uncovered, to anger that she had trusted the woman as a confidante, and her only friend. A small, satisfied smile tugged at her mouth. Her file was ready; tidy, precise, and filled with details no one could ignore. She slid a sheet of paper from her bag and circled the first name; the pen leaving a hole in the page. That one would fall first. A car pulled into the lot beside her, the squeal of its brakes snapping her attention back to the moment. She folded the paper, slipped it into her pocket, and reached for another sip of coffee, her expression calm. Just another local enjoying her morning, or so it would seem.

Several miles along the winding road, she tossed the cup through the open window and parked in a grassy turnout near the trailhead. She smoothed her shirt over her plump figure, yanked her hat down low, and secured her earbuds. She considered a jacket as the mist danced over the ridge, obscuring the trail hidden below the tree line. The spring weather was teetering on the edge with a promise of warmer days, but enough fog to filter the sunlight and cast an eerie gloom over the landscape. Determined that the warmth would win the battle, she tossed the windbreaker in the backseat and proceeded toward the trail.

Two men laughed by a truck, and her insecurity made her halt by the water fountain. Pretending to tie her shoe, she strained to hear their remarks, certain they were full of judgment and cruelty. The man patted the protruding belly of his friend, bringing another round of hoots and hollers. Realization washed over her. They were sharing a good-natured joke that didn't involve her, she continued up the path. Heat prickled the back of her neck, and she assumed it was activated by the angst of coming close to having it all, until the rug was pulled out from under her.

The first mile seemed more difficult than usual, and the heat radiated through her scalp, blinding her with sweat. She took a swig of water from her bottle and contemplated turning back. The rugged five-mile trail was challenging, but she had become accustomed to the steep hills and normally could complete the circuit in under an hour. That stupid barista had probably given her whole milk instead of soy, never able to complete an order without a mistake. She had learned to live with the exhaustion rooted in her bones, but the hollowing weakness felt different. It stole her breath, crept from her toes upward, numbing her legs into gelatinous stumps.

"Are you okay?" a young woman asked as they passed at the hill's crest, her outfit aggressively bright and coordinated.

"I'm fine," she snapped, pushing past, seeking the shade towards the lower part of the curve. Checking her watch, she rubbed her eyes as the numbers blurred. Her heart hammered, a sharp pain twisting low in her abdomen. She forced herself forward, determined to finish the loop and return for her shift.

"Hey, I was hoping we could talk."

The man stood with the sun behind him, his face erased in light. His voice drifted, unfamiliar and distorted, the world pitching around her. Panic burst free in a spray of nonsense. She shoved past him, desperate to escape the noise and the spinning. Her feet slapped the trail, vibrations rattling up her spine. A bench appeared ahead, and she willed her legs to cooperate.

She collapsed forward, hands on her knees as the trees blurred into green ribbons. A feeling of queasiness washed over her, and she stumbled to the edge to empty the contents of her stomach. She brushed the back of her hand across her mouth, choking on the remnants of the acrid bile as the world spun around her in a euphoric haze. Her ears hummed with the vibration of the muffled sounds of nature. The weight of her resentment faded as she tipped into darkness, finally surrendering to the weightlessness she had been chasing.

2

THE SOCIAL CIRCLE

"Shelby! You look amazing," the petite woman sporting a fashionable streaked haircut squeezed her tightly.

"Thank you," Shelby answered, wincing at the hug that pressed against her feeding tube port, making her abdomen throb. She tried to say the woman's name, but the word slipped away, the brain fog blunting memories of people she had known for years. She glanced around the table and winced at the familiar faces with names she couldn't recall. One ran the daycare. Another worked for a jam and spice company. The restaurant manager smiled and the head chef welcomed her back to her usual seat. She knew the complicated love life of the barista and the surly disposition of the woman she was serving. The newest addition, the gorgeous wife of the woodworker, hadn't arrived yet. These were her friends, the ones she depended on, and supported as they navigated their own struggles. The daily coffee ritual before work had slipped into memory, leaving her feeling adrift and alone.

Her husband, Alan, noticed the pain reflected in her eyes and eased her into a chair safely away from full body contact. Her German Shorthaired Pointer, Gus, silently slid beside her, looking at ease, but obediently on alert. Alan had become adept at reading visual cues, knowing the illness often stole her words before her thoughts which made it difficult for her to communicate her state of mind. For the past couple of months, Shelby had kept her bright disposition, even making jokes to the nurses in the ICU throughout her lengthy stay. Alan had learned to mask his emotions, hiding his fear from Shelby and keeping the trauma she didn't remember between himself and their closest friends and family. He disentangled himself from the memory of her on a ventilator and asked, "Are you happy to be visiting your friends finally?"

Shelby slid her hand in his. "This is wonderful. Thank you for bringing me here today. It was an excellent incentive to get through the radiation procedure this morning."

Alan leaned down and kissed her forehead gently. "Shelby Bean, you are the most resilient woman I know. You're halfway through treatments and you're doing great."

"One third and I still have a huge surgery looming," she whispered.

"It will be a breeze," he teased, swallowing his own terror about the proposed eleven-hour procedure. "You've come tremendously far already and proven you're one tough cookie."

"Yummy, a cookie sounds amazing," Shelby giggled.

Alan chuckled, grateful for the levity, relieved she could still meet fear with humor.

"Wow, the short haircut is super flattering on you!" A beautiful blonde woman plopped in a chair at their table and leaned toward Shelby for a side hug.

Shelby tousled her short hair, styled to cover the thinning strip down the center, and smiled at the exuberant woman who was an investor in the resort. "Thank you for recommending your hairdresser. He came to my house and cut my hair in the kitchen. It was a shock to go short, but I feel rather chic now."

She bit her lip and glanced at Alan, a silent signal he recognized when she was having trouble with names.

"Thank you for arranging it, Casi," Alan said smoothly. "It was a nice perk for Shelby to have a personal stylist."

Shelby laughed. "But in the humidity, I appear to have a pompom for a head." She leaned toward Casi and said, "I'm doing the old man comb-over now to hide the bald bits."

Casi smiled and grasped her hand. "Take it from a former model, your health is more important than your looks."

"You still look like a supermodel," Shelby stated, eyeing the gorgeous woman clad in a shell pink silk top and dove gray pencil skirt.

"Chemo has affected your vision," Casi giggled as she glanced at her elegant gold watch with diamond accents. "It's time for me to make my way to Seattle. I have a business meeting at ten." She directed her attention to Shelby and said, "Please don't worry about your job. The Board has assured me they will reinstate you whenever you're ready. You're an exceptional event coordinator, and the resort needs you to come back."

"My replacement will not be pleased to hear that," Shelby said. "She worked hard to get the promotion."

Casi shrugged. "Kristen is temporary."

"I've heard she is precise," Shelby said, cautiously hand-picking her words.

"More like a whiner who involves herself in everyone else's business," Casi corrected. "As investors, we have input in the operational aspects. We are a big family here, ready to help as needed." She smiled at Alan. "Call Kyle or Jake if it's man stuff."

Alan grinned. "Like drinking beer and talking about how needy our wives are?"

Casi flipped the side of her hair back in fake disapproval. "Whatever works," she giggled as she melted into the embrace of her handsome husband.

Kyle kissed her cheek and turned to Alan. "Can you come to sports night?"

Alan hesitated, but Shelby asserted herself. "Yes, he can. I'm learning to do more by myself, and it's good for him to be with friends. In fact, I'm walking around the lake today."

"Just the lower mile," Alan quickly explained.

"Amy typically runs the rim trail before working at the wood shop. Would you like me to text her and have her meet you?" Kyle asked.

"No, I'm fine. Amy has enough to do with her upcoming wedding to our nephew," Shelby's voice faltered.

"Riley said they would postpone it if you're not well enough after surgery," Alan stated.

"That's silly; it's their day." Shelby noted the angst in Alan's expression and quickly rephrased her comment. "I'm eagerly anticipating attending. I already have the dress, and it's several sizes smaller than the last proper outfit I wore." She cast her eyes downward at her black yoga pants, slung low on her hips to accommodate the J-tube port, and Alan's oversized t-shirt that had become her standard attire. "The upside of cancer is I've already lost forty pounds!"

"Remember, your oncologist wants you to focus on your strength, not weight loss," Alan chimed in.

Shelby made a face and continued, "Which is why I'm hiking the trail today." She extended her wrist to show them her fitness tracker. "My doctor said the surgery is like running a marathon. I'm exercising to improve my strength and lung capacity. I have my service dog, Gus, with me in case anything happens."

Their focus shifted to the dog they hadn't noticed, clad in a bright orange harness. Kyle chuckled. "That looks like Alan's hunting dog, dressed up in a fancy vest."

Alan smiled. "After everything that happened, he won't

leave her side. He seems to sense when she needs help before I do."

The owner of the coffee shop smiled as she presented an assortment of pastries. "Shelby, you must try the Supreme Croissant. It has a pistachio filling. The pastry chef at the restaurant makes the dough, because it's super hard to figure out, but I follow this group on Instagram, and I have mastered the pastry cream."

Alan frowned, figuring everyone was aware Shelby was on a feeding tube and was unable to eat solid food, but Shelby smiled. "Thank you. These pastries look amazing!" She chose the golden croissant studded with pistachios. "I'll just take a tiny bite and save the rest for later. I'm walking the trail, and I want to feel my best."

"Are you diabetic? I must be cautious because I had gestational diabetes with both of my pregnancies," Lia sighed.

Shelby broke off a crumb and placed it on her tongue. "Oh my, that is divine." Lia beamed with pleasure, not noticing most of the bite ended up in Shelby's cupped hand to be discreetly discarded later. "I react differently to food, especially sugar, now. I'm working with a nutritionist to come up with a plan." Shelby shifted her hand to the left of her abdomen over a bulge under her T-shirt. "Once I get rid of Joey Kangaroo, I'm back on actual food."

Alan laughed. "That's the name of the pump for her feeding tube. Our lives revolve around the nutritional schedule." He checked the time on his watch. "Shel, we had better get you to the trail before we need to reconnect you for the afternoon again."

Shelby jumped up, grabbing the chair as she wobbled, and everyone leaned in to come to her aid. "I'm fine. I caught my foot on the table leg," she assured them, annoyed that she hadn't made a more graceful maneuver. "I'm excited to enjoy a bit of freedom before I'm back in the recliner, hooked up to the feeding apparatus while Alan hovers around me, consulting his medication schedule." She caught her breath, seeing the hurt in her husband's eyes. "I'm kidding, darling. I couldn't have made it this far without you. Now, let's get walking so I can prepare for our next adventure in recovery." She eyed the platter of baked goods and glanced at the name tag on the owner's apron. "Lia, can I take the croissant to go? I want to enjoy it later when I drink my tea and read my true crime stories."

Alan realized she was being polite, and he would end up eating the pastry. Luckily, his tall build allowed him to indulge without putting on weight, much to Shelby's dismay, since she always had to be cautious. He regarded her slimmer figure, and his heart ached with the realization she was finally achieving her weight loss goals because of cancer. "Shelby has a new obsession with crime. I'm encouraging her to read less grue-some literature."

"I enjoy solving mysteries. It gives me something to do with all the time I spend sitting around." Shelby sighed and consid-ered it was one of the few things she still had control over in her life. Alan handled all the household chores, medication, and doctors' appointments. She had been told her only job was to breathe and keep a positive attitude. It seemed simple, but she yearned to return to work and the daily duties, even the mundane ones that used to annoy her. Spending every minute focused on her health felt endless and draining. She craved an unexpected event to break through the heavy silence of her prolonged illness.

"Let's get walking," she said brightly. "I have a marathon surgery to train for."

As they headed toward the door, Shelby let herself linger for just a second. The vibrant group of women, the ordinary routine, a fragile return to normal. She didn't know why the moment felt heavier than it should.

3

LOONS ON THE LAKE

Shelby stared out the window while Alan drove, taking in the charming village of Blackberry Falls with fresh eyes. The towering redwoods lining the road dwarfed everything around them, their massive trunks rising like silent sentinels, while delicate birch trees swayed in the gentle breeze beside them. Wildflowers dotted the landscape in bright blues, yellows, and purples, creating the impression of a living painting carefully arranged for her benefit. The scene felt impossibly vivid, almost unreal, as though the saturation had been turned up too high. Birdsong filtered through the open window, and somewhere ahead, a pair of squirrels chased each other across the road before disappearing into the trees. The beauty pressed against her chest until her eyes burned. This was home. And somehow, after everything, it felt new again.

"You okay, Shelby?" Alan asked softly, lifting one hand from the steering wheel to gently grip hers.

She blinked back tears and smiled. "It's silly, but I'm overwhelmed by the magnitude of the natural beauty around us." She gestured toward the waterfall cascading down the granite mountainside, splashing into a pool before trickling into a creek scattered with smooth boulders. "I forgot how much I've missed all of this."

Alan tilted his head as he waited for pedestrians to cross the road toward the farmer's market, which had just opened for the season. The brightly colored tents covered tables laden with fresh vegetables and baked goods. "Do you want to check out the market instead? Don't walk the trail if you're not up to it. We can still do your mile as we circle the vendors."

Gus sat with his head on the console between the seats and glanced between them, waiting to see what decision was made. Shelby rubbed his soft ears, still lost in thought. "Maybe we could stop after you pick me up?" She turned to face him. "Please don't interpret this negatively, Alan, but I need a few minutes by myself." She noted the dismay on his face and continued, "I appreciate everything you're doing for me, but it's not fair to give up your friends and work, to sit around all day to be my caregiver." She straightened her posture. "I want to wander along the path and get lost in my thoughts. You should make your way to the office like we agreed and pick me up in an hour. Then we can go to the farmer's market and get interesting ingredients for dinner."

"You can't eat solid food."

"For goodness' sake, Alan. Please stop sulking. I'm trying hard to stay positive, but you're making it difficult," she stated.

"You're right. The home nurse said we should find ten good things each week to focus on, and I'm doing the opposite." He maneuvered his vehicle into a parking spot by the trail. "If you're in the mood for it after your walk, we'll stop by the market, and you can help me make a great appetizer to bring to sports night at Kyle's. Everyone misses your incredible treats."

"That is the perfect solution," Shelby praised. She stepped out of the car, shrugging into her lightweight windbreaker. The jacket was baggy and dull, another casualty of weight loss and practicality, but it fit easily over her feeding tube without rubbing, which felt like a small victory.

Gus hopped down eagerly while she patted her pocket before Alan could speak. "Cell phone. Glucose tablets. Band-Aids. ChapStick. Cash. Dog treats. Poop bags. Whistle."

"What's the whistle for?" he asked.

"In case a pervert approaches me."

Alan snorted. "I doubt we have many of those here. But I'm glad you're prepared. " He smiled warmly. "You look fantastic, Shell Bell."

She flashed him a wink and gave a playful sway of her hips as she guided Gus toward the trailhead. Before stepping onto the path, she glanced at her fitness tracker, confirming her heart rate was steady.

"I'll meet you in an hour," she said, waving. "Plenty of time to walk and sit by the lake. I hope I see a loon. It's been a long time since I've heard one."

Alan watched her go, pride and worry warring in his chest.

Shelby smiled as she walked. The weight she had lost made movement feel easier, lighter. Even with one damaged lung and a compromised immune system, her body responded eagerly to the rhythm of motion. Gus trotted beside her, happy and alert. The feeling was monumental, changing her outlook. The walk was not just exercise. It was proof. Proof that she was still capable of taking up space in the world outside her living room and hospital rooms.

Gus trotted beside her, equally thrilled to be outside exploring. She contemplated the ten good things to write on her list. The home nurse was scheduled to come towards the end of the week, and she would be pleased Shelby had diligently done her homework. Alan always wrote the same things starting with the fact that he was glad Shelby was his wife. She smiled to herself at what a good, solid man he was. He was handsome in an ordinary way, not the type that warranted a second glance when he passed by, but kindness emanated from him. She and Alan were a wonderful match, and their twenty-plus-year marriage had been quite easy. Until cancer. That would be number one on her list. Alan was an amazing caregiver. He was patient and sweet even when she was throwing up or stuck full of needles like an old pincushion. Next would be Gus. His loyalty and companionship had gotten her through the arduous nights and eased her pain. His taut body wrapped tightly around her legs while she lounged in the armchair, and the rhythm of his heartbeat calmed her. It had been excruciating to be away from them both during her time in the hospital, and she had often cried herself to sleep. She would add the nurses to the list. They certainly had been compassionate and caring. Her family would be noted, even her sister Willow, who was chronically self-centered, sent her funny memes and odd bits of news to cheer her up. She was also thankful for her friends, who always looked out for them and dropped in to bring baked goods and flowers while offering to help Alan with the household chores. She smiled with satisfaction that her list was halfway complete and decided the next five things should be new and exciting.

A distinct coo filtered through the air, and she smiled. The call of the loon was like a reward, a small promise that things might soon be alright. She strolled to the edge of the path and gazed at the water, spotting the black and white birds floating through the gentle mist rising from the lake. She inhaled deeply, smelling the damp earth and pine needles as she absorbed the beauty of the scene, punctuated by the hues of blue and green of the lake and foliage. Shelby checked her mileage and was delighted to realize she had made it to the half-mile mark without being winded. She had an abundance of time to relax by the lake and enjoy the tranquility. Gus stretched out on the sand as Shelby settled herself on a bench. "Smell the roses, and blow out the candles," she repeated the mantra as she did the breathing exercises the specialist had taught her. The crisp scent of the water mixed with the earthy foliage in a heady symphony of early spring's best offerings.

She snapped a few photos, sending one to Alan with a message about the loons. A breeze ruffled her honey-blonde hair, cold against her scalp. She realized she had forgotten a hat and, mindful of her radiation sensitivity, turned back toward the trail.

Shelby checked her heart rate on her fitness tracker; glad it reflected how she felt. Often a low reading would scare her into an episode, and she would be required to retreat to her chair to recover. In the beginning, it had been a pleasure to sit all day and watch a mystery or read books. She had even found a site on Instagram that had a cold case of the day. It was exhilarating to unravel the clues and try to solve the crime. Plus, it took her mind off not working, which had been a severe blow to her lifestyle. Eventually, she got bored with the sedentary routine and started insisting on getting out for walks as soon as the weather permitted.

Shelby strolled along the path, tingling with happiness. She smiled and greeted people she recognized, pausing for brief discussions during her walk. She grinned at the group of teenagers gathered on the sandy beach of the inlet, daring each other to jump into the still-icy lake. Children's laughter from a nearby playground filtered through the trees, and she smiled at people walking by, some with dogs, and others in deep conversations with friends. She had timed the walk perfectly. The warmth of the sun extracted the deep chill that had settled in her bones, and the trail wasn't bustling yet with the throngs of people that would make her feel rushed.

Gus remained on her left side, keeping pace with her gait, wagging his bobbed tail. As they rounded the final bend, he barked and stalked what she assumed was a squirrel. "Leave it," she ordered. He continued to edge forward. His ears flattened, muscles coiling as he went rigid on point. His back legs quivered, indicating he had located something he wanted to investigate.

"Gus, come on," she coaxed, tugging lightly on the leash. "We're having such a good walk."

Shelby stumbled forward, heart rate spiking as she tried to see what he fixated on. At first, it looked like discarded clothing tangled in the ditch below. Gus jerked harder, and before she could let go, she was pulled from the path, crashing into the blackberry bushes.

She cried out in pain when her knee struck a rock, tearing the material and piercing her delicate skin. Gus returned with a shoe, and she extracted it from his mouth, not understanding how she had lost it. She examined her feet and noticed her shoes were still on and tied. When it dawned on her that the garment held a person, she yelled and flung the shoe in the direction of the shrub, grasping Gus's leash tightly before he could retrieve it again. A shiver traveled down her back, and she struggled to make sense of what was happening. Using all her strength, she pulled herself out of the undergrowth and scrambled to the trail. Her fitness tracker beeped with an alarm that her heart rate was dropping, and Shelby realized she had only moments to react before she collapsed. Disregarding her broken nails and bloody hands, she grabbed her phone from her pocket. She clicked the emergency button and sobbed. "What did I do? Alan will be extremely upset with me," she wailed, concerned that her poor husband would be traumatized by her appearance.

"Ma'am, are you okay?" the voice asked.

"I think there has been a mishap," was all Shelby could manage before the world went dark.

4

TRAGEDY ON THE TRAIL

"Can you hear me?" a gentle voice asked.

Shelby became aware of sound before meaning. Concerned tones overlapped with the rustle of movement. It felt achingly familiar. The sensation dragged her backward into hospital corridors and half-remembered conversations held just beyond her reach while she floated in and out of consciousness. The terrifying helpless suspension. The haunting feeling of being physically present but not fully mentally aware.

A nudge of a wet nose accompanied by a slight whine caught Shelby's attention. Gus loomed over her, muscles taut, eyes locked on her face with an intensity that bordered on fiercely protective. His tail twitched once, then stilled, as if he was afraid, she might disappear again if he moved too much.

"I'm okay, baby," she whispered, though the words felt more like a promise she was trying to make true. She threaded her fingers into his coarse fur, grounding herself in his warmth and unmistakable presence.

As her vision sharpened, the scene rushed back in fragments. A paramedic crouched close, one knee planted on the dirt. Yellow caution tape snapped in the breeze. A ring of stunned hikers clustered farther down the trail, murmuring in low, unsettled voices. And then the memory crashed fully into focus.

The body. The unnatural angle of limbs. The way the clothing had blended into the earth until her brain finally rejected the illusion. Her stomach tightened painfully.

"Slow breathing," the paramedic said calmly, watching the monitor attached to her finger. "Do you know if you hit your head?"

Heat surged to her face as he checked her scalp. She was acutely aware of how she must look. Hair thinned and uneven from treatment. Clothes hanging loose in a way that made her feel older than she was. Her pants were torn at the knee, the fabric crusted with dried blood.

"I have cancer," she said quietly, offering the explanation before he asked. The effect was immediate and practiced. The shift from assessment to sympathy. "Esophageal." She touched her throat as he reached for a juice box. "I can't use straws."

His expression flickered. A moment of recognition passed through his eyes before he swallowed whatever personal association the word brought up.

She waited patiently as he finished his checks, bracing herself for the familiar discomfort of the blood pressure cuff. When the numbers stabilized, relief washed through her with surprising force. As he helped her sit up, she became aware of the watching crowd again, of being seen when she least wanted to be.

As he helped her to her feet, she heard heavy footsteps, out of rhythm because of the slight limp from an old basketball injury. "Shelby! What happened?" Alan yanked her into his arms, hoisting her from the trail as if she was a small child.

"Ouch, Alan," she cautioned, as the feeding port tugged against his belt buckle.

"I'm sorry," he winced. "I was in my car waiting for you…"

"You didn't go to the office," she chastised.

His face was etched with guilt. "I couldn't, Shell. I figured it wouldn't take you an hour to walk one mile, and I worried you would wait too long at the completion of the trail. There weren't any benches there, and I preferred you not to sit on the ground." He glanced at her tattered appearance and scanned the level surface of the trail. "Did you pass out? Didn't the fitness tracker show your heart rate was erratic? Are you dehydrated?" He glanced at his wristwatch. "Our priority is to get you home and hooked back up to the feeding tube."

The paramedic watched the scene with interest and asked the dreaded question. "Should you have been walking alone if you are not medically fit?"

Shelby wanted to slap the concern off his boyish face for making Alan feel worse and trampling the sliver of independence she had fought for. She silently lamented the unfortunate turn of events that stole her freedom. She had longed for this walk to prove to herself she could still move through the world without being monitored. The adrenaline drained quickly, leaving a bone-deep exhaustion in its wake. The grim reality of what had happened settled heavily over her. Gus pulling her insistently toward the gully. The image of the body. The knowledge that this walk, her first real independent outing since treatment began, had ended with her sprawled unconscious on the trail. She had planned carefully. Chosen a mild day. A familiar path. She had even timed it to avoid crowds. Shame crept in alongside the fear. A quiet, corrosive thought she hated. Alan had been right to worry. She had wanted to prove something and instead had shown how fragile she truly was.

"I didn't trip." She took a slow breath and waited as a police officer ambled toward them, not wanting to repeat herself.

The dreadful events that had unfolded had taken the wind

out of her sails. She longed for a hot bath, gin and tonic, and a couch cuddle with Alan while they watched a movie. Unfortunately, none of those things would happen. She was only allowed a quick shower, and then Alan would methodically change the bandages and clean her feeding tube. Today he would also need to locate, sanitize, and cover all the new scrapes she had gotten. Even trace amounts of germs that enter her body could cause serious damage to her fragile immune system. As for the cocktail, alcohol was no longer allowed. She might have small sips of water and occasional apple juice, consuming it in a shot glass to prevent a mess. Her gaze briefly moved to the juice box on the medical bag, and she understood Alan would have a conniption if she drank it. It was probably full of sweeteners and would send her blood sugar soaring, prompting a whole new level of testing and balancing. Finally, couch cuddles were a thing of the past, too. After she was clean and patched up, she would settle herself in the armchair and get reattached to Joey Kangaroo. His constant whirring and beeping kept her company while her exhausted husband finally dragged himself to their bedroom to get a few hours' sleep before one of her numerous alarms beckoned him awake.

The detective walked around the yellow caution tape, nodding to the crime scene investigator taking pictures of the hillside. He scanned Shelby and Alan and eyed Gus cautiously. "Keep your dog close," he ordered, as if Gus had caused the turbulent scene.

Before Shelby could respond, Alan took the leash. Gus sat obediently at his side, calm despite the surrounding chaos.

"Alright," the detective said, eyes tracking the activity behind them. "How are you involved in this?" His annoyance showed through, thinly veiled, as he stifled a yawn. He looked at Shelby as if she were just another interruption, a middle-aged woman with innocent brown eyes and tears she couldn't control.

Shelby noted the sheriff department emblem and considered his demeanor, wondering if he was irritated, he had been assigned to an accident in a small town rather than a more exciting crime in the city. Or was his brusque tone a coverup for deeper insecurities? She was unfamiliar with the detective. He wasn't in Alan's group of friends, and she didn't recall him from the resort. He had a head like a potato with a swoop of dark hair, which would not have gone unnoticed. His rounded features were offset by keen, assessing eyes that missed very little.

Alan likely had the same idea when he enquired, "Sam's on a fishing trip, but where is Carla, or Ben?" He glanced at the officer's badge. "Why is a detective from the Sherrif's office here for a simple fall?"

"There's a memorandum of understanding when a body is involved," the detective replied evenly. "County sheriff handles the investigation."

"A body?" Alan gestured to Shelby. "She's a little scraped up, but she's hardly a corpse."

The officer scowled and pointed toward the crowd gathered at the trailhead. They parted to allow rescue workers through with a stretcher containing a mound in a black bag.

Alan's jaw dropped, and Shelby gulped. "That's why I fell, Alan. Gus pulled me over there, and I tumbled into the blackberry bushes. It looked like a heap of clothing. But then I noticed the legs, and they were bent in a peculiar way."

"It's definitely a body," the detective confirmed without emotion.

"Who is it?" Alan strained to hear what people discussed as the crowd dispersed.

The detective turned away, no longer interested in Shelby. "Can't say. We'll be in touch if we need anything."

Alan scanned Shelby and turned to the paramedic. "How did this all come about?"

He shrugged. "We got a call from a passerby who noticed your wife unconscious on the trail. By the time we arrived, a runner pointed out that there was a body in the ditch. Your dog was riled up but wouldn't leave your wife's side. It's been a frenzy of activity with Parks and Rec, the crime scene investigator, and that surly detective."

"Are you aware of what happened to that other person?" Alan asked, grimacing at the body on the gurney.

"Nope, we just take care of the living," the paramedic laughed, making Shelby shudder.

5

CHEMO AND COMMITMENT

T he medicinal smell of the room combined with the fragrance of chicken soup being heated in the microwave, blended into a nauseating infusion. Shelby was eager for the procedure to end, not because it hurt, but because she wanted to return to her crime novel. The bulky ice gloves made it impossible to operate her tablet. Earlier, Alan had turned the pages for her, intuitively syncing with her reading pace, pausing at the slightest flick of her eyes. He never rushed her, even when the pages slowed as fatigue crept in.

He had been especially vigilant that morning. Attentive in quiet ways. Adjusting pillows. Checking the angle of the IV line. Repeating reassurances he had already offered. She suspected yesterday's events at the lake had rattled him more than he admitted. He likely welcomed the moment she fell asleep, grateful for the temporary escape from replaying images neither of them wanted lodged in their minds.

He had carefully fitted the ice slippers and gloves recommended to prevent neuropathy while the nurse hung the chemo drip. The premeds worked quickly, as they always did, coaxing Shelby into a soft, hazy sleep within minutes. Alan must have secured her tablet and gone for coffee during the forty-minute infusion window. Her niece, Stella, had offered to teach Shelby how to listen to audiobooks or podcasts, but Shelby resisted. Alan's presence mattered. His quiet efficiency brought her comfort. She didn't want Alan to think his silent role in this monumental illness was insignificant.

Shelby glanced at the clock, grateful for a rare stretch of uninterrupted thought. She and Alan had been married for over twenty years, and he had always been her anchor. That role had hardened into something heavier after the diagnosis.

We found a mass.

The words still landed with startling clarity. It had been a routine endoscopy. Preventative. Responsible. Two months later, her life revolved around appointments, medication schedules, and carefully rationed energy.

She had Googled obsessively in the early days, consuming information until every possibility ended the same way. She and Alan had clutched each other through the first night, crying and making promises neither could guarantee. She had begged him not to share the full diagnosis with her family, especially her mother, who had recently moved into a retirement community in Bellingham. Shelby became adept at editing the truth. Weekly video calls stayed buoyant. Cheerful. Carefully curated. Optimism had always been her superpower. It served her well as the events manager at the Blackberry Falls Resort. No rainstorm, blown generator, or emotional bride could derail her. She thrived in chaos, smoothing it into something seamless. She had built her career on competence, calm, and connection.

Now, someone else was organizing the perfect day for eager young couples. The thought surfaced gently, without bitterness. Shelby was genuinely grateful. Kristen had stepped in willingly when Shelby took medical leave. She handled logistics meetings, and endless emails. It was no small thing, and Shelby appreciated the continuity.

Still, gratitude came bundled with something sharper. Envy, perhaps. Shelby missed the work more than she had expected. Missed the buzz of planning. The satisfaction of execution. The feeling of being needed outside the confines of illness. She told herself it was natural to feel displaced, even resentful, when another person occupied the life, she had been forced to pause.

Kristen was capable. Exceptionally organized and eager. Sometimes overly so. Shelby had noticed, over the past few weeks, that Kristen's texts had grown shorter. More formal. Updates arrived without the warmth Shelby remembered from earlier conversations. She brushed it off as workload stress. Anyone would be overwhelmed stepping into her position. Still, there were moments. Like yesterday morning at the coffee shop. Shelby frowned faintly, replaying the scene. Kristen had arrived after most of them were seated. She had hovered near the counter, collected her drink, and slipped out without joining the table. No smile or quick wave. It had stung more than Shelby expected. She told herself she was reading too much into it. People got distracted. Kristen was busy managing her job, Shelby's job, and probably feeling the pressure of scrutiny. Shelby inhaled, releasing the thought. She hated second-guessing people. It felt unfair.

Alan returned just as the chimes signaled the infusion stage change. The nurse swapped the bag efficiently, her motions practiced and calm.

"Two down and four to go, Shelby Bean," Alan said brightly.

"I swear I hear those bells in my dreams," Shelby yawned and regarded the pump while the nurse set the timer for the final round.

Alan slid off her slippers and gloves and tugged on warm

socks, which weren't necessary in the mild weather. She had become overly sensitized to heat and cold, though, so she relied on Alan to maintain the optimal temperature.

She smiled at him, noting the weariness that had crept into the creases on his handsome face. His tall frame slumped with the burden of caring for her and the trauma they had recently faced. Not having children of their own, they had doted on her extended family while her sister flitted about as a flea market artist once her children became young adults.

They had settled into a lovely life, balancing family, work, and travel, enjoying a close relationship with common goals. The week Shelby was diagnosed with esophageal cancer was a blur of tears while they relayed the news to family, friends, and employers. Alan meticulously took notes while Shelby worried about stocking the freezer and planning events, convinced this illness was only a speed bump on their journey.

Shelby had ignored the excruciating backache that took her breath away and told Alan it was from stress. Waking up two weeks later in the ICU, she was only informed she had minor surgery but needed to focus on her healing, especially her breathing, as she prepared for radiation and chemotherapy. Shelby knew they were withholding information, but the fear in everyone's eyes suggested it was best if she just obeyed. She had barely been able to walk when she left the hospital, and Alan had created a chart on a whiteboard and secured it to the wall in their living room to document all the medications essential to her recovery. That was the initial stage of sensing she was losing control.

"Still pondering what occurred on the trail yesterday?" Alan asked.

Shelby noticed he had finished tying her shoes and was expecting her to ease out of the recliner. "Everything seems unreal at this moment." She knew she needed to clarify, given his lack of awareness of her earlier reasoning. "I mean, we finally got a handle on this cancer thing, and I was making progress toward healing and preparing for surgery. Then, wham! A body by the lake!"

Alan chuckled at the imagery. "It's surreal."

"Did you hear any news or the identity of the victim?" Shelby shuddered, imagining the person enjoying a pleasant day at the lake, then it abruptly ended. Death had occupied her thoughts lately, sharpened by her own vulnerability. At least she had an opportunity to fight. She couldn't fathom being plucked out of life in an instant.

"No word on either," Alan said.

She stared at him blankly, having forgotten the question. Her focus drifted these days, and she counted it a victory when she followed an entire conversation. She brushed it aside, not wanting him to assume she wasn't up to her next request. "Can we pop into the coffee shop? I have no desire to answer a million text messages about how I'm doing after yesterday's ordeal."

He shook his head. "That's why we set up the group text so you can reply once. You get exhausted after treatment. It's best if we go home." He gathered her belongings and chuckled at the title of the book on her tablet as he powered it off, *Crime doesn't pay.* "You want to chat with your coffee gals and hear the latest gossip, don't you?"

Shelby laughed. "Remember, I'm high on steroids. I won't crash until Friday."

Alan laughed, knowing the current routine, and dreaded the 24-hour mark when the nausea would swoop in and take her down for another day or two. "Let's live it up today, then."

6

COFFEE AND CLUES

"Shelby! How are you?" Gail practically sang as she spotted her at the door.

The women immediately widened their circle, chairs scraping against the worn wood floor as they shifted to make room. Someone reached out to steady Shelby as she eased herself down, a dozen familiar hands ready before she even asked.

Alan lingered behind her chair, taking in the scene with a small, grateful smile. "I'll give you an hour to get caught up on our small-town mystery." He checked the time on his watch. "If she throws up, that's your issue. I'm headed to the office to pick up papers and sign checks."

Gail waved a hand dismissively. "I have kids, and I run the daycare here. Vomit doesn't bother me."

"No food," Alan said automatically. "She's already anxious, and I don't need her having an episode."

Gail opened her purse and rummaged inside. "She can have hard candies, right?"

"Sure," Alan agreed. "That's fine."

He leaned down, placing a tender kiss on the top of Shelby's head before straightening. His smile softened for just a second longer than usual, then he was already turning, heading for the door. He hoped he could get to the meeting while she was distracted by her friends. Normally he slipped out while she napped after chemo, but yesterday's events had left her buzzing with restless energy. Sleep had not been an option.

He also suspected the police would want to finish questioning them, and he wanted a few uninterrupted minutes with Sam before any outside detective arrived. Some conversations were better had quietly, between friends.

Once Alan was gone, Shelby found herself the center of attentive gazes. She explained that she had not been injured in her fall the day before, only shaken by the discovery of the body. She walked them through what she had seen, what Gus had done, what had drawn her attention to the gully in the first place.

Her background in reading crime reports kicked in automatically. She stuck to facts. Clothing. Position. Location. Timing. She wanted it to be known, if the police asked later, that she was a reliable witness. Not one of those people who scrolled through their phone and missed everything important.

"Was the person a man or a woman?" Lia asked, resting her chin in her hand. "I can't believe Shane didn't see them beside the trail. He's completely oblivious."

"I'm pretty sure it was a female figure," Shelby said. The image surfaced with uncomfortable clarity. "She was wearing black leggings and blue Hoka runners. She was partially hidden by blackberry bushes in the gully. If Gus hadn't pulled me down there, I would have walked right past her."

"That's a serious walker," Gail said thoughtfully. "Anyone wearing Hokas isn't casually wandering."

The table murmured in agreement.

"What's your perspective on what happened?" Mary Ann asked. The slim brunette folded her arms loosely, curiosity bright in her eyes. She and Gail were fixtures at this table, watchers as much as talkers.

"Well," Shelby said, smiling despite the heaviness settling in her chest. She leaned forward, lowering her voice instinctively. "The body was lodged in the ravine, face down." She paused, letting the image settle. "It was an awkward position. That's what makes me believe she fell from the rim trail above."

"Is it possible she was jogging and tripped?" Jocelyn asked. She cradled her mug in both hands, staring into the coffee as if the answer might be swirling there. "Have the police said whether it was intentional?"

Shelby noted the question but not consciously. Jocelyn always asked reasonable questions. It was part of her job to anticipate problems before they escalated.

"It's odd they brought in the county sheriff's office," Shelby said. "That makes me think they suspect foul play."

A subtle shift rippled through the group. Chairs creaked. Someone sucked in a breath.

"What did Sam say?" Lauren asked, pulling out a chair beside Shelby. "Since Garrison retired and Carla only works nights, I can't imagine Ben would be much help if there's a full investigation."

"Alan will call him today. You know how reserved he generally is. He refrains from getting involved in things that aren't our business," Shelby said.

"Falling into a ditch and finding a body is pretty much the definition of your business," Gail laughed. "What happened after you passed out?"

"I'm not sure," Shelby shrugged. "I woke up, and the trail was swarming with people from Parks and Rec, police, and even a crime scene investigator! I wasn't out very long, but they said a hiker saw me pass out and called it in."

"Do they know who it is?" Lia asked. She quickly surveyed the patrons in the coffee shop.

Before Shelby could answer, the bell over the door chimed, and Casi walked in. She scanned the room quickly; a habit Shelby had seen countless times in the past. A woman used to living life on the edge. Her movements were precise and efficient. She spotted the group immediately and dragged a chair over with a bright smile.

"I know who the dead woman is," Casi said casually.

The table erupted.

"Who?"

"Do you really?"

"Seriously?"

Casi laughed, settling back, clearly enjoying the moment. She took a sip of coffee, letting the anticipation swell.

"A tourist?" Lauren ventured. "They don't understand how difficult that rim trail is, especially if they go onto an unmarked path."

"And it rained a few days ago," Gail added. "Mudslides are common near the waterfalls."

Shelby watched Casi closely. Her posture was relaxed and there was an unmistakable gleam in her eyes.

"It's not a tourist," Shelby said slowly. "Unless they were staying at the resort, Casi wouldn't know their name."

"Very good," Casi said.

Shelby continued, feeling an odd prickle along her arms. "That means it's someone we all know. You don't look upset."

Casi shrugged. "I'm sorry she's dead. But I won't pretend I liked her."

"You like everyone," Lia said.

Lauren's eyes widened. "Kristen Martin?"

Shelby's hand flew to her mouth. A ripple of shock vibrated through the group. "Why don't you like Kristen?" She asked once the murmurs subsided.

"I didn't think she was a good fit for the company," Casi said evenly. "And no, before anyone asks, I didn't kill her. It's most likely an unfortunate accident. This is a small town, not a big city where it's not unusual for a person to be randomly murdered."

"How did you determine it was her?" Jocelyn asked.

"I got a call from the waitstaff yesterday afternoon, and they were in a panic because Kristen was absent and there was a group from Japan scheduled to do an event," Casi explained.

"The Maki family reunion. I booked that months ago," Shelby lamented. "There was a lot of coordination since they had relatives coming from numerous locations worldwide."

"Correct. Kristen understood that the event needed to go smoothly. We devoted considerable time to these partnerships, and they had a three-day itinerary before they headed to Banff."

"I forwarded all my notes and event details," Shelby lamented. "We had extensive conversations about the planning." She frowned at the thought that Kristen's lack of follow up lately was because she hadn't wanted to disturb Shelby. It made her sad to think her illness had caused a potential issue with an important client.

Casi sighed. "Kristen wanted to alter the menu and rearrange parts of the itinerary. She had only been in the position for a little over a month, and she didn't have the experience to handle those changes, but she felt she could prove what an asset she was to the position. She described herself repeatedly as a progressive employee who is results driven."

Shelby noted the way Jocelyn's jaw tightened at the mention of missed work, inaccurate files, and forgotten responsibilities. Jocelyn had always hated chaos.

Shelby regarded her hands, picking at her brittle nails. "I guess she wanted to become permanent in management. That's understandable, since we don't know how long it will take me to recover and my position can't be held indefinitely."

Casi placed her hand on top of Shelby's. "We will hold your

job until you are ready to come back. No one will replace you. Kristen understood her move up was temporary. If she had excelled at it, we could have created another position within the organization for her in the future."

"That would be the Board's decision, not yours," Lia asserted.

"True, but the Board wants what is best for profitability and the image of the resort, especially internationally. Shelby has worked efficiently with the team and understands the value everyone brings to an event like the reunion. Honestly, if any of Kristen's eco-recycling ideas had merit, we would be compelled to try them. Unfortunately, she only appeared to possess the ability to dissect what others did and tell them how wrong they were," Casi countered.

"I agree. I spent months planning the menu and recipe testing," Lauren added. "I specifically created it to be seasonal and highlight local ingredients. Kristen felt it should be eco-friendly and even talked to our produce vendor about what methods our partner farms used for growing, production, and transportation."

Shelby nodded, understanding Lauren took her job as head chef seriously and would not have welcomed advice on menu planning. "Casi, are you sure Kristen isn't just angry that you didn't listen to her? Maybe she quit and wanted the event to fail as a punishment to you?"

"That's what I originally thought, too. I had to leave a meeting in Seattle to facilitate the event. I was there until well after midnight," Casi said. "I'm not even an employee of the resort, so I wasn't happy to be filling in last minute. Kyle's not pleased I'm putting in a gazillion extra hours on top of my full-time job, but..." Casi glanced at Shelby, not wanting her to be uncomfortable about taking medical leave. "Anyway, I planned to go to Kristen's house and confront her. I'm tired of walking on eggshells, waiting for her to have a meltdown because things didn't go her way. It was completely inconsiderate to treat our clients like that and possibly ruin future relationships with them. We have many events booked over the summer, including Riley and Amy's wedding. It's not the time for her to go off script and invent new ways of doing things."

Shelby sighed, understanding everyone was already going out of their way to fill in for her while she recovered, and Kristen's disregard for a client caused enormous stress on the staff. "If she wasn't home, did it look like she had gone away, perhaps?" She recalled a recent documentary where the family thought harm had come to the wife, even accusing the husband. It turned out she had gone to Vegas with a friend to 'recharge her emotional battery'.

"Her car wasn't at her house," Casi blushed. "Okay, I peeked in the window, and I saw cats lounging on the couch. Even a bad person doesn't leave a pet."

"Maybe she was just misunderstood." Lia said. "You guys can come across as a bit overwhelming with your tight friendships, and she could have felt left out."

"Give me a break, Lia," Lauren snapped at her sister. She made air quotes and said, "If her little feelings were hurt because she didn't fit in, it's still not okay to mess up a client's event. I can't understand why you feel the need to defend her when she was always criticizing how you run this coffee shop and making stupid suggestions on your menu."

"Maybe I should offer more gluten-free options," Lia lamented.

Lauren leaned forward to make her point. "This is a resort, Lia. People come here to indulge. They have healthy options on the spa menu and at the restaurant. You already have a variety of milk choices that most people don't want, and it's killing your budget."

Casi moved on from the sisterly spat, familiar with Lia's sulking and Lauren's stern rebuttals. "When I called Kyle and informed him, I had to work the event, he told me Amy said she saw Kristen hiking the rim trail."

Mary Ann chimed in. "Casi, that's still a gigantic leap from Kristen not showing up at work and identifying her as the victim found in the ditch."

Casi shrugged. "I was unaware of the body until this morning. Jake mentioned it while we were having coffee, which was very unpleasant."

"I hope he didn't say it in front of the children. They're too young to be hearing morbid details like that," Gail stated.

Lia jutted her bottom lip out, annoyed by the interference of Jake's first wife. "That's funny because you all thought my boys were better off living with their father than with me."

Casi cringed, not wanting to start up the argument again. "Lia, Shane had three little girls he was raising on his own. Your bungalow couldn't handle five kids. Plus, we all agreed the boys should live with their sister since they are close in age." She sighed. "No, the kids were across the street with Anna, getting ready for school, and they didn't hear it. You know how Jake is. I had a mouthful of cereal, and he asked if I had heard about the chick who took a header off the side of the rim trail and ended up in a heap."

"That sounds like Jake," Gail laughed.

Casi nodded. "It struck me as odd that Kristen was absent from work and wasn't at home. I drove to the trailhead on my way here and, sure enough, Kristen's piece of crap car was parked there."

Shelby looked around the table. At the hands wrapped around mugs. The glances that lingered too long or darted away too quickly. And one, who stared at her coffee as though it might betray her if she looked up.

Shelby gasped. "If Amy saw her on the trail, and she had been there for about thirty minutes before she greeted me..." She looked at her fitness tracker, attempting to recollect the exact time. "Oh my, that indicates she likely fell somewhere in that hour! I wonder if the police know who she is?"

"Hopefully she had ID on her," Mary Ann shivered. "It would be terrible to be identified through dental records."

"Casi, maybe you could go to Seattle and confirm it's her? That would be sad for her family to do it." Lia said.

"Yuck, no!" Casi gagged. "I'm not looking at a corpse."

Lauren raised an eyebrow. "I'm sure they will figure it out on their own. What I'm curious about is how she ended up dead?"

7

HOLDING THE LINE

Sam steered his small aluminum fishing boat toward the weathered dock at the lake's edge. The sun hung low, casting a golden glow across still water in the remote Canadian wilderness. Pines and spruce framed the shoreline, their reflections rippling as the boat glided in. The scent of pine and damp earth filled the air, and the distant call of a loon echoed across the lake. He cut the engine and let the boat drift the final few feet before it bumped gently against the dock. He stared across the water, letting the quiet settle into his bones.

He glanced at the live well, two decent-sized trout shifting beneath the surface, and hesitated. He had come here to relax, but the thought of cleaning fish had lost its appeal. He tipped the well and released them, watching them disappear before stepping onto the dock. Wood creaked under his weight as he tied the line and slung his cooler over his shoulder, pausing to absorb the scene. The lake glowed softly, unchanged by time, and moments like this eased the weight of town life and his duties as chief of police in Blackberry Falls.

Sam packed away his fishing gear with a sigh. The past week had been wrapped in silence, free of distraction. His daughter had left with friends for a last getaway before exams swallowed her final weeks of high school. She had also announced she would skip the family summer vacation, opting instead for a backpacking trip through Europe before college in Spokane. Sam thought she should get a part-time job, but his wife insisted she would have plenty of time for work later. Sam wasn't entirely sure what a sustainability major entailed, but Heather made most parenting decisions, which suited him fine. It left him time for hunting and fishing once work was done. Heather had encouraged him to join her on a family visit to California, but Sam claimed she would enjoy it more without him. After twenty-five years of marriage, they had learned compromise kept things peaceful.

Sam paused while stowing lures, his fingers brushing the beaded edge of a bright green spinner. It had been Jason's favorite. The boy would fish for hours, calling out with delight whenever he got a bite. Jason should have been preparing for college with his identical twin, Jen, but a car accident three years earlier had shattered their family. They had survived in different ways. Jen retreated into friendships. Heather buried herself in real estate. Sam knew Jen carried crushing guilt for leaving the party early with her boyfriend, leaving Jason to accept a ride from a friend who had been drinking. Heather blamed herself for ignoring the underage partying, turning a blind eye to alcohol and recreational drugs because it had seemed harmless in the days when they were young.

As police chief, Sam had been called to the scene, unaware his son lay in the twisted wreckage at the bottom of the ravine. He had seen brutality in his career, but nothing compared to holding his child one last time.

The irony was they had moved from Tacoma to Blackberry Falls when Heather was pregnant, seeking a quieter life in the town Sam had grown up in. After high school, he rushed toward city excitement. College and the police academy in

Seattle followed, later moving to Tacoma for work experience. In their early thirties, twins arrived. The suburban promise was held for fifteen years. Sam rose to chief. Heather earned her realtor's license. The twins thrived. He was not prepared for losing half of that life in an instant.

Friends and family moved beyond comfort into quiet acceptance, knowing grief never truly left. Barbecues, sports nights, and town events filled the calendar, moments of near normalcy. Then a glimpse, a father fishing with his son, a laughing family on vacation, and the darkness returned. Heather stayed through his drift into alcoholism and his slow climb back. There were no ultimatums. She understood his pain and weathered every storm beside him.

Sam exhaled as he loaded the final piece of equipment into his truck. The trip had ended early after a supply run into town, where a single bar of reception delivered urgent messages from Officer Carla Nguyen reporting a woman's body along the lakeside trail. Out here, silence was the point. No calls. No responsibility. Jen knew to contact Heather in emergencies, and Heather managed their lives with the precision of an air traffic controller.

With Garrison retired, the department was stretched thin. Sam felt guilty leaving, but before tourist season swelled, he needed the escape. Carla worked nights handling DUIs and bar fights. Ben Tanner was fresh from the academy, eager but inexperienced. Sam kept him on low-risk calls until he found his footing.

At the lake, Sam had taken one final cast to clear his head. Now, six hours of road awaited him. He planned to return calls once he crossed the border, where service improved. Messages from Alan, Ben, and Heather stacked up.

At the border, Sam scanned texts while idling in line. Ben's frantic messages were riddled with errors, nearly indecipherable. Heather's clear explanation finally revealed the truth. A woman had been found dead, not Shelby. Relief flooded him, sharp and immediate, and he was grateful to be alone. The guilt followed close behind. He imagined Heather's anxiety over Shelby's fall and the discovery that followed.

The stress sparked an urge for a drink, and he briefly considered returning to the cabin. The small log home, built by his grandfather on Shuswap Lake, had always been a refuge. Heather hated it and saw no point in escaping when they already lived in a small town with a beautiful lake. She didn't understand the draw of solitude, or how bigger cities lured people with temptation they couldn't seem to resist.

Sam had hosted an annual fishing trip since moving to Blackberry Falls eighteen years ago. The group expanded to include the Jensen brothers, then Shane. They bonded over meals and shared histories. Sam nearly canceled the year Jason died, but Alan insisted the break would help. Later Sam realized Alan was pulling him away from grief and the inevitable drinking that followed. After that, alcohol disappeared from the tradition. Conversations grew quieter, more intentional. An undefined support group for men, silently protecting each other from the challenges of life, and the demons within themselves.

Sam smiled at the image of Jake recounting his two failed marriages, before settling down again with a spirited third wife. And they were all shocked when Kyle traded bachelorhood for a swimsuit model from Los Angeles. Then there was Shane, the Canadian outsider, widowed young, navigating blended families and loss with stoic grace.

As the line crawled forward. Sam plucked out his phone and called Alan.

"Hey, how's it going?"

"Pretty good. You get my message?" Alan asked.

"Yeah. How's Shelby holding up?"

"She's alright. She's already Googling every way a person

can die falling off a cliff," Alan said with a laugh. "She didn't like that detective from Seattle. Says his head looks like a potato."

Sam chuckled. "Sounds about right. Hopefully he's just there to check boxes. Falls happen. Have they said if she's local?"

"Nothing official yet," Alan replied. "But Casi told the coffee group it was a woman from the resort, Kristen Martin."

Sam frowned. "How does Kyle's wife know that? Did she see her fall? What are the actual facts?"

"She connected a few dots. Kristen was filling in for Shelby during her medical leave."

Sam exhaled. "Let's hope it's not murder. County resources are already tight, and my budget barely covers overtime. If Seattle's involved, things will get messy."

"And the coffee shop crew will feast on it," Alan said.

"Yeah," Sam replied softly. "They always do." As the call ended, Sam merged onto the highway, already shifting back into duty, and sudden unrest in Blackberry Falls.

8

BLUNT FORCE

"Are you feeling alright?" Alan asked, noting Shelby's cheerful disposition as he walked with her along the corridor of the cancer center. "You were up pretty late last night on your laptop."

"I'm sorry. Did the light bother you?" Shelby asked.

The living room was adjacent to the main bedroom, and the electric recliner had become her home base, even for sleeping. The doctors insisted her head always remain at a thirty-degree angle to avoid aspiration, since that's what had landed her in the ICU to begin with. They had plenty of space to set up her monitors and machinery, like Joey Kangaroo, and predicted it would be more convenient for her to access the bathroom during the night and not bother Alan while he tried to get a few hours of sleep. Unfortunately, the slightest buzz or alarm kept him checking on her a good portion of the night.

She had to haul the whole contraption she was tethered to when she ventured to the bathroom. She had learned to maneuver the feeding pump and pole like a reluctant dance partner, catching the tubing on door handles with maddening frequency.

She hated what their home had become. Medical supplies filled the dining room. Nutritional drinks were stacked in cases against the wall. The worst addition was the plastic bucket for sudden bouts of vomiting. Alan cleaned it without comment, resetting the space as though dignity could be restored by routine.

In those early weeks after the ICU, visitors had been barred completely. Shelby's immune system was too fragile. She missed her friends fiercely but appreciated the distance when she felt so awful. It was easier to be brave in text messages than face people while vomiting blood or sitting hooked up to a feeding pump with greasy hair and blotchy skin.

It had been especially hard on her niece and nephews. Shelby insisted they continue living full lives, promising she would ask when she needed help. Dylan's kitchen haircut had been a rare treat, though she cringed at the state of the house. He pretended not to notice, likely having been coached by Casi in advance.

Alan smiled, recognizing the inward drift of Shelby's thoughts. As terrible as it was to acknowledge, the discovery of the body had jolted them out of the singular focus on illness. Something external had intruded. Unknown, urgent, and unsettling. Although, he begrudgingly admitted it brought much-needed excitement into their lives. "It didn't bother me. I got enough sleep," he lied.

"After I finish radiation..." Shelby began, then paused, the thought branching into too many directions at once.

"You want to stop by the coffee shop and dissect the new clues?" Alan asked, a grin tugging at his mouth.

"Bingo." Shelby laughed.

Alan leaned down and kissed her forehead, keeping his touch light. He wanted to shield her from everything, but too much care now felt like another form of harm. He swallowed his own fear, his loneliness, his exhaustion. His friends offered support in fragmented ways, but he didn't dare unload the magnitude of what he carried. If he opened that door, he might not survive the flood.

"Since you're still riding the steroid high," he said carefully, "we can swing by. Sam got back late last night. He might want to talk to you."

"I would rather talk to him than the potato head," Shelby muttered.

She waved goodbye and disappeared into the changing room. As she passed a woman standing nervously by the door, Shelby smiled automatically. Two weeks ago, this hallway had been foreign. Now it felt strangely familiar.

"It's not that bad," Shelby offered.

The woman looked up hopefully. "Does it hurt?"

"No, it feels a bit like a sunburn after, but there's no actual pain." Shelby said as she changed into a hospital gown. "What type of cancer do you have?"

"Breast cancer, stage 2," the woman said tearfully. "You?"

"Stage 3 esophageal cancer," Shelby replied, recalling her oncologist's words that she was borderline stage 4, but they hoped they could reduce the tumor with chemo and radiation, and she could be considered a candidate for surgery.

"Wow, I had an uncle who died from that." The woman shook her head sadly. "I didn't know there was a cure."

"There are numerous new treatments," Shelby said, having given up on internet searches at the advice of her oncologist and finding a Facebook support group instead. She nodded as her name was called and followed the technician to the small room down the hall. She untied her gown and settled it around her hips, still not used to disrobing in public. The technician aided her while she positioned herself on the table and adjusted the pillow that had been specially formed for her to use. He checked the light lined up on the targets tattooed on her chest and stepped into the next room. Shelby closed her eyes and imagined lying on a beach, beginning to giggle at the thought of sunbathing topless at her age.

"Stay still, please," the technician said into the microphone.

Shelby stayed as rigid as possible, listening to the whir of the machine as it rotated over her body. There was a slight warmth from the radiation, and she hoped the lady with breast cancer was having a good experience as well.

"All done," the technician announced twenty minutes later. He helped tie her gown behind as she wobbled toward the door. She was unwavering in her decision to go to the coffee shop and willed herself to use the steroids remaining in her body from the chemo the day before.

"Great job, Shelby. You've almost completed the week, and then you only have eighteen more treatments to go," the technician noted as he held the door for her.

She beamed at his words, thinking her only job had been to stay still. "I'll see you tomorrow," she said, knowing Fridays seemed to be when the nausea hit, and it was challenging to remain flat on the table for even twenty minutes.

"All done?" Alan asked as she met him in the waiting room. Shelby smiled and gave him a hug, leaning into his solid frame. When she had been released from the hospital and came to the oncology clinic, she could barely walk down the hallway that seemed miles away. Alan had offered to assist her with a wheelchair, but she was determined to walk even if it meant hanging on to him to keep from falling over. It had been a surreal experience to be inside a center she never knew existed, surrounded by people fighting this deadly disease. It certainly gave her a different way of looking at life and an appreciation for all the amazing things around her.

They drove to the coffee shop with minimal conversation; each lost in their own thoughts. Sam caught up with them as they made their way through the parking lot. "How was the treatment, Shelby?" he asked.

"Not bad. I'm practicing being a pinup girl with the sexy poses they make me do. I might give Casi a little competition," she teased.

Sam swung an arm over her shoulders. "You have a great attitude. I love the haircut too. Nice for summer."

"I can share the name of my hairdresser," Shelby teased, eyeing his thinning hair.

Sam chuckled and propped the door open for her, bracing himself for the onslaught of questions the minute he stepped into the building. He held up a hand as all five women started talking at once. "Wait, one at a time. I was away on a fishing trip, and I'm just getting up to speed."

Lia arrived with a tray of coffee drinks and handed them out while everyone got seated, waiting for Sam to take a chair at the head of the table. Shelby looked wistfully at the cappuccino before sliding it over to Alan. Lia still didn't understand that she couldn't eat or drink, but she appreciated that she was included. "Alright," Sam began, stopping to take a sip of coffee. "The local authorities have confirmed the identity of the victim."

"Kristen Martin?" Lauren asked ahead of anyone else. "How did you determine it was her?"

"Apparently the police department is not as perceptive as your friend, Casi." He glanced around the table. "Where is she?"

"At work in Seattle," Gail stated, setting down her phone. "I texted her that the identity was confirmed."

"Very good. We wouldn't want her falling behind," Sam joked. "Although Kristen did not have identification on her, forensics was able to run her fingerprints to find her identity."

"Oh? Did she have a criminal record?" Jocelyn asked.

"Not that I'm aware of," Sam said cautiously. "It matched her driver's license print."

The group nodded in agreement. And Gail raised her hand. "Do they know the time of death?"

"Good question," Shelby said, checking it off her list.

"We have an estimated number given the timeframe she was last seen and when her body was discovered..." Sam started.

"Time of death was between 9:30 am and 10 am," Shelby asserted.

"Correct." Sam looked at Alan and smiled at Shelby's animated excitement.

"Have they determined how she died?" Mary Ann asked.

Sam hesitated, determining the most optimal approach. "The coroner has determined the factor leading to her death as blunt force trauma to her head." He waited for the collective gasps to extinguish before continuing, "We aren't certain if she slipped and hit her head on a rock or met with a trauma before the fall."

"Like murder?" Lauren asked.

"We aren't ruling anything out at this time," Sam said.

"But who would do that? We don't have killers in this town," Lia professed.

"The pathologist is still running tests to see what may have caused the fall. It could end up being as simple as she tripped and got too close to the edge," Sam explained.

"Oh!" Shelby exclaimed. "Gus brought me her shoe when I fell in the blackberry bush. Maybe her shoelace was untied, and she tripped over it. That can be very dangerous."

"I've tripped over my shoelace," Jocelyn noted.

"Plus, she was jogging, which would definitely send her over the edge," Mary Ann said. They became animated and shared similar stories of tripping and the perils of untied shoes.

"Will the sheriff's office still be investigating?" Jocelyn asked, rubbing her hands together. "It's very unsettling."

"They are involved for now. Nobody will be interviewed

without me, Carla, or Ben present," Sam confirmed. He noted Shelby's eyelids flutter and nudged Alan. "For now, how about we all get much needed rest and pick this back up once we have more information?"

"One more question," Shelby yawned. "Has any evidence been found that would suggest foul play?"

Sam met her gaze, weighing honesty against fear. "Nothing definitive. Yet."

9

ALWAYS CONNECTED

"You're okay, Shell Bell," Alan soothed as he stroked her hair.

Shelby clung to the bucket with sweaty palms, preparing for another violent wrench of her stomach. Since the feed tube led to her lower intestine, the only thing coming up was blood tinted bile. Alan steadied his phone over the contents to snap a photo. "Gross, Alan, no one wants to see that!" Shelby croaked.

"I'm sending it to the oncologist. Do you think I should show the surgeon, too?" He asked.

Shelby lurched forward as another wave of nausea hit her. Alan lovingly wiped her face with a towel and moved the bucket away to clean and sanitize during the reprieve. He glanced at his watch, anticipating the next episode. He inserted a pill under her tongue and patiently waited for it to dissolve before asking, "How about a popsicle?"

"Oh, that sounds nice," Shelby said, perking up at the suggestion. "It might help alleviate the bitterness of the anti-nausea medication."

Alan unwrapped the lemon-flavored treat, following the

doctor's orders to avoid grape and cherry flavors because they made it difficult to determine if there was gastric bleeding. He handed her the popsicle and went to work cleaning her feeding tube before injecting a syringe full of water while she was distracted. "Not too fast," she cautioned. "You'll make me have to pee."

Alan chuckled, slowing the pressure. He refocused his attention on the click of the side door closing. "Stella?" he asked with confusion. "When did you get to town?"

"Hey," Stella said, trying not to cry. She noted the weariness in her uncle's expression and the deep circles under his eyes. His shirt was wrinkled, and he was disheveled, like he hadn't slept in days. "I didn't mean to disturb you. Work has been slow, and Casi suggested I come home since the campaigns don't really pick up again until after summer. I took an Uber from the airport."

Shelby regarded her niece's thin frame, cautious not to comment on her weight, being well versed in the brutality of the modeling world through Casi. "I can make up the guest room for you."

Stella shook her head, turning away as the tears sprung free. "I'll stay with Amy. She needs my help with the wedding, anyway. I'm devastated you're sick. Are you feeling any pain?" Her breath caught in her throat. The house didn't feel like home anymore. It felt like a hospital. The vibrant life of the bungalow had been replaced by an unfamiliar hum of machines and the weight of illness.

"I'm better than I look." Shelby waved a hand over her rumpled attire, pale skin, and spikey hair. "Fridays are my bad days, but it's a cakewalk after that."

Alan glanced at his phone when it vibrated. "Hey, good news! The presence of blood in the vomit is from the tumor breaking down. That means the chemo and radiation are working."

"Hallelujah!" Shelby cheered.

"That's wonderful," Stella agreed, as she stole a glance at the living area and cringed at the cases of nutritional feed stacked against a back wall while the dining room resembled a medical supply closet. She realized Alan was doing everything possible to keep the house up and Shelby had to focus on healing, but it was shocking to see the normally pristine environment in disarray. There was a medicinal odor in the air that mingled with last night's pot roast dinner, which she guessed her uncle had reheated in the microwave. She recalled Shelby telling her on one of their frequent calls how she had stocked the freezer with Alan's favorite dishes, hoping to lessen the burden on him when he became the caregiver. They had spent hours on the phone planning easy meals to reheat. She smiled, remembering the laughter they shared while attempting to explain to her aunt how to download recipes from Instagram. It had made Stella feel involved, even though she was several states away.

Alan grimaced as he noted her concern. "These past few weeks have been hectic, and keeping this place in order was the last thing on my mind. My focus was staging this section with everything she needs and providing a clear path to the bathroom and the recliner.

Shelby giggled. "It's imperative to clean the bathroom every day because I'm radioactive. I probably glow in the dark."

Alan chuckled. "It's a preventative measure. We don't have young children or old folks to contaminate." He regarded Gus stretching at Shelby's feet. "You're a useless guard dog. You let a stranger come right in the back door."

"I'm only a stranger for a bit. I promise I'll fall back into the rhythm of this family in no time." Stella stroked Gus's ears. She remembered when he was a tiny puppy, whining to be held and played with. Six years had gone by quickly as she graduated high school and set off to LA to pursue a modeling career. As she petted Gus, the softness of his fur reduced her anxiety, and she felt the weight of regret lift from her shoulders. She turned to Shelby. "You looked after me and the boys when we were little, and my mom was overwhelmed. We all want to be available to assist you guys now."

"Speaking of which," Shelby grinned. "Tonight is a sports thing at Kyle's. Alan hasn't been there for weeks. Would you mind staying with me so he's not afraid to leave me alone? He'll take care of all the nasty stuff before he leaves."

"I don't need to go, Shell. They have one every week. I'll catch the next one," Alan protested.

"I don't want you to pass up the chance to gather evidence. I'm sure Sam will be there, and he might divulge a little clue." Shelby shifted her focus to Stella. "Did you hear about the body at the lake?"

"No! Did he drown?" Stella asked.

"It was a woman," Shelby clarified. "The cause of death was blunt force trauma to the head! Can you imagine?"

"Ugh, that's violent. Did someone hit her?" Stella asked.

"We aren't sure," Shelby shrugged, handing Alan the stick from her popsicle. "Maybe you could help me set up a sleuthing station at the desk. I'm having trouble with the internet."

Alan directed Stella to the side with the pretense of getting her a glass of water. "She's struggling a bit with her memory right now."

New tears filled Stella's eyes, turning them into a liquid aqua color. "Does she have dementia?"

He sighed. "No, it's from chemo. It's like she's in a fog for a few days after. It clears over the weekend, then we're back for treatment on Wednesdays."

"I like how you say we," Stella said. "I'm thrilled she's not alone in fighting this battle. She's the strongest woman I know, but she deserves a hero to look after her."

"I'm doing everything I can to earn that title," Alan said, straightening Shelby's blanket as it slipped to the floor beside Gus.

Shelby reached out for Stella and offered her a sleepy smile. "Fridays are my bad days. It's vomit and naps for twelve hours."

Stella kissed her cheek gently, ignoring the repetition of the bad days. "Riley warned me to come on the weekend. I should have listened. It's unfortunate that the lady died, but it's kind of exciting that we can try to solve a real live crime in person. It will be like old times when we would run around the neighborhood in the summer, finding all the clues you guys planted for scavenger hunts." Her face lit up at the memory of long summer days and the games they would play until the sun went down. She realized she was nostalgic about her childhood when things were simpler, but also for knowing how strong and healthy her aunt had been. The gravity of the situation settled heavily on her shoulders. She followed her uncle to the kitchen as he discarded the empty cartons of nutritional supplements. "How are you holding up?" she asked.

Alan sighed, running a hand through his graying hair. "I'm doing my best," he said, his voice breaking unexpectedly. "It's harder than I ever thought it would be." He glanced at Shelby. "It isn't the caregiving that bothers me. You know I am prepared to do whatever is necessary for her." His voice wavered as he continued, "I just wish I could take her pain away and make her well again."

"Would it be okay if I stay here?" Stella asked. "I want to feel useful, and I can still help Amy after she gets home from work. It's important to me to be close to you guys and be part of her recovery process."

Alan smiled. "I've gotten pretty good with this work from home routine, but I'm sure Shelby would like it if you could take her on a few errands, maybe even for a walk? She feels like I hover, and it drives her crazy."

"I would be happy to do that. Now get on your way to Kyle's and bring back clues for our investigation." She filled the kettle and set it on the stove, discreetly wiping the counter and organizing a tray with pills. "Aunt Shelby, can you still drink tea?"

"Tea sounds lovely," Shelby said.

"Lukewarm," Alan interjected. "She's sensitive to temperature." He reached above Stella, towering over her five-foot ten frame, and selected a box on the top shelf. "Apple cinnamon is her favorite. Normally, she prefers a berry blend in the spring, but that may be too acidic right now, and we are avoiding anything with added color."

After Alan left, Stella brought Shelby tea, clearing a spot on the table. She sat cross-legged on the sofa, feeling suddenly exhausted from a day of travel and an emotional reunion. The soft hum of the feeding tube pump brought a strange comfort to know she was here with her aunt, even if things were different.

"Remember when you used to sit here and watch the sunset with me?" Shelby murmured. "You always talked about seeing the world outside Blackberry Falls. How does it feel to have started a new life in LA?"

Stella took a sip from her cup and thought of LA, the glittering lights, the cameras, the endless hustle. "It's everything I wanted. However, I suppose it doesn't feel as significant now. Being here with you feels more real."

Shelby smiled, noticing the childlike quality of Stella's features. The memory of the little girl perched on the sofa many years ago tugged at her heart. "I'll get through this, Stella. Don't give up on your life because you're worried about me."

Stella sniffed back tears and directed her gaze out the window. "I have no desire to be like my mom and run away when things get emotionally challenging."

"You only have her good bits in you," Shelby assured her.

"You're creative and thoughtful. But you are your own person, too."

Stella nodded. "Part of me wishes I could be a little girl again, even for a day. Wouldn't it be wonderful to time travel to our favorite memories and get to relive them?"

"It would be divine!" Shelby agreed. She sank back in her chair and smiled. "Did I tell you that when I was in the hospital, your grandpa was there with me? I was in a lot of pain after my lung thingy happened. I felt him rubbing my back, and then he tucked the sheets around me perfectly snug, like he always used to. It was amazing to have him there with me when I felt isolated and afraid." She noted Stella's concern. "I'm aware he wasn't physically there. I have no doubt it was the anesthesia or the multitude of drugs they had me on, but it was real to me and brought me tremendous comfort. He couldn't communicate during his final year of life, but then when I needed him the most, he was there for me. That's the power of memories and connection, Stella. We'll always be together, no matter what happens."

10

———

SUDDENLY SUSPECT

Shelby blinked awake in confusion. There was an odd smell in the vicinity that she couldn't decipher. It was a mixture of savory herbs and furniture polish. She took a deep breath and smiled, recalling Stella had arrived the night before, and a quick glance confirmed the house was sparkling clean.

"Good morning, sleepyhead," Stella called, coming to plant a kiss on her cheek. "I managed to get most of the house organized and started a load of laundry. Would you like me to add that robe in with the darks?" She eyed the stained garment Shelby had lived in recently.

Shelby yawned. "That would be excellent. Today is shower day, and I even get to wash my hair." She patted the frizzy dome. "What is that delightful aroma?"

"Grandma's chicken soup. I made a clear broth for you, and I've already checked with the advice nurse, and she said you can have it lukewarm and take small sips. I'll add vegetables, noodles, and chicken for Uncle Alan. I don't think he's been eating properly," Stella said.

Shelby smiled at the young woman with porcelain skin, a

glossy chestnut brown shoulder-length haircut, and stunning gray-green eyes. Although Stella was doing well in LA as a model, Shelby still saw her as the precocious little girl with an infectious laugh. She was wearing one of Shelby's aprons, wrapping it around herself with fabric to spare. She always seemed at home in the kitchen, happy to whip up coffee cake or bagels on a whim. Shelby was pleased Stella had seized the chance to work as a model, especially with the guidance of Casi, who had excelled in the field. She hoped Stella would follow Casi's example and know when to leave the glamorous life behind and find a more fulfilling career.

"Something smells incredible." Alan entered the room with a yawn. "Holy cow, is it nine already? I can't believe I slept that long."

"That's the first time in months you've been able to sleep through the night," Shelby said.

Alan turned in panic and regarded the empty supplement bag. "Didn't the alarm go off when the food ran out?" He tapped Joey Kangaroo to check if it was working.

"It did, and I turned it off," Shelby answered. She raised her hand as he began to protest. "It's Saturday, Alan. We can go off schedule and add another round earlier in the afternoon. I wanted you and Stella to get a proper night's rest. I certainly won't starve overnight."

"Breakfast is ready," Stella said, setting a plate with toast, eggs, and sausage at the table for Alan before handing Shelby a small cup of broth.

Shelby took a sip before Alan could caution her to drink it slowly and stifled a cough as the liquid went down too fast. She felt his hand rubbing her back, already anticipating her choking. Stella looked alarmed, and Alan chuckled. "She got a bit too excited to taste it. She has a stent to open her esophagus, but it's still partially blocked." Shelby nodded, not revealing that even drinking caused pain in her sternum, but the overwhelming desire to have the flavors in her mouth overruled the negative outcome.

Once she regained the ability to swallow, Shelby asked, "Alan, what exciting tidbits did you learn last night?"

"The Mariners need to step up their catching in the outfield if they want to win a game," he teased, and noted her eager expression. "Sam only mentioned that a note was found in Kristen's pocket, which might suggest a lead."

"Oh my! Like a suicide note? Do they think she jumped?" Shelby winced.

"He didn't say anything about her mental state, only that she gave the impression of being a mostly healthy woman in her early forties," he confirmed.

"Why did they say mostly healthy?" Shelby asked.

Alan shrugged. "I guess she was a little overweight, not enough to be obese, but they are considering it a possible factor."

"Like maybe she suffered cardiac arrest because she wasn't fit enough for that level of exercise?" Stella asked.

"Possibly," Alan commented.

"See? This is why I need to lose weight!" Shelby exclaimed. "I refuse to be labeled as a pleasantly plump middle-aged lady. If I die, it will be something aggressive like cancer, not because my flab kept me from walking on a trail properly."

"Middle-aged would be correct if you plan to live to one hundred and four, which is a great goal," Alan teased. They turned their attention to a sudden knock at the door, and Alan strode over to answer while Gus trotted beside him to investigate the visitor. "Sam, hi..." Alan paused upon catching sight of the detective at his side. "I assumed you were coming to say hello to Shelby. Our niece, Stella, is in town as well."

The detective pushed past him without waiting for an invitation. He stopped in his tracks when Gus growled and blocked his advancement into the room. "Sorry, Alan, the detective had a few questions for Shelby since she found the body. Do you mind if we come in for a minute?" Sam asked.

Alan nodded, directing Gus to his bed as they entered. "Stay, Gus," he said. The dog monitored the stranger, stretching himself from his bed to contact Shelby's sock-clad foot to ensure she was safe. She leaned over and caressed his ears, assuring him she was fine. Alan regarded his breakfast cooling on the counter. The perfectly over-easy eggs, now coagulating into an unappealing yellow blob. "Can I get you coffee?"

"No," the detective positioned himself on the sofa near Shelby. When Gus growled again, he coughed to clear his throat. "Can you take the dog outside? I'm not comfortable with him here."

Sam started to protest, but Alan grasped Gus's collar. "Come on, boy, it's time for you to eat, anyway."

Sam exhaled and poured himself a mug of coffee, adding sugar and cream. He resented the intrusion of the detective in his friends' home but wanted to ensure they followed proper procedure since most of his cases over the years were thefts and drinking offenses. With only a few more years until retirement, it was important that it didn't appear to the authorities that he couldn't handle a minor investigation because of personal connections to the townspeople.

Stella sat near her aunt, taking over Gus's duty to protect her from the surly detective. "My aunt is not well. What questions were you interested in asking?"

The detective looked at his notes, not making eye contact. "What time were you on the trail?"

"About 10 o'clock," Shelby answered with precision.

"Exactly? You didn't get there a little earlier...considering your condition? It could have taken a considerable amount of time to reach the half mile marker by the lake," he said.

"I'm fully capable of walking," Shelby scoffed. "As for the time..." she extended her fingers and grasped her phone. "It would have been around ten fifteen. I know this because I snapped a photo of a loon on the lake and shared it with Alan. I believed it was a stroke of luck that I saw several after I told him I hoped I would. See? There's the timestamp on the picture I sent. It was right after that Gus located the poor woman. It was Kristen, correct? I didn't realize back then, but I believe it was confirmed."

"Yes." The investigator shook his head, not expecting a highly detailed response. "And Gus, that's your dog, grabbed the woman?"

"He did no such thing!" Shelby gasped.

"He's a hunting dog," Alan added. "He probably caught the scent and went to investigate. He doesn't grab things; he points until given a command to retrieve."

"Although you weren't there to witness that," the detective said. "Your wife was walking alone even though you've stated she's unwell."

"Walking is part of her therapy. She wanted to do one mile by herself. We had several people along the trail report that she was fine, and I was parked at the one-mile mark." Alan's cheeks blistered with heat at the accusations.

"Right, that would be Amy, your nephew's fiancé, and Shane, who is he? Someone's second husband?" he said. "Did you seek their assistance in ensuring the welfare of your wife, or did a concerned citizen feel it was necessary to have individuals supervise her walk?"

Sam stopped Alan from answering, seeing he was about to snap. "Detective Sanchez, are these questions necessary? This isn't a wellness check, and I can assure you, Shelby Kincaid is completely capable of walking one mile, even with cancer. We look out for each other in this community, and if a friend stopped and said hello on a lovely stroll by the lake, I hardly think that constitutes a crime."

"True enough. It appears by all accounts Mrs. Kincaid was

able-bodied enough to chat with her friends at the local coffee-house and then go for a leisurely walk around the lake with a high-strung animal." He leaned forward. "One might ask then if she had the strength to push an unsuspecting woman off the ledge of the trail?"

"That's enough!" Alan leaped up in a frenzy. "Shelby did nothing of the sort, and you're in our home mocking her illness."

Sam stood and intervened. "Detective Sanchez, it might have been prudent to have shared this information with me before coming here. Do you have the audacity to accuse this woman of hiking a steep incline, attacking the victim, then returning to another path to engage with two witnesses, and fake finding a body all within forty-five minutes? Even an Olympic athlete wouldn't be capable of accomplishing that."

Shelby sensed the intense burn of the acid as her anxiety flared. She reached for her fitness tracker from the basket on the table beside her and held it up to Alan. "Can you go to Tuesday's results? It tracks my heart rate which will indicate when I became upset."

Alan took the device and located the information. "Hey, you did well, Shelby. Your numbers are level. Whoops, that must have been when Gus got riled up." He turned the dial to the detective.

Detective Sanchez rolled his eyes. "You seem to possess an abundance of convenient ways to document your whereabouts on that day. Were you anticipating being a suspect?"

"Every person can be a suspect. What ties them to a murder is motive. I had no reason to want Kristen dead," Shelby sat back with satisfaction.

"I see you enjoy engaging in amateur detective work in your spare time?" The detective pointed to the stack of books by Shelby's chair. "In real life, it's a lot more difficult to get away with murder."

"If I wanted to kill a person, I would probably choose poison. Weapons are messy, and I must say, shoving a person off a cliff, especially in my condition, could have unpredictable results."

The shock rippled through the room when Detective Sanchez laughed. "Okay, you win that one. I have a question, though."

"Fire away," Shelby said, making a mental note to ask Stella later what she thought of the detective's oddly shaped head.

"We found a sneaker with bloody fingerprints. The shoe belonged to the victim, but the blood was not a match." He pointed to Shelby's chipped nails and scratched arms.

"When Gus dragged me into the blackberry bushes, it tore my pants and scratched my arms. My nails are brittle from chemo and got wrecked in the fall." She sighed at the memory and noticed the detective waiting for an answer. "It's probably mine. The blood, not the shoe. I like that brand, mind you, but I've taken to wearing more color as I age. Pink would have been my choice, conceivably. That would be delightful. Dark blue seems like a wasted opportunity to have a bit of pizazz."

The investigator slouched in his seat, suspecting it would be a while before she finally got to the point. "How did your blood get on the shoe?"

"Gus brought it to me. I assumed it was an arbitrary discovery. He does that. We've collected more socks, gloves, bits of paper, and even a pair of underwear once. Remember that, Alan? It was hilarious. They were a very racy pair. We set them out on the front gate so the owner could collect them without embarrassment. I must admit I peeked out the window though, and it was a man who took them. I wonder if he was returning them to his wife. Or maybe he had a fetish?"

The investigator sighed. "Back to the shoe. The dog retrieved it because he's into footwear and lingerie..."

"Obviously I was confused and hurt. When he offered it to

me, I grabbed it. That's when I noticed the woman in an unusual position. I threw the shoe away and called for help," Shelby finished. "Test it for canine saliva, and I guarantee it will come back positive."

"I believe there has been a mishap," he read from his notebook. "That's an understatement."

"Well, I was in shock. I hesitated to jump to conclusions and say she was dead. I didn't even realize it was a woman until later, when I thought about how she was dressed," Shelby said.

"Before you hung up, you said *What did I do? Alan will be upset with me*," he read. "That almost sounds like a confession."

"Shelby, why would I be mad at you?" Alan lamented.

"It was very unsettling to be looking at loons one minute and toppling over into a ditch the next." She looked at Sam. "Alan has been an incredible caregiver. It was extremely difficult for him to let me walk that trail on my own. I had spoken to the chaplain at the hospital, and I shared with him that I was finding it difficult to have lost control over every aspect of my life. I could no longer work, which was more than just the actual job. It altered my daily life, chatting with friends, and being a part of something bigger, like booking significant events for our clients. I wasn't allowed to drive or go out in public for fear of germs. My tasks around the house were taken over because of my inability to do them. The final blow was that I couldn't eat." She gestured to the machine. "I can't even have coffee and a scone with a friend. I'm tied to this damn thing that does everything for me." She exhaled. "Anyway, the chaplain said to stay focused on the things I could do. I spend my time attempting to solve crime stories and deduce who did it. I'm intrigued by the psychology of what makes a relatively normal person commit an unfathomable crime."

"Why were you speaking to a chaplain? Don't they only come around in end-of-life situations?" The detective asked.

"Oh," Shelby said, looking at the horrified faces of her

niece, husband, and friend. Silence reverberated through the area with a deafening aftershock. The detective cocked his head, confused by the reaction. She extended her arm and gently touched his hand as if he was the one who needed comfort after the accidental revelation. "Some things are better left alone. Now where was I?"

"Alan was mad?" he offered.

"Disappointed would have been the better word," Shelby clarified. "He's tried hard to fix me up and piece me together again. Are you married?" she asked.

"Divorced," the detective replied.

She pursed her lips, not wanting to judge another person's relationship, but sensed that it might be where his careless attitude originated. "There's a lot of pressure on a husband when his wife is sick. He's expected to make everything right and be the rock. We don't have children." She gestured to Stella. "But we've been there as much as we could for our niece and nephews."

"One is getting married in September?" The detective asked, surprising himself that he was interested. There was a quality about Shelby that was incredibly endearing. He couldn't help but want to hear more of her misdirected, wayward stories.

"Yes," she praised his attention to detail. Shelby tapped her bottom lip with her finger. "If her shoe was found in a separate place than her body, that could be the reason she fell. Either she tripped on the lace or, if she was running, maybe she slipped out of her shoe and tumbled over the edge?" She faced Stella. "That's why I don't wear open back shoes anymore. I was rushing to get a contract for a client, and I rounded the corner too abruptly. I went one way, and my shoe went another way. It was quite funny but awfully embarrassing in front of a crowd. Do you remember when I threw those shoes out, Alan? I said, there would be no more of that craziness."

"You loved those shoes until that day," he agreed.

Shelby looked toward the detective. "My sister, Willow. Well, she started out life with the name Wendy, but suddenly in high school she aspired to be called Willow. She worked as a cocktail waitress, and she could wear the highest of heels. Holy smokes, what a sight." She raised an eyebrow. "What was the subject we were talking about prior to bringing up high heels?"

The detective checked his notes, having gotten lost in the rambling story that piqued his curiosity about Willow. "We found a note in her possession, which seems to be a list of people who had wronged her. Can you explain why your name was listed first?

"Goodness, that's a lot to take in." Tears sprang into Shelby's eyes. "I've never done anything unkind to anyone ever in my life." She looked at Alan for confirmation.

"Certainly not! Everyone loves Shelby," Alan insisted to a round of nods. "But if Kristen compiled a list like that, wouldn't it give her the motive to hurt those people? Why would Shelby harm her because Kristen didn't like her? I don't understand the intent." Alan examined his watch and noted Shelby's flushed cheeks as moisture beaded on her forehead. "I need to test her glucose level and get her back on her feeding tube. This had been a lot for her to take in. She has an excellent reputation within the hotel, and there's not a single person in town who will claim otherwise." His nostrils flared with annoyance as he bent over his wife in a protective stance and grabbed the monitor from the basket and unzipped the case. He meticulously opened an alcohol wipe and cleaned Shelby's ring finger, giving it a squeeze before holding the pen to the tip and clicking the button to release the needle. Shelby winced, knowing the sting was temporary, but her fingers were raw from continuous testing. Alan directed her hand towards the test strip on the monitor and waited for the result. "It's high, Shell," he said, showing her the reading. "One unit of insulin," he said, strolling to the fridge to retrieve the pen and twisting the dial.

"But Alan, it hasn't been five hours since Joey Kangaroo ran out. You know the nutritional drink has glucose."

Alan hesitated with the pen in hand. "But if it's high and I reconnect you, it will only increase. That kind of spike isn't good for you. Your body is already using all its energy for healing."

"I know, but if it gets low, I feel wobbly. I wanted to spend time with Stella baking for the girls at the resort as a pleasant treat," Shelby complained.

Stella rested her hand on Alan's arm. "Remember, I gave her the chicken broth? It had carrots and onions in the base. Could that affect the reading?"

Alan winced. "Yes, you're right. Let's hold off and I'll check it again later." He regarded Sam and detective Sanchez. "Shelby needs to rest now. I trust you got the information you came for."

11

A BRIDE AND A BODY

"What's the story of the Kincaids?" Detective Sanchez asked as they drove.

"Are you finally appreciating that relying on long-term relationships with people in a tight-knit community is more effective than big city style interrogations?" Sam chuckled.

He smiled. "I wouldn't go that far. Shelby might be an anomaly, but we all have a dark side. If we feel threatened, there's no telling what we might do."

"What happened to your ex-wife?" Sam chided.

"She's alive and well and taking me to the cleaners for every dime," the detective scoffed. "Speaking of liars, what's the big secret about Shelby's illness? Her husband hovers around her like she might croak at any minute. That doesn't jibe with letting her walk on a remote trail by herself."

Sam shrugged. "It's only a secret to Shelby. After she was diagnosed with cancer, she ended up in the ICU. She thought her back pain was due to stress, but it was an infection in her lung caused by aspiration. She ended up on a ventilator for a few weeks, and the doctors prepared Alan for the worst. The oncologist advised him against sharing the information with Shelby because they didn't want her to feel defeated. Her spirit is extraordinary but knowing they didn't think she would make it to even begin chemo would be a serious blow. Alan asked us to support her in her recovery by staying positive and believing she'll beat it."

"Wow, that's tough!"

"It hit Alan hard. Shelby is his entire world. We were all concerned that if she died, he wouldn't make it either."

"He's a suicide risk?" the detective questioned.

"Probably not, but he would be the type to die of a broken heart. They don't have kids, and they have a unique relationship between themselves. It's an amazing partnership," Sam explained.

"She seems to have a strong connection with her niece and nephews. Where are their parents?" the detective asked.

"The father checked out a while ago. He was a hockey player who chased more than the puck, if you catch my drift. Shelby and Alan were there from the beginning, providing stability while Willow dabbled in various artistic careers. None of them ever panned out. She's in Arizona now, at a hippie compound with her new boyfriend. The eldest nephew, Robert, works at a craft brewery in Bellingham, owned by Casi's family. Riley is an apprentice at the Jensens' wood shop."

"He's marrying Amy, who we are on our way to see," he confirmed.

"Yes, she's the receptionist at the same location. That's how they met," Sam stated.

"Just what I would expect in a rural area," the detective joked.

Sam laughed. "True, but we like our soap opera romances and coffee shop gossip better than big city crime, drugs, and homelessness."

"And yet we are investigating a murder," the detective said.

"Possible murder. It might all add up to nothing more than being in the wrong place at the wrong time. We don't get many killings around here. Mostly drunk driving and domestic disturbances," Sam stated as they walked up the narrow stone path leading to Amy's bungalow, with the fragrance of freshly cut grass and blooming flowers wafting through the air. The house was small but charming, painted a pale yellow with white trim. Whimsical wind chimes dangled from the porch, tinkling gently in the breeze.

"Are there hanging baskets full of flowers in every corner of this town?" the detective asked, taking in the expansive porch with hand-hewn furniture adorned with playful pillows, and bright pots billowing with blooms.

"It's the local ordinance," Sam joked, rapping on the front door.

A lovely woman with soft auburn curls dancing about her cherubic face smiled as she opened the door. "Hi Sam."

"Hello, Amy. This is detective Sanchez," he made the introductions. "May we come in? We have a handful of questions for you. It won't take long."

Amy frowned. "Is Jake, ok?"

Sam chuckled. "No connection to Jake. It's about Kristen Martin. We heard you might have talked to her on the trail the other day."

Amy stepped aside and kept the door open. "Please come in. Excuse the mess. I'm sending out invitations this weekend." They entered the charming bungalow that was styled straight out of a Home and Garden magazine. The aroma of freshly baked cookies mingled with cleaning products. Oversized furniture in various shades of blue accented a feminine room brimming with floral prints and framed photos. The space was bright and meticulously organized, with billowing curtains framing the windows and an array of wedding magazines spread across the dining table. A stack of invitations sat on an antique pine table beside neatly printed envelopes. "I'll have them in the mail on Monday," she said, pointing to one with Sam's name.

"I'm uncertain if I can come," the detective joked.

"Oh, I..." Amy blushed.

"He's teasing, Amy. Big city humor," Sam assured.

"How well did you know Kristen?" the detective asked.

"Um, not well," Amy chewed on her cheek. "Would you like lemonade?" She made her way to the kitchen without waiting for a reply. She came back with tall glasses on a tray beside a plate of cookies. She turned the pitcher to hide a crack on the rim, embarrassed by the defect but proud to display the antique set that looked like a family heirloom. She filled the glasses and set them on coasters featuring photos of Blackberry Falls.

"Thanks, Amy. This is delicious," Sam said, taking a long sip.

"Try a cookie," she urged. "It's Shelby's recipe."

Sam took a bite and smiled. "Strawberries and cream. I haven't had these in a while."

"Riley loves them. He said they were his favorite ones that Shelby made when he was a kid. Please, have a seat," she gestured to the sofa as she sat in an armchair.

They sat on the puffed cushions and toppled together as the stuffing compressed under their combined weight. Sam clung to the arm of the loveseat, avoiding the awkward contact as Detective Sanchez struggled to wiggle forward. "Can you tell me what you know about Kristen?" Sam asked.

"She was temporarily replacing Shelby while she was on medical leave." She shrugged.

"Sure, but how about on a more personal note?" Sam continued. "She was handling your wedding. How was that going?"

"Fine, I guess," Amy looked away. "Actually, Shelby had

done all the work. We had already booked the venue before she got sick." Tears welled in her pretty hazel eyes. "We suggested moving it a month out to make sure Shelby was healthy enough to attend, but Kristen said there weren't any openings."

"Did that upset you? Was Kristen being unreasonable?" the detective pushed.

"No, it was fine. Shelby is doing great with her treatment. She assured us she would be there. Lauren has the perfect menu and even ordered special wines for pairing." Amy beamed. "The cake is from a bakery in Seattle."

Sam leaned forward slightly, the creases on his face deepening. "Amy, we understand you spoke with Kristen not long before her accident on the trail. Are you able to enlighten us about that conversation?"

Amy's expression faltered for a moment, but she quickly composed herself, brushing a stray curl behind her ear. "Yes, we talked, though I didn't consider it significant at the time. She seemed... distracted, maybe a little stressed." She hesitated, her fingers tracing the rim of her glass.

"Did you discuss the wedding?" Detective Sanchez asked.

"No, it's odd. I've seen Kristen a few times at the resort, and she's very professional, but she acted like she didn't recognize me on the trail." Amy laughed. "I like to have fun while I work out. I listen to music and do jogging sprints." She prodded her thighs under her cotton dress. "I'm trying to lose weight before the wedding. I was tempted to try one of those weight loss drugs they show in all the commercials, but Casi said the most effective approach was hiking the trails and eating healthy." She turned toward the detective. "Have you met her? She has an incredible figure! She was right, because I've already lost ten pounds."

Sam reached over and patted her hand. "You look wonderful, Amy, and you'll be a beautiful bride."

"Thank you," she said. "I was completely absorbed in my

thoughts while I was on the trail, and I wouldn't have even noticed Kristen except she was staggering a bit, you know, like a drunk person might do? I didn't recognize her at first because she had her hat down low. I inquired if she was okay, and she kind of snapped at me. She was sweaty although she had just started the trail. I told Riley about it after they found her body." She blanched. "I may have made a mistake by not calling for help when I saw her! I assumed she was just working out intensely. She's lost a bunch of weight, and I see her on the trail a lot. You know how you keep to yourself while you're exercising?" she asked, glancing over their portly shapes that didn't indicate they went to the gym.

Detective Sanchez scribbled notes on his pad and looked up. "Did she say anything specific about anyone? Did she seem afraid?"

Amy shook her head, her brow furrowing in concentration. "No, not afraid. Just... distant. Almost like her mind was elsewhere." She paused, glancing at the invitations on the table. "I was completely preoccupied with my wedding plans; I didn't even think to press her about it."

Sam's gaze lingered on Amy's face, reading her subtle expressions. "Did Kristen mention anything about an argument or tension with anyone?"

Amy's eyes widened slightly. "No, not directly. But since you brought it up, I saw her arguing with someone near the front desk a few days earlier. I didn't catch what they were saying, but it looked tense. I didn't recognize the other person."

The detective nodded. "And you didn't overhear anything?"

"Sorry, no. I just assumed it was work-related. You know how things can get at the resort with all the events." Amy looked away; her attention drawn to the bridal magazines.

"Were they male or female?" Sam asked.

"It was a lady," Amy said. "About my age. Heavy set. It was

probably nothing. Maybe a bride who was unhappy that Shelby wasn't there to manage her wedding."

"Thank you for speaking with us, Amy. We won't take up more of your time. I know you have a lot to do today," Sam stood, taking another cookie from the plate.

"Why did she ask about Jake?" Detective Sanchez inquired when they made their way back to the car.

"He's had a few run-ins with the law. A bar fight and drunk and disorderly. Nothing major and no charges," Sam said, glancing away.

"What are you leaving out?" Sanchez asked. "Do I need to run his name through the system to find out the real story?"

Sam sighed. "Two years ago, there was an issue with Lauren's ex-husband and Casi. Jake went crazy and beat him to a pulp. No charges were officially filed."

"An affair?" he questioned.

"No," Sam clenched his jaw.

"Ok," Sanchez said slowly. "Then why did Casi's brother-in-law take care of it instead of her husband?"

"Because Kyle would have killed him." Sam shrugged. "Jake is very protective of his family. He knew what he needed to do to get justice for Casi and keep his brother from taking it too far."

"Could Jake be a suspect in this case?"

"I highly doubt it. He's on his third wife, and she keeps him in line. He's a hard worker with a bunch of kids. I can't imagine he would have any connection with Kristen," Sam stated.

"He wasn't on the list, but I'm still wary of small-town bad boys. Sometimes the reputation fits the crime," Detective Sanchez said.

12

POSTMORTEM

"Any new information for us?" Detective Sanchez called as he strode down the long, sterile hallway, his footsteps echoing off white tile that had lost its luster, fading to a dingy clinical eggshell.

The woman at the end of the corridor did not look up. Short dark hair cropped close to her head, she moved with purpose, the curve of her figure disguised beneath a white lab coat that mirrored her professional manner. She flipped a page on a clipboard and sighed before responding. "Oliver, I'm already working on the weekend," she said flatly. "I don't need you prowling around the coroner's office like you're in a police procedural. I told you I cannot establish the cause of death beyond blunt force trauma. We're still analyzing bloodwork to determine whether there were contributing factors that caused the fall."

"Or if she was bludgeoned?" Sanchez offered.

She shot him with a razor-sharp look. "Let's not jump to conclusions."

She finally turned her attention to Sam, her expression softening just enough to become approachable rather than irritated. She extended her hand. "Dana Mercer. Chief medical examiner."

"Sam Adakai," he replied, shaking her hand. "Chief of police in Blackberry Falls."

Her gaze flicked to the notebook he carried, then back to his face. "You're out of your jurisdiction and into my world. What do you need?"

Sam nodded toward the file tucked beneath her arm. "Any insight into Kristen Martin's general health? A witness described her behavior as unsteady. Possibly intoxicated. Alcohol could explain a misstep near the edge."

Dana's lips curved slightly. "No alcohol in her system."

"Damn," Sam muttered. "I'm struggling to believe this was a violent attack in the middle of the day on a public trail."

Dana flipped open the folder and adjusted her glasses as Sanchez attempted to peek over her shoulder.

"Knock it off, Oliver," she said without looking at him. "This is above your pay grade and your IQ."

"Ouch," Sanchez said. "Throw us a bone. All we've got is a list of names of people she apparently hated."

Dana hesitated. Then she glanced over her shoulder before lowering her voice. "This stays off the record."

"It's just us," Sanchez assured her, leaning in.

"We found traces of semaglutide in her bloodstream," Dana said.

Both men frowned.

She sighed. "Diabetes drug. More recently marketed for weight loss. It stimulates insulin release and suppresses appetite."

She winked at Sanchez. "You might need a prescription."

He patted his stomach defensively. "This is muscle."

"Could that explain a fall?" Sam asked.

"Unlikely," Dana said. "She had been taking it for at least a year. Her body adjusted. Blood levels suggest she was due for another dose around the time of death."

"Would that cause symptoms that would make her unsteady?" Sanchez asked.

"No," Dana replied. "If anything, it would only increase appetite."

She flipped to photographs. "She had muscle wasting in her limbs. Known side effects. Also increased risk of cardiac events, organ failure."

"And?" Sam prompted.

"And none of those occurred," Dana said bluntly. "She died from a fractured skull. Why she went over the edge is your problem."

"Thanks, Dana," Sanchez said. "I owe you dinner."

"You owe me much more than that," she replied, already walking away.

Outside, Sam glanced at Sanchez. "So. Old flame?"

"In the past," he chuckled. "And hopefully again. That's twice weight loss drugs came up today. Do you think there is a connection?"

"Who else mentioned them?" Sam asked.

"Amy said she considered it," Sanchez said. "Decided not to upon hearing Casi's advice."

"Smart," Sam said. He pulled out a laminated document. "We can skip ahead to Casi."

Sanchez snapped his fingers. "Exactly. Former model. Beauty guru by default."

They pulled into a sprawling home overlooking the lake. Stone pillars framed the entrance, and floor-to-ceiling windows reflected blue water beyond.

"Jake and Kyle built most of it themselves," Sam said. "Wait till you see the view."

Kyle answered the door, brow furrowed. "Why are you knocking? You usually just walk in."

"I'm not alone today," Sam indicated the detective behind him. "Is Casi home?"

Kyle turned toward his wife, wondering if he should intervene as she walked toward them. "Is this police business?" she asked.

"What did you do now?" Jake teased as he wrangled two little boys in the kitchen while a girl with strawberry blonde hair about the same age sat at the counter drinking juice.

"Do you live here, too?" Sanchez asked, stepping into the home without an invitation.

"No, but I should start charging him rent because he's always here," Kyle answered. "He has the house across the street."

Detective Sanchez perused the kitchen, finding interest in the stack of blueberry pancakes dripping with butter. "I take it you aren't on a diet in this household?"

Casi tilted her head, looking svelte in leggings and a T-shirt that conformed to her shapely figure. "Are you in the habit of coming into people's homes on a Saturday and asking rude questions?"

Sam stepped between the sultry blonde and the detective. "Whoa, he didn't mean to imply anything." He jutted his thumb toward the detective. "He's from Seattle. They're short on charm."

Casi scowled. "I'm from Vancouver and lived in LA. What is the reason for your impromptu visit?"

The detective scanned the large living area with a fieldstone fireplace and a breathtaking view of the lake. "Sorry to intrude. We just wanted to clarify a few facts. I've heard you might know something about where to get weight loss medication?"

She folded her arms across her chest. "Why would I need that?"

Kyle's face lost color. "Who said that? Katie was the one..."

Casi stepped in front of Kyle and gave him a look to halt the conversation. "I work for a skincare line. We have no affiliation with the weight loss industry."

Sam cleared his throat. "Actually, Amy said you had advised her not to use medication but to eat a healthy diet instead." Before Casi could respond, he continued. "Since you're a former model and people trust your opinion on beauty topics, we thought you might have heard about a trend of using medications to aid in weight loss."

Casi surprised them when she laughed. "You want me to be the narc who blabs how women have access to drugs without going through a doctor?"

"Snitches get stitches," Jake called from the kitchen.

Sam smiled. "It's likely unrelated to the case. It's just the second time today we heard about these drugs." He paled when he realized he might be revealing confidential information.

Casi poured a substantial quantity of maple syrup over her pancakes. "We all knew Kristen was taking the drugs. Is that what killed her?"

"Wait, how were you aware? Was she open about it?" Sam asked.

Jake placed pancakes in front of the detective. "She's smarter than she looks. Not much gets by her."

Casi shrugged. "Within a few months she dropped around thirty pounds. She was never pleasant, but she turned into a nasty bit..." she noticed the children listening and said, "witch. Her temper was off the hook, and she became very secretive, making little lists, and sending emails to clients without informing managers. We all noticed it, and we were glad that she didn't join us for coffee anymore."

"Did you see her the day she died?" the detective asked.

"Briefly. She skulked into the coffee shop and ordered a

ridiculously complicated drink, then gave Lia a bad time for messing it up," she reported.

"She complained about the coffee?" Sam asked.

"Not verbally, just with an evil eye that indicated she was unhappy before she even tasted it," Casi said. "I didn't acknowledge her because we had already had an argument about stuff, and I vowed to wait it out until Shelby could come back and then Kristen would be out of there."

"What stuff?" the detective said.

"Work stuff," she remarked brusquely. "It's not associated with her demise, I assure you."

"How can you be sure?" he pressed.

She leaned forward. "Kristen created an inventory of people she disliked with a declaration of retaliation. When someone is that miserable, it's not jaw dropping when they kick it."

"Sounds like she had some enemies," the detective challenged.

"She was her own worst enemy. No one knew or would have cared about her stupid list," Casi said.

"But you knew about it," Sanchez said.

"Yes, because she was foolish enough to jot it down on a notepad in the office. I noticed the indentation when I worked at the party the other night and needed to take down a phone number. I could see my name written on it, so I was intrigued. I colored it over with a pencil and saw the whole ridiculous thing. I went over to her house later that night, and I planned on firing her," Casi said.

"For writing the list?" Sanchez asked.

"I'm not twelve," she huffed. "Blowing off an event was cause for dismissal. Ultimately, it would take approval from the Board, but I wanted to tell her I was recommending it."

"Why not just let her be surprised?" he asked.

"I don't play games, especially in business," she said. "I wanted Kristen to hear from me how her attitude was poisoning the organization. Her list referred to revenge, and I would not stand by and allow her to harm my friends, especially Shelby, whose name was at the top." She straightened, the practiced composure returning instantly. The former model who had learned young how to control what the world was allowed to see. LA had taught her to fight for what she wanted. Blackberry Falls had given her restraint. "You should consider that she wasn't just cataloguing people she disliked. She was documenting leverage."

Sanchez leaned back slightly. "That's a serious assumption."

"It's an experienced one," she corrected. "People who feel powerless find ways to be in control. Kristen wanted more than she deserved. She had a victim mentality."

Sam shifted uncomfortably. "You're starting to make this sound more sinister than a simple fall."

Casi narrowed her eyes. "Reality can be dark."

Jake held out the syrup. "Casi's lived on the wild side," he offered lightly. "Life before small towns and pancake breakfasts."

"Shut it, Jake," she warned.

Sanchez seized the opening. "Care to share more?"

Sam stepped in smoothly before Sanchez could push. "We're not here to reopen your past."

Casi smiled, slow and knowing. "Good. Because I didn't invite you to." She reached for her coffee and took a deliberate sip, eyes never leaving Sam. "Kristen wasn't as isolated as she wanted people to believe. And maybe she dabbled in things she shouldn't have." She smiled again, that polished, dangerous smile that had once sold magazine covers and now closed deals. "And just maybe, someone got tired of her little games."

Kyle cringed, realizing her words could be perceived as a threat. "Sam, do we need a lawyer?"

"Doubtful," Sam said with a grin. The detective frowned at him, hoping they had just heard a confession. "Casi went over there around midnight after the event ended. She was fired up regarding the list and Kristen's perceived incompetence and intended to have a serious discussion with her."

"Sounds like a motive to me," Sanchez said.

"Except Kristen had already been dead for about fourteen hours. A murderer would have known," Sam concluded.

13

———

CLEAN SLATE

"Happy Sunday," Casi announced brightly as she stepped inside.

Alan glanced at the open door and laughed. "We will need to start locking it. People keep letting themselves in."

"I come bearing gifts," Casi said, holding up the pink bakery box, "and I hear they're only murdering people on the trails these days."

"They might expand the perimeter," Alan deadpanned. "Start canvassing the neighborhood."

"Unlikely," Casi replied, slipping out of her shoes and setting the box down. "Killing a person in their home is messy. Too many personal variables. Outside is easier."

Shelby blinked from her recliner. "That's... disturbingly logical."

"The trail is ideal," Casi continued. "Naturally contaminated. DNA everywhere. You couldn't design a better location."

Shelby nodded thoughtfully. "High traffic, unpredictable footfall, and overlapping evidence streams. I'm surprised more crimes don't happen there."

"Kyle says it was the make-out spot of his youth," Casi added.

"I'm sure he was very popular there," Shelby chuckled.

Casi turned her attention fully to Shelby. "How are you today?"

Shelby smiled meekly. "A bit rough. Pain here." She gestured toward her collarbones. "They say it's the stent adjusting."

Casi's expression softened, but her eyes sharpened. "You shouldn't be in pain and bored. That's a terrible combination."

"I've exhausted my crime novels," Shelby admitted. "Even the murders blur together."

"Then you need a palate cleanser," Casi said, handing her the box.

"Casi, I'm sorry, but she still can't eat. I can freeze it until later," Alan said, reaching for the box.

"Let me just smell it," Shelby protested, opening the lid. She laughed and withdrew the lavender T-shirt with the looping scroll of a design on the front. "What does it mean?"

"It's the Sanskrit symbol for *Breathe*," Casi said. "You mentioned that was your only job right now. You were looking less than fashionable in Alan's shirt the other day. I thought you might like one that fits properly. It will be nice and light for when you head back out on the trail."

"I love it!" Shelby said, holding it to her chest. "I'll wear it to chemo on Wednesday. I've been dressing like a frumpy old lady in dark oversized clothes." She turned to Alan. "Perhaps I can take a walk after I'm done. I've been watching the weather channel all morning, and it looks like we're in for several nice days coming up."

Casi regarded the drizzle outside the window and hoped the forecast was correct. "Where's Stella?"

"She got here on Friday, but she went to help Amy finish her invitations. The poor girl was worried she wouldn't get them done in time to mail tomorrow. She's very rigid with her schedule. It seems bride syndrome has kicked in."

"Amy is super organized. That's one of the things they love about her at the wood shop." She grasped Shelby's hand. "You got your nails done. I thought you couldn't get a manicure yet?"

"Stella did them," Shelby remarked, waving her hand. "She was very gentle and used natural products. She gave me a pedicure too."

"That's fabulous. I'm sure she's happy to be home for a bit. She asked about getting a waitressing job at the resort. What do you guys think about that? It would be a great way for her to make money while she's here," Casi stated.

"That would be a wonderful opportunity," Shelby agreed. "It would be beneficial for her to keep busy. I want her to have fun, not be my caregiver."

"That job is already taken," Alan teased.

"Correct, and no one can replace you," Shelby beamed.

Casi smiled. "I'll tell her to talk to Jocelyn this week. I know they need more help. Lauren said it's already been incredibly busy, and we have a multitude of events booked." She turned her gaze toward Alan. "If you're interested in going out for the afternoon, I can hang out with Shelby."

"I'm fine," Alan shrugged.

"Let me rephrase that," Casi laughed. "Can you go watch sports with Kyle? I want to talk about girl stuff with Shelby."

"What are your qualifications as a caregiver?" he asked, calculating the time left on the feeding schedule and Shelby's overall condition.

"I can fetch water, give positive affirmations, and call 911," Casi shrugged. "People seem to think I'm good with babies, and I haven't dropped one yet."

Alan chuckled and tugged on a ball cap as he planted a kiss on the top of Shelby's head. "I'll return in a couple of hours.

Don't do anything crazy." He regarded his list on the white-board, mentally confirming everything was complete.

Shelby waited until she heard his car back out of the drive-way. "Is everything okay at work? I could come in a few afternoons."

"We're fine, but I'll keep that in mind. I wanted to have a conversation with you about my visit with the police yesterday," Casi explained.

"The detective from the sheriff's office?" Shelby asked. "Don't you think he has a lopsided head?"

"It's the way he wears his hair short on the sides and longer on top, like a garnish," Casi giggled.

"Oh, that's it!" Shelby agreed.

"He came by with Sam. They were trying to play good cop, bad cop, but they had the rhythm all wrong. They accidentally revealed that Kristen was taking weight loss medication, and I'm sure they weren't supposed to spill the beans on that," Casi said.

"Oh, then it's true! I wondered about that. She lost weight quickly and got awfully crabby." Shelby said. "I considered bariatric surgery in the past." She cast a glance at her feeding tube. "I opted out because it seemed risky. Who knew I would get a similar surgery due to cancer? I'm afraid I'll never have the capability to eat properly again." She sighed and cocked her head. "Do they think that's what killed her? I've heard there can be side effects."

"They gave the impression that it was something else, but they seem to be investigating it as a murder," Casi said.

"Do you think there really is a killer running around town? Why would they target her?" Shelby asked.

"They tried to be sly about a list but failed on that one too," Casi laughed, pulling a note from her handbag. "Your name is at the top." She quickly pulled the paper back. "I'm sorry. I forgot we aren't supposed to upset you. That was very insensitive."

"I'm not upset, more like intrigued. Let me see the details." Shelby extended her hand. "I wonder if there is an order to this or if she wrote it randomly? It's not alphabetical."

"It appears she wrote it down by date of the imaginary offense. It's chronological," Casi said.

"Oh." Shelby's eyes widened. "But what did I do?"

"By my calculations, you're on top because you're patient zero," Casi laughed.

"Like a virus," Shelby frowned.

"Pretty much. Once you were diagnosed with cancer, Kristen moved into your position. She had already been employed with the company, but the promotion came with a lot more responsibilities," Casi said.

"That benefited her," Shelby pointed out.

"It did, except you didn't die, which meant you would come back and take the job she felt she deserved," Casi said.

"I'm very selfish for living," Shelby chuckled. She squinted at the paper to decipher the smudged combinations of letters and symbols. "I don't understand. What does that signify?"

"I'm not sure." Casi captured an image of the content with her phone and enlarged it. "Do you have something to write on?"

Shelby eyed the large whiteboard on the wall. "Perhaps we should start listing clues. It seems you figured out more details than the cops did, with a lot less information."

Casi took a photo of Alan's directions on the board and hovered over it with a towel. "Speak up if you don't want me to erase it. Alan invested a great deal of effort into this, and I know he's incredibly methodical."

"That's because he's a fiduciary advisor. Numbers are his life," Shelby laughed. "I'm tired of those rules, anyway. Half of them don't apply anymore. He keeps trying to test my blood sugar, but it's supposed to be at least two hours of fasting, and he forgets that my nutritional feed is glucose-based."

"Why do they do that if you can't taste it?" Casi asked.

"It's designed to be taken by mouth or as a liquid supplement for feeding tubes. Glucose is the body's primary source of energy. Most people get enough from regular food, which is converted into glucose from sugars and starches during digestion and absorbed into the bloodstream. Insulin helps it enter cells to be used for energy, even breathing. It's crucial for the brain, and I especially need that."

"You sound like Google," Casi teased.

"That's because I memorized the pamphlet," Shelby laughed. "It was by mistake. I had nothing to read in the hospital without my tablet, and the diabetic counselor left me a leaflet. It was before I started chemo, so the information got stuck in my head."

"Why do you need insulin if you have elevated blood glucose levels? Wouldn't you just have tons of energy?" Casi read the board with the blood glucose numbers and how many units of insulin would be needed.

"When the body doesn't need glucose right away, it stores it as glycogen in the liver and muscles, or converts it to fat," Shelby explained.

"Huh, but you're losing weight already," Casi said.

"I've leveled out," Shelby frowned at Joey Kangaroo. "They won't let me reduce the number of cartons because it's the perfect combination of calories, protein, nutrients, and glucose. I'm not allowed to lose more weight until after surgery."

Casi erased the board. "It's a good thing Alan is in charge. These numbers and rules would have my head spinning."

Shelby regarded the clean space. "It was nice for Alan to have the perception of power over this cancer. I'm ready to gain a bit more independence."

"Great, shall we put the roster of names? We can add things

about each person as we go over their interactions with Kristen, specifically in the past couple of weeks. You should definitely come to the coffee shop on Wednesday, and you can begin your investigation." Casi stepped back and regarded her work. "I'm uncertain about my ability to replicate the symbols. I wonder what her intentions were with all this secret spy stuff?"

"I can't imagine what she had in mind or what most of this means, but if this list was important enough to create, it might have been motivation to kill her because of it," Shelby stated.

14

FRACTURED TRUST

"I don't understand," Alan said, his voice tight as he stared at the whiteboard where his meticulous medication chart had once lived. In its place sprawled a chaotic constellation of names, arrows, symbols, and question marks that looked more like a conspiracy theorist's wall than a caregiving plan.

"Casi and I were going over the collection of names, and we needed a place to put them so we could continue to add clues," Shelby explained.

"You could have used a notebook," Alan suggested.

"Yes, but we wanted a large visual to help us piece together the sequence of events," she said. "There are a lot of new clues and motives keep popping up."

"That's the job of the police, Shell Bell. I know you like your crime stories and solving mysteries, but genuine investigative work is a lot more complicated than that," he said.

"The police can continue to do the boring part," Shelby laughed. "Casi and I reasoned we know the residents of this town better than the police do, even Sam."

"I don't know if I like your involvement in this. What if the killer strikes again?" Alan ran his finger over colorful circles containing clues. "This is permanent marker."

"We became engrossed in designing our clue map, and I didn't realize we used the markers from the desk," Shelby explained.

Alan frowned. "It took me a considerable amount of time to create the medication list."

"Casi snapped a photo before she erased it. I forwarded it to your phone," she said.

He stared at his phone and grunted. "I'll blame Casi if your medication times get messed up."

"For goodness' sakes, you've been doing this for weeks. We finished the antibiotic regimen. It's straightforward now," Shelby scoffed. "It could be an opportunity for me to take more responsibility to free you up."

"I enjoy doing it," Alan said, turning to a sudden interruption at the front door.

"You like being the one in control," Shelby muttered.

"Hello," Alan said, looking past the two police detectives on the porch. "Where's Sam? Is this a follow-up about the woman at the trail? Shelby's resting right now. We just got home from radiation."

"The Chief is taking care of local business today. This is detective Ames," Detective Sanchez said. "She has questions about Kristen Martin." He eyed the whiteboard. "Engaging in a bit of amateur crime-solving?"

Shelby laughed. "Since chemo, details don't stay in my head for long. I needed a visual to see what's what."

Detective Ames stepped forward, annoyed to see the list on the board. "It seems you have information that was only known to the police."

"There was another copy of the list," Shelby stated, not elaborating.

"Hmm, perhaps the police chief is too close to this case,"

Ames said, scowling at Gus. "Could you please take the dog outside?"

"He's not aggressive," Alan said.

"I have allergies," she said. Alan tapped his thigh for Gus to trot over, giving one last glance to the intruders before he was taken to the backyard. "Thanks," she said curtly, opening her notebook.

"I really don't think I have anything else to say in addition to what I've already mentioned," Shelby said, feeling suddenly tired.

"That's fine," Detective Ames said.

Detective Sanchez nodded. "We've confirmed the times you were at the lake, Mrs. Kincaid, and it wouldn't have been possible for you to be on the rim trail and return to the pathway below during the time Ms. Martin fell."

"Or was pushed," Detective Ames stated.

"Then why are you here?" Alan asked, disapproving of the way the detectives looked around the house, picking up medications and reading labels. "Please don't touch those. I have a particular order for keeping Shelby on schedule," he said, lamenting the loss of his whiteboard again.

"Actually, we are here to ask you a few questions." Detective Ames said.

"Me? I don't have anything else to contribute to what Shelby already told you," Alan said.

"You can start by telling us about your relationship with the deceased," Detective Ames said.

"Alan didn't know her," Shelby said. "She worked with me. Until I got sick, he never knew most of my coworkers unless they were the wives of his friends."

"She never came to bring you flowers or a homemade casserole? Some small-town gesture of kindness, perhaps like coming to see how your husband was coping while you were in the hospital?" The detective said.

"I doubt it," Shelby said. "Kristen wasn't that type of friend." She noted Alan's face turning pale and the detectives' eyes reflecting a glimmer of suspicion. "If Kristen brought a meal to my poor husband while I was receiving medical care, I'm sure it was meant to be thoughtful, just like everyone else in town who has supported us." Shelby gulped as she remembered how Casi suggested Kristen might have been disappointed that she didn't die so she could keep her job, which made her become number one on the list. But why would she console Alan? He wasn't involved with the resort.

"Are we disturbing your thoughts?" the detective asked, obviously waiting for an answer and noticing Shelby had drifted away.

"I apologize. I'm exhausted and quite nauseous," Shelby said, swallowing acid as it arose in her throat. Shelby's vision fractured, colors bursting at the edges. Heat surged through her body as the room swam by in waves.

"Nauseous?" Alan repeated. "That rarely happens until Friday. Should I get your medication?" He froze, feeling unprepared for the unusual timing of the symptoms.

"We'll be quick," Detective Ames said. "Or Alan could accompany us to the police station in Seattle while you relax."

"It's necessary for me to stay here with my wife," Alan fumed.

"Ah, then explain how you knew Kristen Martin," she repeated.

Alan shifted his gaze downwards, and Detective Sanchez expedited the questioning in case Shelby got ill, noticing she had gotten pale, and beads of perspiration were erupting on her forehead. "Mr. Kincaid, we know you've been meeting with Ms. Martin in private at a motel, not the resort, since your wife became sick. During her hospitalization, it has been reported that Ms. Martin was at your home quite often."

"Alan!" Shelby gasped. "Tell them they're confused. I'm sure it's that nosy Mrs. Gregory up the street making up these lies. That woman has nothing better to do than gossip about the neighbors."

Alan rubbed his neck. "Um, I did meet with her, but it's not what you think."

"Really? We're thinking of several scenarios. One being that you were carrying on an affair while your wife was hospitalized. It's not unusual for a man to turn to someone for comfort when he's distressed. Maybe Kristen wanted to continue the relationship once Shelby got well, and you had to shut her up?"

Alan blanched. "That's outrageous!"

"Then could you clarify what you were doing in those covert meetings? We would also like to know what you were doing on the trail on the same day Ms. Martin was found dead there?"

"I was waiting for Shelby," Alan combed his fingers through his hair. "I promised to be at the last point on the trail to pick her up."

"Except you were seen leaving your car, and a witness saw you having a heated argument with Ms. Martin during the period she would have fallen." Detective Ames stepped toward him. "You can tell us the truth. Maybe she got upset and fell? You wouldn't be responsible for her death."

"No, that's not what happened," Alan stammered.

Stella entered quietly into the cozy kitchen through the side entrance, not wanting to interrupt the conversation in the living room. She couldn't place the police officers and assumed they were following up on the accident at the lake. She noted Shelby appeared to be at an odd angle, partially slumped in her recliner as her uncle explained something to the detective. Stella's heart raced as she noticed her aunt's face was pale, and her breathing was shallow. "Aunt Shelby?" Stella called softly, approaching her. "Are you okay?" Shelby glanced at Stella with a bewildered, detached expression. Stella quickly located the glucose monitor, and Shelby's eyes rolled back as Stella pierced her skin before placing a bead of blood on the test strip.

Alan turned to the soft moan escaping Shelby's lips. "What's going on?" he asked, wondering why Stella was hovering over her.

"Her blood sugar is fifty-two!" Stella stated. "She could go into a coma."

"She didn't say she wasn't feeling well," Alan swiftly moved to her side. "Should I get her glucose tablets? Normally, she takes a few when she feels a bit off." His hands shook as he searched through the basket for the bottle.

"She can't communicate effectively when her sugar is so low. We need to bring it up quickly," Stella returned with a small bowl of sugar mixed with water to make a paste, placing a spoonful directly under Shelby's tongue. "This is the fastest way to get it to enter her bloodstream. Let this dissolve and then swallow," Stella said firmly, kneeling beside her aunt. "It'll help you feel better."

Alan hung back, feeling helpless as he gripped the bottle of tablets in his hand. "How much sugar should we give her?"

"My mom usually needs about a tablespoon or two to bring her back up," Stella reasoned.

After two doses of sugar, Shelby's breathing steadied, and her eyes focused on the surrounding faces. She mustered a weak smile. "Thank you, Stella," she murmured. "I was completely consumed by these questions; I didn't notice the symptoms."

The detective surveyed the scene. "Are you a nurse?"

"My mom has hypoglycemia, and she can decline quickly. I can recognize the signs in an instant." Stella stated.

"Mr. Kincaid, It would be a wise idea for you to come with us to the police station in Seattle," Detective Sanchez said. "We need to clarify a few more details and the Blackberry Falls precinct isn't properly equipped for the task."

"I need to stay here to take care of my wife," Alan said.

"Like you attended to Ms. Martin on the rim trail?" Ames uttered with a sneer. "Was the plan to run off together, but then your wife survived? Was Kristen's demise a result of an accident, or did she jump when you refused to leave your marriage?" She eyed Shelby. "Maybe this act of caring for your wife is an attempt for you to have control of her medications, and no one will be surprised if she suddenly fades away. You're a fiduciary advisor, right? I imagine you are quite excellent with numbers. What type of life insurance do you have on your wife?"

"That's enough!" Alan yelled.

"Go with them to Seattle," Shelby said. "For once in my life, I'm not comfortable with you here."

15

THE WEIGHT OF SECRETS

"Aunt Shelby, do you really think Uncle Alan could be capable of murder?" Stella asked tearfully. He was the closest thing she had to a father, and she couldn't fathom losing him.

"Of course not," Shelby laughed.

"But you said you didn't feel comfortable with him," Stella said.

"I needed those people out of my home," Shelby explained. "I was in the midst of an episode, and they kept coming up with ludicrous ways Alan could have killed Kristen and farfetched reasons why."

"But now he's down at the police station. Do you think they will arrest him?" Stella asked.

"He's better off there," Shelby said, patting her pockets. "Where's my phone?"

"We can't let him go to prison," Stella wailed, searching the counter.

"Don't be silly. He wouldn't answer their questions because he didn't want to upset me. He's been in protection mode since my diagnosis. He was squirming around, looking like he was about to pass out, for goodness sakes," Shelby said.

"You don't believe he was in a romantic relationship with Kristen?" Stella asked.

"Oh, lord no!" Shelby laughed. "Your uncle has been in love with me since the fifth grade. He was all arms and legs, like a Great Dane puppy. Thankfully, he grew into those limbs, and it served him well when he was a star basketball player. I still made him wait until we graduated college before I said yes to a date, though."

"Why did you wait until then? Didn't you like him?" Stella asked.

"I wanted to have fun and go out with a few boys first." Shelby smiled. "I knew once I began dating Alan, we would get married. We were always meant to be together. He might admire how another woman looks occasionally, but he's not interested in anything beyond that. He loves me for who I am, and he's committed to our marriage. He's a good-hearted man." She sighed. "If I recall correctly, Kristen's mother passed away last year from cancer. I realize the promotion to my job was a helpful tool in her healing, but I can't comprehend why she felt like a victim or what this talk of retaliation was about."

"Here's your phone," Stella said, extracting it from the seat cushions. "Why do you believe he was meeting Kristen?"

"That's why we need Sam. I'll bet he knows," Shelby said.

"Do you think he'll tell us?" Stella asked.

"Not a chance. He's known Alan even longer than I have. They were thick as thieves since they were little boys," Shelby said. "It was peculiar that the detectives came without him. They thought they could rattle Alan if Sam wasn't here."

"It seems to have worked," Stella stated.

"They will try to shake him down, but Alan is as honest as the day is long," Shelby quoted. "I'll call Sam and have him go to Seattle. He won't stand for these shady police procedures."

ALAN RETURNED a few hours later with a sheepish smile, full of apologies and concern for Shelby's health. He looked disheveled, having a nervous habit of raking his fingers through his hair as if it somehow sparked his thought process. His shirt and been tucked in and out so many times it had become misshapen and hung loosely over his slim hips, giving him the appearance of being lopsided. Stella kissed his cheek as she left for work, and Shelby looked him up and down. "Did they torture you?"

"Only mentally," Alan sighed. "Shelby, you know I didn't have a thing with Kristen. That was just nonsense."

"I know you aren't a killer or a cheater," Shelby stated. "It's time to be honest, though. These secrets aren't healthy. You want to protect me, but I'm more anxious now than when I was diagnosed. Am I dying and you're trying to keep me in the dark?"

"No!" Alan's expression shattered, releasing the pain he had internalized for months. "That's just it..." He poured a glass of water and pushed a footstool over to sit beside her. "You almost did, Shell. I was devastated, and I didn't know what to do."

"Did you really have an affair?" Shelby swallowed, wincing at the discomfort in her chest. "Perhaps I would prefer to remain ignorant of this. We can get through my treatment and then talk about it later." She nodded to indicate the topic was off limits for now.

He extended his arm to hold her hand. "We'll talk about it now. You're right, this anxiety isn't good for either of us." He brushed a tear from her cheek. "When you went in for your back pain, they did two surgeries to help your lung. They ended up removing a portion that could not be re-inflated. You coded, and they put you on a ventilator." A sob caught in his throat. "I was completely lost. I couldn't sleep, and I was a mess at work. I told them I needed to work remotely so I could schedule my time around visiting you at the hospital. I sat at the end of your bed and rubbed your feet, begging you to wake up."

"Oh," was all Shelby could muster, not being prepared for the severity of her ordeal.

"When you woke up, you went into Atrial Fibrillation twice where your heart was beating erratically. Do you remember that part?"

"I remember being on the floor with that nice nurse, Morgan, holding my head in his lap. The cardiologist declared I was sturdy and should be fine," Shelby said, thinking it was an insult about her weight at the time, but maybe it was intended as a compliment.

"Right, he didn't have the best bedside manner," Alan smiled. "That's when the chaplain came to speak with you." He exhaled. "I saw how you responded to him, and I asked Sam if he knew a place where I could get help, too."

"That was an excellent idea. He certainly would know how to handle tough things like that," Shelby agreed.

"He told me about a grief group that gathered in a banquet room at the motel on Brook Street. I didn't know who Kristen was back then, but she recognized me," he said.

"Was she there because of her mother?" Shelby asked.

"We aren't really supposed to discuss it outside of the group, but I suppose it's irrelevant now. Yes, she was having trouble accepting that her mother was gone. She had been her caregiver for years and put off dating or having a family of her own. She was struggling between loneliness and resentment for what she sacrificed. One of the group rules is to keep topics general, but we are encouraged to meet up in pairs to work through deeper issues. She visited the house to bring information about chemo and things like advanced directives. It helped me a lot to talk with her and the group." He bit his lip. "I started to feel guilty when you made a miraculous recovery, and we were suddenly back on track to begin the regimen. I was hesitant to share my good news when people were still dealing with terrible losses. When you came home, I didn't need them like I did before. I wanted to be supportive, but I had a full plate with so many special medical needs."

Shelby laughed. "I am a handful right now."

He inched forward and put his forehead to hers. "I'll take every minute of caring for you as a gift." He looked up in horror. "You've been off the feeding tube for way too long! You're behind on your schedule."

Shelby squeezed his hand. "Alan, breathe. I won't starve. First, tell me if you met up with Kristen on the trail like they said."

"I did," he squeezed his eyes shut. "After I dropped you off, I thought I should get a walk of my own in. I've been very lazy lately. I took the rim trail, figuring I could do a quick lap and be back at the car before you completed your mile."

"Show off," she giggled.

"I made it to the peak of the trail and saw Kristen coming the other way. I tried to backtrack because it was awkward to interact with her in public. She's a very private person, and I wasn't sure if I should acknowledge her," he sighed. "She had tried to contact me a few weeks ago. It was non-stop phone calls, and I was apprehensive she may have taken my interest in her mental health the wrong way.

"The snitch said you had a heated argument," Shelby recalled.

Alan laughed at her choice of words. "I have no idea who reported that. When I realized Kristen had seen me, I decided it might be wise to have the discussion out in the open. I asked her if we could talk. I figured we could walk the trail and meet you at the bottom and tell you about the group we belonged to. It seemed like the perfect way to broach the subject."

"That sounds reasonable," Shelby said. "It would have been nice to speak with Kristen about her mom's journey through cancer. I look at it differently now, and I wish I had been more supportive."

"I had hoped that would be the outcome. Instead, she became irate and talked gibberish. She behaved as though she had no idea who I was and was infuriated by my presence. She lashed out at me and shoved me out of the way," Alan reported.

"Oh no, I hope you didn't accidentally push her off the trail!" She covered her mouth with her hand.

"No! I reversed and jogged towards the car and left her there. I considered she might be on drugs, and I had no intention of being caught up in a public display. I assumed she would calm down, and we could discuss it later. I even went to the group the next day hoping she was there."

"But she wasn't because she was dead," Shelby cringed.

Alan chuckled. "Well, that's blunt, but accurate." He grasped her hands. "When you didn't show up at the last part of the trail and I saw the ambulance..." he shivered with emotion. "I speculated maybe she had attacked you. She was behaving so strangely. At the sight of the cuts and blood on you, I almost had a heart attack."

"I must confess it's a bit surreal to get attention when you're sick or suffering a loss. I've certainly been treated wonderfully by all the nurses, doctors, and people coming around to ensure my well-being. I didn't consider how it might have felt for Kristen when no one cared about her losing her mother anymore. Even her attempts at being revolutionary at work were met with skepticism and doubt, as she was constantly compared to me. It probably was comforting when you paid attention to her in the group." Shelby patted Alan's hand. "You're immeasurably kind, and a wonderful listener. Then she's thrust to the background again when I was healthy enough to come home."

"That could be true, Shel, but you were seriously ill. That's different," Alan said.

"She was closer in age than I am to most of the ladies at the resort, yet she was rarely included in the coffee meet ups or social events. I can only imagine how lonely she must have felt." She tilted her head. "I'm curious if she threw herself over the edge. Perhaps she just intended to experience a minor fall to garner sympathy, and it went utterly wrong when her head struck a rock."

16

MUFFINS AND MOTIVE

"We should leave it to the police to handle," Lauren urged.

Heads nodded around the table and Shelby sighed, "I'm convinced they're grasping at straws. I mean, they took Alan to Seattle and interrogated him for hours. It's ridiculous, he's just...you know, Alan. He's hardly an adulterer or a murderer, for goodness sakes."

"He definitely lacks motive," Gail agreed. "What actions do you believe we can take that the police can't? Is Sam involved again? That was sneaky that they questioned Alan without him present."

"I did not care for that female detective either. The potato head stood back and let her spew all kinds of wild theories," Shelby said.

"Was she his superior?" Mary Ann asked.

"It seemed like it. I get the titles mixed up." Shelby exhaled. "I know Kristen wasn't exactly well liked, but she was a member of this community. We're obligated to find out if it was an accident or if someone hurt her. Wouldn't you want us to do that if it was you or your friend?"

"Kristen was my friend." Jocelyn shook her head.

Shelby reached over and squeezed her hand. "I realize you had a coffee group before we worked together. I'm honored I was included once you relocated here."

"I was never included in the original group," Lia stated, setting down a tray of blackberry streusel muffins.

"Probably because it was Gail's group of friends and you weren't exactly welcome after you slept with her husband," Lauren chastised.

Gail laughed. "That's all water under the bridge. Let's not revisit our past mistakes. I'm not proud of how I treated Jake at the end of our marriage. As the group founders, Mary Ann, Jocelyn, and I are happy that you all joined us at this beautiful new location. Heck, we even let Casi in, and we didn't like her in the beginning."

Mary Ann smiled. "Thankfully, we have all grown up a bit and realized the error of our ways." She turned to Shelby. "What do the police think happened to Kristen?"

"They are all over the place. This doesn't seem to be a major case for them. They would prefer to classify it as an accident and be done with it," Shelby explained.

"Perhaps that would be best," Lia said. "I only know what I've seen on TV, but it seems like they dig into people's personal lives when they're investigating a crime. That seems uncomfortable."

"Are you hiding a big secret?" Lauren teased her sister. "There's much that happens around here that could be considered scandalous."

"You wouldn't mind if they asked you about Dalton?" Lia said.

Lauren scowled. "My ex-husband is in jail, and everyone knows it. Maddy and I are fine without him." She grabbed a muffin and tore it in half. She generously spread it with jam before taking a bite, settling into her chair with a sigh.

Mary Ann rubbed her temples. "I don't know. I'm not saying we shouldn't try to help, but what if we make things worse? Imagine if we come too close and expose ourselves to danger?"

The group fell into silence, each of them weighing the risks. Lia glanced nervously around the coffee shop, concerned they might be overheard. "We don't know who we're dealing with. If we become too involved, we could be next."

Gail bit her lip, tapping her finger against the rim of her coffee cup. "But if we wait for the police, we could lose our chance to discover the truth. What if they miss something?"

Lauren nodded. "Maybe we don't have to do it alone. We could gather more information, be smart about it, and hand over anything we find to the police. That way, we don't put ourselves directly in harm's way."

Shelby smiled when Casi walked in, tapping away on her cell phone. "Let's ask an expert. Casi, should we consider trying to figure out what happened to Kristen or let the police do it?"

Casi looked up from her phone. "Why am I the expert?"

"Jake and Kyle claim you're the world's best snoop," Gail teased.

Casi threw her head back and laughed. "Ok, well, that's true." She regarded the group. "Even though I'm the newest resident of Blackberry Falls, you guys have included me in your clique. We owe it to Kristen to ensure the police are given the proper information, to ensure they are thorough." She gave them a wry smile. "And if we unearth anything unrelated that doesn't have any association with why she ended up dead, it stays with us."

"That's a suitable compromise," Shelby agreed. She took a notepad from her purse with a yawn. "Sorry, I have about an hour before nap time. Alan is even more regimented about my schedule since I had my last episode."

"Is he still perturbed that I erased his precious whiteboard?" Casi giggled.

"He maintains it's your fault that he got rattled when the police were questioning him. He doesn't like his routine altered," Shelby said. She taped her pen to the open page. "Where should we begin?"

"It might be a good idea to duplicate the list of names and then write motives," Casi suggested.

"What list?" Gail asked.

Casi looked at Shelby. "Should we tell them?"

Shelby nodded. "Apparently, Kristen created a roster of names of people she had an issue with. It was a convoluted plan for retaliation. My name was first."

"Because she was engaged in a secret relationship with your husband?" Gail joked. "What number was I?"

Shelby laughed. "Casi and I figured out that I was first because I'm getting better and will eventually take my job back." She smiled at Gail. "Your name wasn't on it."

"Wow, that's rude," Gail said.

"What about me?" Mary Ann asked. "I didn't really know her."

"You're not there either," Casi confirmed. "It's Shelby, Lia, Lauren, Jocelyn, and I'm last. There are weird symbols and letters by each name that we haven't figured out yet."

Lia looked up from her coffee. "I didn't do anything."

"Um, none of us did," Casi stated. "It obviously seems to be about people she had direct contact with. Gail works at the daycare, and Kristen doesn't have kids. Mary Ann is in our coffee group but doesn't work at the resort."

"What about Anna?" Gail asked about Jake's third wife. "She looks like she could be a killer. I bet she would be crafty though and poison the victim rather than shove them off a cliff."

Casi laughed. "Anna would hire a hitman. She couldn't be bothered to do it herself. But consider the list probably isn't who killed her. Someone could have been protecting us or trying to hide information we might have had that could potentially expose them for another crime."

"Then Gail could be the killer and be covering for an acquaintance on the list," Jocelyn surmised.

"True, but she lacks motive," Shelby said. "Her ties are to Jake because they have kids, and Lia since she's been babysitting her boys from the time they were born."

"It's not because I lack the ability to look after my own children," Lia pouted.

Shelby blushed, and Gail rushed to defend her. "That's not what she meant. But she's correct that I lack motivation. If Kristen hurt my kids, or your boys, that would be another story. I would take her down in an instant."

"We are getting ahead of ourselves," Shelby said. "I have our five names…"

"But why is my name on there?" Lia lamented.

"Lia! It isn't a list of possible murderers," Lauren said. "How would Kristen know who was going to kill her before it even happened?"

Casi suppressed a laugh. "Obviously, any of us could be a murderer. In my opinion, we need to figure out why the list was created and go from there. We can establish connections and patterns and determine what is related to the list and decide if we should turn over evidence to the police."

"Shouldn't we tell the police everything?" Lia fretted.

"Not if it's unrelated to the case," Casi asserted. She noticed Lia fidgeting with the strings on her apron, which indicated she was feeling stressed. "Look, Lia, we don't even know if Kristen was murdered. It's more likely that she tripped and fell. If the list is a personal vendetta, why do we want the cops involved?"

"Right, it comes down to motive," Shelby said, forging ahead with the original conversation.

"For instance, Shane could have been mad that you had a

conflict with Kristen. He was at the lake. Maybe he did it," Casi teased.

Lia's eyes watered. "Shane wouldn't do that. He's too sweet."

"I'm sure your second husband isn't a killer," Lauren joked. "Maybe it was Jake? He can be unpredictable."

"Jake's too busy working and raising kids to worry about what Kristen was up to," Gail said. "Plus, if he had a problem with her, he would let Kyle fix it as always."

Casi smiled. "Kyle is very diplomatic and a good brother. He would be more disciplined in his murder technique, though. Plus, he only just discovered the existence of the list, and it was the day after she was killed." She studied the piece of paper carefully. "Hey guys, there's another entry at the bottom. I didn't notice it before because I stopped with my name."

"Whose name is it?" Gail asked.

"I hope it's me. I want to be included with the cool kids on the killer list," Mary Ann joked.

"It's only an initial, but it's underlined a few times, which makes me think she was super mad. I can only see what looks like an S." Casi turned to Shelby. "You need to obtain access to the original document to properly unravel this mystery."

Shelby nodded. "I prefer not to compromise Sam's position and make our friendship awkward." She tapped the pen on the paper. "Maybe I could have Alan ask him to take a photo?"

"A picture would be great," Casi said.

Shelby circled a number on the paper. "Hey, does this look like a date?"

Casi tilted her head. "If it is, it's the same as the Board meeting. It's the quarterly review. Kristen was creating a lot of turmoil among all the employees at the resort. I'm curious if she had something planned for that night. She's been very secretive and asked a lot of questions about who oversees what."

"She's not a member though. What would it matter?" Lauren asked, turning to look at Casi.

"Quarterly board meetings are public, and anyone can attend. Technically, as an employee, she's considered a stakeholder and would be allowed to ask questions during the open forum," Casi declared.

Shelby glanced at her notebook. "Do you think that was the meaning of this list? She mentioned retaliation. Perhaps she planned to expose secrets about each of us during the meeting!"

Casi sat back in her chair, her arms tightly folded across her chest, her brow furrowed in thought. "Not only are the meetings open to the public, but they are recorded and uploaded to YouTube. It would be the ideal opportunity to embarrass or punish an employee without consequence for herself. She could use the information to be protected as a whistleblower rather than a snitch. Or it could have been included as an anonymous item of discovery."

"Do you believe she was shrewd enough to do that?" Gail asked.

"The burning question is, what did she feel she had on each of us that was worth that much effort?" Shelby stated.

17

BLURRED BOUNDARIES

"I'm not comfortable doing this," Alan said, wiping the sweat from his forehead. "Why can't you use the list Casi has? It seemed adequate enough to jot it all over my whiteboard."

"We've discovered her copy is smudged and might be missing crucial information," Shelby said as she reclined in the chair and waited to have her blood drawn.

"Please allow the authorities to handle this, Shell," Alan pleaded. He moved aside while the nurse inserted the needle into Shelby's vein and watched the red liquid fill the vial. "Maybe I could call Sam and see if he can take a picture."

"Great, can you do it now?" Shelby asked.

"It can wait until after your chemo," Alan said.

"It might take Sam most of the day to complete this task," Shelby warned. "You know he's about as fast as molasses in winter."

Alan chuckled. "He's already annoyed with the detective from the county. I'm sure he's not highly motivated to have another conversation with them regarding this case."

"You have a few minutes while I wait for her bloodwork if

you want to step out and make a call now," the nurse suggested, realizing Shelby would insist her husband called his friend for whatever list she was referencing, but wanted to discourage use of the cell phones in the treatment area.

"I can see I'm outnumbered," Alan said. He picked up a blanket and smoothed it over Shelby as he kissed her cheek. "Don't get up to any mischief while I'm gone." He walked to the elevator and took it down two floors. The memory of their first trip to the cancer center flooded his senses as he walked down the hall, seeing the scared faces, scarf wrapped heads, and families comforting each other. The center was nestled in the hills, tucked away from the chaos of regular day-to-day life, which gave patients comfort and anonymity in the serene surroundings. He clicked on Sam's number as he used his foot to activate the automatic door and step out toward the parking lot, not wanting to disturb anyone undergoing treatment.

"Hey, Sam," he said. "No, I'm fine. I explained everything to Shelby about how I was attending grief counseling, not having an affair." He laughed at Sam's response that, of course, Shelby knew he wasn't seeing Kristen and had only allowed the police to interrogate him as a punishment for not telling her the truth initially. "Yup, I told her about being on the respirator too. You were right, it's much less stressful to be honest about every-thing. She's doing well, and I can't believe what a trooper she is with these treatments." He paused and said, "Yup, we are halfway through it. Then she'll get a break before surgery. Which is why I'm calling. Shelby is insisting she needs to see the original list that Kristen made." He moved aside for a lady with a walker. "Honestly, Sam, I'm unsure of the reason behind her need for it. I'm worried she's taking this crime solving thing too far, but it's keeping her entertained while she does her treatments. I mean, it can't hurt, right? Your Sheriff buddy already told her about the list and how her name was on it. Plus, Casi has a copy that is now plastered on my whiteboard."

He shook his head. "I didn't let her use it. I came home from Kyle's, and the damn thing was erased and reinvented as a crime headquarters." He held the phone away from his ear while Sam laughed. "Can you just capture an image of the list? You can send it to me and delete it from your text history." He fidgeted with a leaf on a nearby bush, feeling uneasy, asking his friend to do something that might be viewed as unethical. He was surprised when Sam agreed, stating that the local authorities had handled the case poorly from the beginning and had hinted they were ready to close it as an accident and move on to what they considered to be more pressing cases.

Alan slipped his phone back in his pocket and activated the automatic door for a man in a wheelchair who was having a hard time reaching the button. He waited for him to go in and then made a detour for the stairs when he noted the line forming at the elevator. He took a quick glimpse at his watch and hoped Shelby hadn't started her treatment yet. Although the first portion was for hydration, anti-nausea, and pain management, and she didn't need ice gloves and slippers until the second drip, he wanted to show they were a team. Admittedly, he had to acknowledge her recent independence scared him a bit, not because he had no desire for her to get well, but he was limited in what he could do to help, and so he focused on excelling at each task. He noticed a group gathered around Shelby's chair through the curtain that had been placed to provide privacy, and his pulse quickened. The oncologist was leaning toward her, giving her a one-armed hug while the nurse held a paper and patted her knee.

"What happened?" Alan swiftly moved next to her. He did a quick scan for injury, noting the cotton ball was on her inner elbow wrapped with colorful tape, as expected. The IV was not hooked up, which was unusual.

"I can't get my treatment today," Shelby wailed. Bright pink blotches welled up on her overly sensitive skin in reaction to the stream of tears. The honey blonde tufts of hair allowed the sunlight to stream through to her scalp, making her appear like a doll left discarded after a young girl had finished playing with her.

The oncologist gave him a sympathetic smile. "Her platelets are low today, which shows she cannot tolerate the treatment."

"Why are they low? Is it something we did?" Alan cringed at the thought that he shouldn't have let Shelby go to the coffee shop and be exposed to hotbed of germs.

The oncologist shook her head. "This is not unexpected. Chemicals in chemotherapy drugs can damage healthy cells in your body that replicate quickly. The cells in bone marrow that produce platelets are particularly vulnerable to damage. A low count is a common side effect. Since platelets are responsible for clotting the blood, a low count could create a problem with healing and internal bleeding." She flashed a smile at Shelby. "This is just one of the side effects. You're doing extraordinarily well, and we want to keep you healthy. Platelet counts often return to normal within 4–6 days."

Alan regarded the scabs on Shelby's arms from her fall and shuddered to think of the harm it could have caused. "What's the most effective method to get them back up?"

"Time," the oncologist shrugged. "Her body is trying hard to heal, and we are giving her drugs that destroy cells. She needs rest, hydration, and to continue with the nutritional supplement." She glanced at Shelby and noted the devastation because of the setback. "I still want you to get plenty of exercise. It won't help your progress to remain in a chair all day."

"Should I buy her a stationary bike?" Alan asked, watching Shelby cringe at the idea.

"No, walking outdoors is fine," the oncologist said.

"But what if she falls again?" Alan gasped.

"Wear pants and a long-sleeved shirt to protect your skin. You're still photosensitive. Go early in the morning or in the evening. Don't forget to wear a hat, too. Maybe you could walk with Alan or a friend so you can have help if there's an issue?" she said, having been informed about the recent mishap on the trail.

"I don't expect to find more bodies," Shelby said, wiping the tears from her cheeks.

Alan smiled at her resilience in the face of adversity. "I'm sure your coffee gals would love to walk with you. It will give you a break from me, and they're always talking about wanting to be more fit. It will provide an opportunity to talk about clues and such."

Shelby nodded, knowing she couldn't be selfish and give into her despair. Her medical team needed her to stay strong, and her husband had already been through enough. She understood his logic of needing to get to the office was a ruse for lifting her spirits. "Will I still finish treatment in time for surgery?

The oncologist regarded her file. "We've allowed time for these kinds of delays and enough of a gap to continue to give your body a few weeks of healing before you do surgery. I don't expect any issues, but remember, this timeline is fluid. We can administer a drug to help build platelets if they don't come up by next week, but we prefer for your body to do it on its own."

"I can't wait to be finished," Shelby sighed.

"Some patients have reported that pomegranate juice and shrimp can improve counts," the nurse interjected.

All eyes shifted to the oncologist. "It's not a medical recommendation, but I don't see that it would hurt to try," she agreed.

"She can't eat solids, but can she still drink the juice?" Alan asked.

"Actually, the tumor has shrunk significantly," the oncologist said. "Why don't we start with half of a cup of juice? Organic, no sugar. You can try eating three shrimp a day. Wild, not farm raised. No seasoning because it could irritate her stomach, but butter is fine." She noted the smile on Shelby's face. "Little bites and eat slowly. She can also have mashed potatoes, especially sweet potatoes, because they are high in nutrients."

Alan nodded, making a list as she spoke. "Let's take you home, Shelby, and I'll go to the store and get everything you need."

Shelby grinned. "Actually, why don't you check and see if Sam sent you that list. I can take a stroll while you're at the store."

"I feel like you're only hearing the parts that benefit your sleuthing plan," Alan chuckled.

"True, but I want to be good and hungry for my big dinner tonight," Shelby laughed. "I'm sure I'll burn a lot of calories figuring out these clues."

18

LISTS AND LIABILITY

Shelby eased into a chair at the coffee shop, assuring everyone she was fine and that low platelets had been anticipated by her oncologist. She moved the conversation back to the list of names, not wanting to dwell on her illness. Casi peered over her shoulder and squinted at the phone screen before reaching down and enlarging the image. "That's definitely a date, and it coincides with the Board meeting. Hmm, the symbols and letters are still confusing, but..." she blanched. "Oh." She briefly scanned the table. "Never mind. The bottom name only begins with an S. We can assume Kristen might conceivably have had a different sort of revenge for them."

"Retribution," Lauren corrected.

"What's the difference?" Lia asked.

Lauren reclined in her seat and chose her words carefully. "Revenge is an emotional response, while retribution is a punishment that corrects a perceived offense."

"That's interesting," Casi said. "Kristen specifically used that wording in her diatribe on Facebook."

"When?" Gail asked, scrolling through the app on her phone. "I don't see any posts that say that."

"Have you added her as a friend on Facebook?" Casi asked.

"No, but I can see her account," Gail stated.

"Only what she has deemed public," Casi said. "This post was about a week ago, and she tagged it as friends only."

"Why are you friends with her?" Jocelyn asked.

"I'm friends with all the employees," Casi smiled. "I like to monitor what people post in case there is anything that would reflect negatively on the image of the business."

"Plus, you're nosy," Mary Ann teased.

"Very true," Casi laughed. "LA has lots of drama, but Blackberry Falls gossip is much more interesting." She lifted her phone and recited Kristen's post aloud. "Retribution seeks justice with fairness and purpose, while revenge often breeds only a cycle of bitterness and pain. I prefer the former to punish those who have wronged me."

"Wow, that's cryptic. When did she post that?" Gail asked.

"Last week," Lauren said, glancing at her watch. "I have a delivery coming soon." She redirected her attention to the table. "Jocelyn, will you be coming to oversee the lunch rush?"

"Yes, I'll be there in a few minutes," she said, pushing her sunglasses up on the bridge of her nose.

"Don't be late," Lauren said. "We have lots of large groups coming in. Remember, Stella is still training." Her gaze drifted to the door as the slender brunette strolled in.

"Hi everyone," Stella chirped, leaning in to plant a kiss on Shelby's cheek. "Uncle Alan dropped me off because he said you needed a walking partner."

"I see he sent a hat and sunglasses for me," Shelby eyed the bag in Stella's hand.

"He said you forgot them on purpose in the car. I'm supposed to make sure you wear them." She displayed a pouch. "He also made me take a first aid kit in case you fall."

Shelby frowned. "It's not as though I exhibit a proclivity toward falling. Gus is the culprit who pulled me into the ditch." She bent over and stroked the dog on his soft brown head.

"I'm supposed to hold on to the leash, too," Stella reported.

"What a worrywart," Shelby laughed as she stood, carefully holding on to the table to steady herself.

"I'll see you later. I'm excited to work my first shift tonight." Stella waved at the group of ladies.

Casi stood and gathered her belongings. "Do you need a lift to the trail? I'm driving past the lower entrance on my way to Seattle."

"Sure, that would be wonderful," Shelby said, wondering how Alan thought they would get there.

"Um, actually," Stella said, fidgeting with her phone.

Shelby frowned. "What did your uncle say?"

"He said you should take it easy, and I should encourage you to walk around the resort where there are people in case we need help."

"He's overreacting to my low platelets, but let's not tempt fate. How about a leisurely walk near the lake on the boardwalk instead?" Shelby said, tucking her clumps of hair under the tan bucket hat.

"That's the perfect compromise," Stella said.

Casi picked up the box of pastries she bought for the office. "I'll walk with you to the boardwalk."

Lauren watched them walk out and pivoted to face the group. "Did you notice Casi was anxious to talk to Shelby alone?"

Gail asked, "Could it be related to the list? I noticed her face when she read the original document on Shelby's phone. She definitely saw something that wasn't on her copy."

"I saw that too," Jocelyn volunteered. "I heard the police didn't think she could have done it because she didn't even know Kristen was dead until the next day."

"Casi is very smart," Lauren said. "That could have been a choreographed display to throw them off."

Shelby stopped when they reached the fork in the path and turned to Casi. "What did you want to tell me that you didn't want everyone else to hear?"

Casi smiled. "I'm glad you're examining Kristen's circumstances. It's suspicious that she had a fall right after she was poised to make waves in the organization."

"You don't think it resulted from natural circumstances?" Shelby asked.

"I doubt it," Casi said. "Kristen was a few years older than me." She laughed when Shelby frowned. "I mean, she was fairly young and had a rejuvenated concern for her health. It's unlikely she just toppled over and fell down the embankment."

"Like me," Shelby remarked.

"Oh gosh, I'm making this worse," Casi giggled. "What I mean is, there seem to be too many people with motives for shutting her up. You saw how Lauren acted about the Facebook post. She knew Kristen was planning to expose some kind of dirt."

"She was pretty nonchalant about that," Shelby said. "Is it possible Lauren could be the culprit?"

Casi shook her head. "It's unlikely, but there are more layers than just someone getting mad and pushing her to her death. As methodical as Kristen was with her convoluted plans, I believe if there is a killer, they were equally calculated. We can eliminate you; Shelby and Alan already cracked under pressure and came clean about his activities."

"How did you learn about that?" Shelby asked.

"Amy's sister works as a dispatcher in Seattle. She overheard Sam yelling at the detectives about how they handled questioning Alan. She told Amy, who told Kyle, and now I know." Casi laughed.

"That's certainly a convoluted gossip chain," Shelby said.

"It's handy when you want to get the nitty gritty," Casi teased. "It makes me less nostalgic for my modeling days when I have small-town drama to keep me occupied."

Stella giggled. "LA sure is like another dimension. They live in a little bubble of their own making."

Casi nodded. "We can eliminate Stella because she wasn't even in town when it happened."

"Maybe I came in early, killed Kristen, then lied about taking an Uber from the airport," Stella suggested. "My motive would have been to protect my beloved aunt from the person attempting to steal her job."

"That's a solid motive," Casi agreed. "But I know Alix took you to the airport after your shoot, and you used the resort Uber account, and it sent me a notification."

"Goodness, you don't miss a thing!" Shelby exclaimed. "Stella and Alan were never mentioned on the list."

"While we're waiting for the police to determine the cause of death, the logical thing would be to ascertain what Kristen had on each person who was listed. It's possible someone attempted to protect them; except how would they know their person was a target when none of us even heard about the list until after Kristen died?"

"It's likely her plan was about exposing lies or corruption. It's possible Kristen would have done it at the board meeting, like we suspected. She wanted to build intrigue with her post on Facebook, but she didn't plan to let us know who was included. I imagine she wanted to blindside us," Shelby said.

"True," Casi agreed. "You're on to something. We might be approaching this incorrectly. We've been consumed with what we might have personally done and forecasting who would protect us from exposure. Perhaps we need to think bigger, like an actual crime that we could be fired or arrested for."

Shelby took out her notebook. "Should we go over the list and determine consequences to aid in our investigation?"

"You and Stella should do it. If you want to have valid information that the police can use as a lead, it's prudent to only have people involved who are completely innocent." Casi paused and reached for Shelby's phone and brought up the image. "I thought Kristen gathered a group of individuals she had a dislike for, but then I realized the symbols represent what she assumes we did wrong. I didn't notice it on my copy, but on this one there's a dollar sign beside my name." Casi winced. "There was a minor commotion in the office last week, and basically Kristen accused me of being a thief."

"That's preposterous!" Shelby scoffed.

"The problem is, from her perspective, it looked like I was embezzling, and she had enough proof to take it to the Board," Casi sighed.

19

WATCHFUL EYES

"Could you elaborate?" Shelby asked. "I mean, I prefer not interfere in other people's affairs, but if you think it will shed light on what might have motivated someone to harm Kristen, then I promise not to judge you or take it any further than this conversation."

"I'm curious to know the authentic story because I've heard you have buckets of money and there would be zero incentive to take it from the company you co-own," Stella said.

Casi led them to a bench beside the lake and perched on a boulder to face them. "I had planned on keeping this to myself, but if it comes out later, it will make me look guilty. I would rather deal with the consequences of my actions now and have it done with."

"Are you planning on telling the Board?" Shelby asked, directing Gus to sit by her feet.

"It would be the best solution. The problem is, it implicates others, and that's why I avoided it at first." Casi exhaled. "Ok, our accountant, Brian, discovered a discrepancy between what Lia was reporting for sales at the coffee shop and what was being deposited. Keep in mind that the system is computerized, which means every sale is recorded, whether it's cash or credit card."

"Lia tends to be somewhat..." Shelby tried to find a charitable word to describe the woman who was often flighty yet easily upset when her relationships were in turmoil. "Distracted."

"That's what I assumed at first. She has two little boys, and even though they live mostly with Jake, they come to her house every other weekend, which, with Shane's girls, adds up to five young children in a three-bedroom home. At the best of times, it's chaotic, but lately she's been short-tempered, and I didn't want to add one more layer to her pile."

"But why is the shortage at the coffee shop your issue? If Brian thought Lia was messing up, why wouldn't he go to Jocelyn? She's responsible for overseeing the accounts at the coffee shop and restaurant, isn't she?" Shelby asked, recalling Jocelyn's insistence that all financial matters be run through her before being sent to the accountant each month.

Casi wrinkled her nose. "Well, I heard the information from Dylan, Brian's partner. He was doing my hair, and he mentioned Brian was in a twist because he had brought it to Jocelyn's attention and she basically sold-out Lia and suggested she was incompetent and inferred she should be fired. You understand the basic structure of our partnership; a group of us invested in refurbishing the hotel, and we elected a board to oversee operations. Lauren is the singular investor who gets paid because she runs the restaurant."

"Lia doesn't get paid?" Shelby asked.

"She does, but she's not part of the investment group. Her husband, Shane, put in money, but his profits are kept separate from what Lia makes as the manager of the coffee shop." She smiled at their confused expressions. "The original concept was to keep the investors separate from employees. The attorneys thought it was a more favorable business model."

"If Lia is short money at the coffee shop, it doesn't affect her paycheck but could impact the investors cut?" Shelby clarified.

"Exactly!" Casi stated. "That was why we had Jocelyn oversee the financial records for the restaurant and coffee shop, although technically her title is the restaurant manager. The revenue is based on food, hotel, and the spa. It doesn't matter if people eat at the restaurant or get a salad at the spa, the budget, vendors, and oversight is unified. Lia wanted a coffee shop, but she's not qualified to handle the larger aspects of running a business and ultimately, it's more efficient to have one person maintain the general finances."

"I'm confused; the coffee shop isn't Lia's?" Stella asked.

"No, just like the restaurant isn't Lauren's. They each manage the daily operations, and it benefits everyone to have a high profit margin," Casi explained. "At first, the discrepancies were minor, under a hundred bucks, but when it rose to several thousand a month, Brian had an obligation to report it."

"How did that reflect negatively on you?" Stella asked.

"That's where things took a turn," Casi cringed. "Kyle told me to leave it alone and let them work it out. He knows I'm busy with the skincare line in Seattle, especially with all the travel I do. He feels I get overly involved with my friends and has suggested I take a step back and allow everyone to sink or swim on their own."

"That sounds like Kyle. He's very practical, and he and Jake have run a successful business for years. I'm sure they understand the intricacies of finance," Shelby said.

"Which was Kyle's platform, but I considered my friendship with Lia as paramount." Casi regarded the lake. "She went through a lot through the years, and she was finally happy with Shane..."

"I've heard things might be on the rocks with them," Shelby said.

"It's complicated. Shane might talk to the guys, but they

don't share information. I believe he has his hands full with working and raising his three girls, but Lia was concerned he was devoting a substantial amount of time to his recent interest in fitness and inventing excuses for coming home late." Casi shrugged. "I figured that was the root of the mistakes Lia was making with the deposits."

"Did you question her about it? If she shared her doubts about her marriage, it's a natural progression to how she was dealing with things at work," Shelby said.

"Except Lia didn't share her concerns with me. I heard about it from Gail, who overheard Shane and Lia fighting in the back room of the coffee shop," Casi said.

Shelby laughed. "Oh my, there certainly is a lot of gossip in this town."

Casi nodded. "My intent was to smooth things over at the coffee shop to allow Lia to focus on her marital issues and not lose her job." She drew in a long, deep breath and released it. "I began going to the resort each night after the coffee shop closed to read the reports. Sure enough, the deposit was short each time. I covered it with my own cash, assuming it would be a temporary fix until I had an opportunity to sit down with Lia and come up with a better plan."

"Did you suspect Lia might be pocketing the money?" Shelby asked. "If no one informed her the discrepancies were being noticed, it could seem like an easy way to generate additional income."

"Honestly, that was my first thought," Casi admitted. "Lia is often jealous of what other people have, and I thought if a few hundred dollars made a difference, I could provide it for her. Jake's wife, Anna, said I should have offered her a loan instead of covering up short deposits," Casi said. "A few weeks ago, I went to talk to Lia about it, but she was already gone. I checked the deposit bag in the safe and, sure enough, it was short. I had brought cash with me that I had planned to give to Lia. I added several hundred dollars to the deposit, thinking it would be the last time."

"What did Lia say?" Shelby asked.

"Unfortunately, Kristen came into the office. She caught me with the safe open and cash on the desk. I tried to explain what I was doing, but she became irate. She revealed she had known someone was stealing and had detrimental evidence she planned on taking to the Board. She called me ridiculous names, and it escalated from there. Jocelyn came in to see what was happening because we were making quite a racket. By that time, I was livid, and I threatened Kristen," Casi sighed. "I told her that no one liked her and if I had my way, her days at the resort were limited and she had better watch her back because I was coming for her when she least expected it."

"Oh, that's a minor dilemma," Shelby gulped.

"Did Kristen say what proof she had?" Stella asked.

"She highlighted the presence of surveillance equipment in the office that I hadn't noticed." Casi gave a piercing look. "You know I'm stellar with technology. That battleax thought she had pulled a fast one because she had the system installed herself, without the approval or knowledge of management."

"Is that illegal?" Stella asked.

"Not technically. The office is considered a public place because it's shared. There should have been a declaration about surveillance being used, and the cameras should have been visible. What really crossed the line is she gathered the footage on a personal computer for her own use." Casi said. "I honestly wasn't worried about my part in it. Unless she modified the footage, the recordings would show me consistently depositing money in the safe, not taking it out. The daily reports would be accurate, and no crime was committed. What concerned me more was her smug look, indicating my accessing the safe wasn't the only activity she had secretly recorded."

"Did she say where the recordings are?" Stella asked.

Casi stood and took a sip of her latte. "Jocelyn asked her that, and Kristen laughed like a maniac. She said they were somewhere very secure, and we would find out at the appropriate moment."

20

SPIES, LIES, AND BLACKMAIL

Shelby looped her arm through Stella's as they walked, needing the closeness of her niece rather than physical support. "What are your thoughts on what Casi told us?" she asked.

"I believe everything she said," Stella stated. "She has gone above and beyond to help me settle in LA, just like she did for other girls. The people who really know her rave about what an amazing person she is. I can't see her risking her reputation for a little money."

"I agree," Shelby said. "It was her idea to create the resort and give numerous residents in this town jobs. I've heard her business does very well, and if she needed money, Kyle has always been generous with her."

"It's illogical that she would track Kristen down at the trail and then make up an elaborate story to cover up a crime," Stella said. "I feel like she would be savvier in committing the murder."

"I talked to Casi at the coffee shop that morning. She had on a gorgeous rose silk blouse with a gray linen skirt. As always, she wore high heels, and her hair was perfectly coiffed. I saw pictures online of the event that night, and she was in the background wearing the same outfit, not a hair out of place," Shelby said.

"It doesn't add up," Stella agreed. "I doubt she changed into workout gear, killed Kristen, changed back, and managed to get to Seattle for a ten o'clock meeting."

"She's severely lacking motive. She's very computer savvy, and if she wanted to access Kristen's files, she could figure it out," Shelby said.

"Wouldn't she want to see the footage from the office if it exists?" Stella asked.

"Casi is aware of her actions and, as nosy as she is, doesn't care about what anyone else did in there. She can explain what she was doing and is highly respected by the Board," Shelby said. "I believe it would be wise to remove her from our suspect list."

"Done." Stella used the stylus pen to draw a line across Casi's name on the image. "Should we go in order?"

Shelby paused at the conclusion of the boardwalk and looked up at the building, majestic against the backdrop of mountains and redwood trees. The location was divine, and people flocked from every corner of the world to relax in the tranquil setting. The building had been a hotel in the early 1900s, sadly left to decay for years when it closed. After the timber industry moved farther north, the draw of a fancy hotel was gone. Although quaint, Blackberry Falls wasn't a tourist destination. Kyle Jensen had originally conceived the idea of restoring the hotel and brought Lauren on board to open a restaurant after a business deal imploded when her marriage failed. Casi had been the brainchild behind creating a group of investors to finance the vision while enticing international guests with a world class spa, incredible dining, and refurbished rooms with a spectacular view. Residents were thrilled to find employment, and the deal turned out to be lucrative for the investors.

"Let's go inside," Shelby urged, longing to walk the hallways of her former job. The coffee shop was on the far side of the hotel near the parking lot, and it had been months since she had enough energy to circle around to the lakeside entrance of the hotel.

"Uncle Alan will be back from the store soon. Shouldn't we head back?" Stella said, hesitating at the signpost directing them to the hotel. "Plus, we have Gus. We can't take him inside the hotel."

"He's considered a service dog while I'm sick," Shelby grinned. "Text Uncle Alan and say I'm feeling good and want to enjoy additional fresh air," Shelby released Stella's arm and posed. "Snap a photo of me by the lake so he can see I'm not fibbing."

Stella complied and read the almost instant reply. "He says we have another thirty minutes. He'll drop by the office and collect a few things before he comes to get you."

"Perfect." Shelby quickened her pace, making Stella and Gus jog to keep up. "Come on, slowpoke, we're on a mission."

Stella giggled. "Be careful your blood sugar doesn't drop. Did you drink your water today?"

Shelby reached into her purse and extracted a colorful water bottle. "Three cups down and five to go," she said, taking a sip.

Stella reached for the large door with the oval pane of etched glass proudly displaying the resort's logo. Shelby stepped over the threshold and stopped to inhale the heady scent of polished wood mingling with aromas from the kitchen nearby. The marble entry was exquisite, giving way to a grand staircase. Although elevators had been installed for safety and better access, guests usually took the stairs to the upper levels to peruse the gallery of paintings and magnificent stained-glass windows along the way.

"You can't eat until you get home," Stella said, watching Shelby lean toward the clattering of pots and sizzle of a grill in the kitchen. "Uncle Alan is very excited about your three shrimp, and I will not be responsible for you choking in the dining room."

Shelby laughed. "The aroma of garlic is enough to appease me for now. Let's drop by the office and gather a few items."

"You had better concoct a better explanation if you are trying to snoop," Stella warned. "With Kristen not here, is there a file you might need for an event? Maybe Casi asked you to consult on it?"

"That will make Jocelyn angry if she wasn't given a heads up. Besides the files and calendar are online," Shelby sighed.

"Do you use your laptop?" Stella asked.

"Yes, I can work on it from my recliner," Shelby said.

"Excellent," Stella walked with her toward the back office. The room had once been staff quarters, but since Lauren was the sole resident on site, a two-bedroom apartment had been converted from lesser used rooms lacking the view of the sought-after accommodations on the other side of the hotel. The office was functional and set up to facilitate several people working together. Most of the tasks required the managers to be in the main rooms of the building rather than sitting at a desk, therefore separate offices had been deemed unnecessary. "Hi, Jocelyn, my aunt forgot her power cord for her laptop..." Stella halted as Jocelyn quickly removed a pint bottle from her lips, capped it, and shoved it in a drawer. She pretended to occupy herself with paperwork.

Shelby strolled past Stella, not mentioning what they had witnessed. She opened drawers along the desk on the opposite side of the room. "It didn't occur to me I had forgotten it, of course, because I haven't needed to turn it on," she said, pretending to search for a cord she knew wasn't there. "You haven't seen one lying around here, have you?"

"It's a Samsung," Stella said. She shifted her gaze towards Shelby with a wink. "Maybe we can check the cameras? They might reveal the location where you left it."

"They've been disabled," Jocelyn said. She leaned against the desk and folded her arms across her chest. "When Casi found out they had been installed, she demanded Shane remove them immediately."

"Why would Shane do it and not Kyle?" Shelby asked.

Jocelyn pointed to the small holes above the curtain rod. "They were hard-wired. Shane is an electrician. He knew how to remove them without damaging the walls."

Shelby scanned the room briefly. "Are you sure he got all of them? How did he figure out where to search?"

"I wasn't here when they worked on it. I assume he had a way of tracing the line." Jocelyn shrugged.

"Do they know where the recordings went?" Stella asked.

"No," Jocelyn huffed. "Look, I know you're not here to find a power cord. I saw you talking to Casi earlier, and I'm sure she told you about what happened a few weeks ago with the big blowup."

"Yes, that's how we learned about the cameras," Shelby confessed. "I'm wondering if what was recorded led to Kristen's death. The police have pretty much given up on it and want to rule it as accidental. As residents of this town, I believe we have an obligation to find out if that's true."

Jocelyn sighed and opened the drawer of her desk. She held up the bottle and sloshed the clear liquid to bring attention to the contents. "I struggle with social situations. Quite often I come into the office and take a little nip to steady my nerves. You know firsthand that I'm excellent at my job. It's not fair if recordings of my consuming alcohol during work hours tarnish my reputation."

Shelby hesitated before asking. "You saw the recordings?"

She shook her head. "No, but when Kristen and Casi got into the big fight, she said there was evidence that would prove illicit behavior at the resort."

"Was she targeting the people on the list?" Shelby asked.

"She said she had been compiling evidence that would prove people were untrustworthy," Jocelyn stated.

"But what was her end goal in revealing that?" Shelby asked.

"I can only speak for myself," Jocelyn said. "Several months ago, she confronted me about my drinking and demanded something from me in exchange for deleting the evidence. I didn't know about the cameras at the time, but she alluded to having concrete proof."

"Can I ask what information she wanted?" Shelby asked.

"We all knew she was using weight loss drugs," Jocelyn said. "Apparently her doctor wouldn't prescribe them because she's not diabetic and was not considered morbidly obese. They were prohibitively expensive without insurance."

"She wanted you to get them from your doctor and give them to her?" Shelby glanced over Jocelyn's solid figure. "Why would your doctor give them to you?"

"She found out I had a connection. He manufactures them in Renton and packages them with name brand labels, so they look like the real thing. It's a new little business around town," she scoffed. "I heard it's a pretty high profit margin."

"Did you arrange it for her?" Shelby asked.

"I gave her the name of a person who could take care of it, and she promised to destroy any evidence. She sent me an email that it was done, but when I saw my name on the list, I wondered if it was a scam to continue to blackmail me." Her eyes welled. "This job is all I have, Shelby. I trusted her to do the right thing." She regarded the half empty bottle. "I ceased drinking for a while, but this latest stress brought me right back."

"It's unlikely the Board will fire you for drinking if you're earnestly getting help," Shelby soothed.

"I hope," Jocelyn exhaled. "Kristen's death didn't benefit me. The videos could still be out there. I am curious to know if anyone on that list is better off now."

"What are you trying to say?" Shelby asked.

Jocelyn pushed a stray lock of hair behind her ear. "Kristen accused Casi of embezzlement. It's easy to figure out that it was a fabrication. If Casi was covering for Lia's shortfalls, maybe someone wouldn't want that information to get out."

"Do you know what day it is?" Shelby asked unexpectedly.

"It's Thursday. Do you have an appointment?" Stella searched through the calendar on her phone, hoping she hadn't missed important details.

"No, I don't. Tonight is the board meeting, though." She pursed her lips. "I'm curious what the agenda is."

Jocelyn shrugged. "They sent an email earlier. There wasn't anything unusual, and no one was scheduled to speak."

"Interesting. Casi said it would be recorded. I'll have to check it out online," Shelby said, redirecting Gus away from sniffing at a corner of the office.

"Can you tell us who supplied the drugs?" Stella asked. "Maybe they were tainted, and that's what caused her death. We should make sure no one else is buying from him."

Jocelyn shrugged. "I don't know the supplier, but the person I asked to arrange the order was Shane."

21

A CONVENIENT SUSPECT

"How was your meal last night?" Stella inquired as she strolled to the coffeemaker to pour herself a cup. Holding the carafe, she turned to Shelby. "Is coffee still on the no list?"

"For now. They promised I can get caffeinated again a few weeks after surgery." Shelby yawned. "I believe that's why I'm tired all the time. I made it for you and Alan, but I love the smell."

Stella added cream to her cup and smiled at her aunt, remembering that she had trouble staying focused and it didn't help to ask her two questions in a row. "So, the shrimp?"

"Oh right," Shelby laughed. "They were delicious! Alan cut three of them into about twenty-four pieces and watched me chew each bit. I even had about a quarter cup of mashed potatoes."

"Wow, fancy," Stella teased. "It must have been amazing to have food in your mouth again. I was thinking about that after the event last night when we had our employee meal. I can't imagine not being able to eat."

"It was tough in the beginning. They refused to even let me

have ice chips due to their concern about my swallowing. It was very much like a dream with everyone floating around, poking me, and whispering." Shelby shivered. "Did I tell you about when I called 911 because I thought I was being chased by the drug cartel? It was traumatic."

"Yes, Uncle Alan told us you had psychosis as an adverse reaction to the anesthesia. He got a call at three in the morning from the hospital saying the police had responded to a distress call."

Shelby laughed. "I don't know why that night nurse allowed me to have my phone. I obviously wasn't in my right mind."

Alan came in and stretched, pleased to witness the contentment as Shelby and Stella sat together at the table in the kitchen. Shelby looked up and smiled. "I was telling Stella how good the meal was last night. What a joy to have the ability to eat again."

Alan planted a gentle kiss on the crown of her head. "I'm glad you enjoyed it. What do you gals have planned for today?" He checked the clock over the stove. "We have radiation in an hour, but you're free after that. The oncologist was pleased you're getting outside. Are you certain that you didn't overdo it yesterday?"

"No, it was enjoyable to spend time with everyone at the resort." Shelby rested her hand on Stella's. "We were thinking of visiting Pike Place today. I want to purchase a gift for Amy's shower in a few weeks."

Alan hesitated at the coffeemaker. "Seattle, huh? You don't think that's far? There are several lovely shops in town."

"We'll be fine. Stella can drive my car, and there's plenty of parking nearby. I won't need to walk too far," Shelby said.

"Take the handicap placard in case you need a spot by the elevator," Alan instructed. "Stella, I'm glad you know the signs for low blood sugar, but let's go over what else to look out for, okay?"

"I'll take good care of her," Stella promised. "Hey, did you watch the board meeting?"

Shelby yawned. "Yes, but it was mostly financial reports, like Casi surmised. Nothing extraordinary."

"What did you expect?" Alan asked. "The Board's role is to maintain financial stability and maximize profits."

"You certainly are good at your job," Shelby laughed.

"WHY ARE you putting on the GPS? I know how to get to Pike Place," Stella said as she backed out of the parking spot at the cancer center. She rolled her eyes. "Are we taking a detour?"

"Just a little one. I have already ordered my gift for Amy. It will just require a moment to pick up. That gives us ample opportunity to have a chat with Shane," Shelby noted.

"Isn't he busy working?" Stella asked.

"He teaches in the afternoon, but he's doing inspections this morning. We can nip in and ask him a few questions without causing a scene," Shelby said.

"How do you know when he works?" Stella asked. She turned to look at Shelby and shook her head. "Did Casi access the Boeing schedules online? She needs to use her tech skills to locate the video files and find out if there is incriminating evidence."

Shelby laughed. "Casi asked Lia and gave me the information. As far as the recordings, the issue is they are most likely on a flash drive and that could be hidden anywhere."

"Do we plan on openly questioning Shane if he is dealing off-market drugs in Blackberry Falls?" Stella pursed her lips.

"Obviously, we will be more discreet." Shelby casually glanced out the window. "I did a bit of digging…"

"On whom? What did you uncover?" Stella asked.

"It struck me that everyone on the list is from Blackberry

Falls, except Casi. She's been here for over six years and has made a big effort to become involved in the community," Shelby said.

"Are you still considering her a suspect?" She inquired.

"Not at all. Did you know Lia met Shane through Casi?" Shelby asked.

"I knew he was Canadian. Did they grow up together? He's several years older than her," Stella said.

"He was married to one of her close friends." Shelby pursed her lips. "Lia told me she died in a car accident."

"That's horribly sad, those three little girls lost their mom. Wait, you don't think Shane had any connection to her death, do you?" Stella asked.

"It's doubtful, but Lia let it slip that Shane was in jail for dealing drugs for quite a few years when he was younger." Shelby raised an eyebrow. "Perhaps he's resorted to his previous tactics to generate extra cash? Casi gave the impression that Lia was coming up short at the coffee shop every night. If Shane is struggling to provide for his family, I'm sure he wouldn't appreciate Kristen threatening to expose him."

"Do you think Kristen knew about Shane's background?" Stella asked.

"If she bought the drugs from him, she might be aware that he's the one manufacturing them." Shelby said, pointing to a sign. "Take the exit."

"Renton?" Stella asked.

"Yes, we're heading to the Boeing plant where Shane works," Shelby explained.

"Ok, but Jocelyn said the person making the drugs is doing it in Renton," Stella stated.

"See? There are too many coincidences," Shelby said as Stella turned into a parking lot. "Jocelyn made it appear as if he didn't have any trouble locating the cameras and disconnecting them. There's a probability he was in on the extortion."

Stella pointed at the guard at the gate blocking the entrance to the buildings. "Now what?" Shelby smiled and took her phone from her purse. She slid her reading glasses on and tapped the buttons with her index finger. "Ok granny, it would be much quicker if you used your thumbs."

Shelby laughed. "I'm not in a hurry, and I'm used to doing it this way." She leaned back in the seat and surveyed the buildings behind the gate.

"Would you like me to give you a boost over the fence?" Stella joked. "Or we could use your cancer card to get the sympathy pass."

Shelby pointed to Shane in blue coveralls walking toward the guard. He stopped and showed his badge, pointing out he was heading into the parking area. "Or we could wait for Shane to come to us."

"How did he know we were here?" Stella asked.

"I told him to meet me in the north parking lot," Shelby said.

"Why would he leave work to come talk to us?" Stella asked.

Shelby opened the car door as Shane approached, looking around in confusion. "I sent a text to Casi. He thinks he's meeting Lia."

"Ugh, that's awkward," Stella cringed. Now you're about to inform him you're aware of his past incarceration for drug dealing. Are you considering questioning him about whether he killed Kristen?"

Shane halted when he noticed Shelby and peered inside the car. "Where's Lia?"

"I have to confess that I asked Casi to send the text for you to meet with us," Shelby stated.

"Why?" Shane shrugged.

"Well, it's actually about Kristen," Shelby started, watching his expression change from friendly to annoyed.

"I didn't know her," he said.

Shelby inhaled deeply. "You understand how things are in Blackberry Falls…"

"Sure, you blame the newcomer," Shane scoffed.

"Not at all. It's more that I'm concerned Lia might become implicated in something without realizing it," Shelby said.

Shane winced. "How is Lia involved? She's too trusting. I warned her to steer clear of all that."

"Can you help us comprehend the situation?" Shelby asked. "We know Kristen asked Jocelyn to find a source for underground weight loss drugs, and she came to you."

Shane shook his head. "It's common knowledge that I have a criminal record for a drug offense." He gestured toward the buildings behind him. "I had to disclose it when I got a job here. I know Casi didn't tell you. I'm assuming it was Lia? She's so naïve."

Shelby quickly weighed the consequences of telling him the truth. "It was said in another context, she wasn't trying to reveal your past. Jocelyn mentioned she came to you to find out about acquiring non-regulated weight loss medications for Kristen."

A wave of shame enveloped Shane, making him appear diminutive. Shelby had an impulse to hug him but restrained herself and allowed him a moment to collect his thoughts. "My ex-wife, Katie, died from using diet pills. She was driving with my girls in the back of the car, and she had a stroke," he said as his voice broke.

"That's devastating! I apologize, Shane. I never intended to bring up terrible memories," Shelby said.

"It's alright," he said, swiping a hand roughly over his eyes. "I knew people would start putting the pieces together. Jocelyn asked me about a guy who makes them, but I refused to be in the middle of it. I gave her the number of a guy from the gym who I know does steroids and tries to hit on women with his wellness package." He glanced into the car as Stella laughed.

"Yup, it is shady. I only did it because I wanted to keep Lia out of it." He fumbled with the zipper on his coveralls. "You know Lia's been struggling to lose weight for a while. It's difficult for her because she's had two children and she's diabetic. It doesn't help that she runs a coffee shop either," he chuckled. "I noticed the same pattern with Katie, my ex. Her body changed after having three kids, but we liked to eat out, and exercise wasn't really our thing. I hoped Lia would join me on the trail, and I included her on my gym membership, but she wasn't interested. I missed all the signs with Katie. When I discovered Lia was considering using something that was potentially dangerous, I flipped out. Of course, Gail heard me chastising her and ran to tell everyone that our marriage was in jeopardy."

"Oh, Lia was taking the medication? Is she still?" Shelby asked.

"That's the crazy part," Shane said. "Lia wasn't taking it. Kristen had persuaded her to obtain a prescription and give it to her, and she covered the cost, which was over a grand a month."

"Why would Lia do that? I didn't think she was close with Kristen," Shelby said.

"Who knows? That's what we fought about. I told her that she was being manipulated by Kristen and, basically, committing a crime. It all came to a head when her doctor stopped renewing the prescription because she wasn't losing any weight, therefore it was pointless," he said.

"Because she wasn't actually taking the drug," Shelby said.

"Exactly. I can't comprehend why Lia was in such a twist about it. Somehow, she felt she owed Kristen the prescription," he said.

"Was she selling it for a profit?" Shelby asked.

"That's what I figured, and I promised to cover the money she would lose if she walked away from the deal." Shane scoffed. "When Lia started coming up short in her deposit nightly, I worried she might have found a shortcut to pay for it. I cut out early from work and went over there so I could count the deposit and make sure it was accurate. Lauren was giving her a tough time and stated that if it continued, she was considering recommending to the Board that they hire another coffee shop manager."

"But Lia is her sister. I'm surprised she wasn't more supportive of her," Shelby said.

"That's the thing..." Shane hesitated. "Lauren appears snippy, but she's super protective of her family. She's in a challenging position because she's the sole investor who also receives a salary for working at the resort. The restaurant means everything to her, especially because she got screwed over by her ex the last time she tried to open a place. I know she feels obligated to make it a success, since Kyle put himself on the line for her to create the opportunity. Casi has the knack of turning everything she touches into gold, which adds pressure on everyone else to step up and do their part."

"Lauren didn't feel Lia was living up to expectations at the coffee shop?" Shelby asked.

Shane shrugged. "Everyone loves Lia. She's sweet and pleasant to work with. Lauren felt she wasn't cut out to be a boss and that the workers took advantage of her."

"How did Kristen fit into that scenario?" Shelby asked.

"A few months ago, Lauren instructed me to install the video cameras. She said someone was up to no good and she wanted proof. Kristen came to me shortly after and asked for the contact information for the medication. I wanted Lia out of the loop. I gave her what she requested and moved on. I didn't realize Casi was unaware of the cameras until she ripped me to shreds over it. I'm unclear of Lauren's intent to install surveillance, but if she got wind of Kristen doing the deal with Lia, she would have gone ballistic."

22

BITTERSWEET

Shelby turned to Stella as she got back in the car. "Did you hear him mention Kristen wasn't the one who had the cameras installed?"

"Maybe she found them?" Stella said. "How else did she get the proof of Jocelyn drinking?"

Shelby opened her notebook and leafed through the pages. "What if we asked the wrong question?"

"What do you mean?" Stella asked.

"When Kristen threatened Jocelyn that she would reveal her drinking problem to the Board, did she reference the video? She may have prior knowledge of Jocelyn's issue, right? It appears Kristen was somewhat of a bully, pressuring Lia to get a prescription and then Jocelyn to give her a contact for off market drugs."

"Perhaps she was simply desperate," Stella said.

"What would lead you to believe that?" Shelby asked.

"Think about it. You've known Kristen for a few years, right? Do you remember ever facing a challenge with her?" Stella asked.

"No, we always worked together well," Shelby agreed.

"Once her mother passed away, she began attending grief counseling and started making significant changes in her life, such as losing weight and focusing on her career goals." Stella shrugged. "Maybe her mom was the bully, and she finally felt free to live the life she wanted after caring for her for so long?"

"The mystery initial!" Shelby exclaimed.

"What is the significance of that?" Stella asked.

"Maybe we're approaching this in the incorrect manner. You might be on to something. Once Kristen was finally free of family responsibilities, she started living life on her own terms and doing things that others got the opportunity to do at a much younger age."

"Like having a boyfriend," Stella suggested.

"Are you dating?" Shelby asked.

"I've been hanging out with a guy named Cris. He's an actor, but I'm unsure if anything will come of it," Stella shrugged.

"You're young. You have plenty of time to find the right one," Shelby said. "Wait, what was the topic we were discussing?"

Stella laughed. "We were suggesting Kristen had a new boyfriend."

"Oh, right," Shelby redirected her attention to Stella. "I need to add that you're a beautiful young woman who is smart and capable of doing anything your heart desires. Don't feel that you need a man to complete you. I would love for you to find a partner who complements you one day, but there's ample opportunity to live your best life right now."

"Thank you." Stella smiled. "I wonder what Kristen's mom told her about finding a man. Do you recall her ever dating?"

Shelby settled back in her seat. "Now that I think of it, I never saw Kristen with a man. The resort has only been open for about three years. Maybe she had boyfriends before that? We're both from Blackberry Falls, but I'm almost ten years older, and we didn't have common interests before we worked together."

Stella started the car and asked. "Are we really going to Seattle, or am I an accomplice to a big, fat lie?"

"I wouldn't put you in that position. I know you adore your uncle. I'll tell him the truth about talking to Shane when we get home. I ordered the gift for Amy weeks ago. We can pick it up on our way," Shelby said.

"What did you get them?" Stella asked.

"I had custom pillows made for the front porch. They are printed with a quote from Robert Browning; Grow old with me, the best is yet to be."

"I love that! She'll be excited," Stella said. "Is it from that store on Dawson Street? They have a lot of fun things. I tried to find a gift in LA, but nothing seemed like the right fit. Amy is the epitome of homespun happiness, and stuff from LA seemed tacky."

"I considered that," Shelby smiled. "I ordered a lemonade pitcher and glasses with her new monogram. Her old set has a chip on the rim, and it should be retired. It was her grandmother's. Perhaps she can use it for a flower vase instead."

"You're very thoughtful," Stella said.

"I try," Shelby said. "That's the primary reason I'm motivated to figure out what happened to Kristen. It bothers me that the police don't regard it as a critical case. If I died, hopefully people would care enough to find out why and not just continue with their lives as normal."

Stella shivered. "Please don't die for another fifty years. I can't bear to lose you."

"I'm doing everything I can," Shelby promised. "I wonder who will claim Kristen's body and plan her funeral? I only knew that she had a mother, she never mentioned anyone else."

"I COULD GO for a cup of tea," Shelby said as they neared the exit for Blackberry Falls.

"Is that code for let's go by the resort and interrogate Lauren before heading home?" Stella teased.

Shelby laughed. "Well, if you insist. Do you work tonight? I don't want to take up your whole day."

"I enjoy spending time with you," Stella said. "It's wonderful to be home and move at a slower pace."

"You'll make good money working this summer, so it's not like you're being lazy. Maybe your boyfriend can come for a week before the wedding, and you can show him the area."

Stella exhaled. "I'm not sure what to call him. He doesn't like labels, so I'm not sure how to define our relationship. Also, he's on hold for a part in a movie. He doesn't like to be distracted by other activities aside from working out and preparing for the role."

"Goodness, he sounds a bit self-centered," Shelby warned. "Although maybe it's pleasant to be home, spending time with your family and friends without worrying about whether he's having a good time."

"Exactly what I was thinking," Stella agreed. "Plus, look at all the extra time I have for sleuthing with you."

"That's definitely a bonus," Shelby agreed. She exited the car and leaned on the door for a minute to steady herself.

"Are you okay? Should we head back and you can take it easy? Stella urged.

"I'm fine. I assumed this Friday would be easier because I didn't have chemo, but apparently my body is still adjusting to the cycle. We'll have a quick chat with Lauren and then I'll take a nap," Shelby said.

The metallic clattering of pots and rhythmic chopping of vegetables greeted them as they approached the back door of the kitchen. As Shelby had predicted, the rapid pace of the lunch rush had slowed to a steady hum of dinnertime prep and mid-cycle cleaning. A dishwasher whirred in the background as the workers refilled the prep stations and cleaned the grill. Lauren raised her gaze from a stockpot, her cheeks rosy from the steam. "Hi, Shelby. Are you back to work already?"

"No, not yet. I miss it dearly, though," Shelby said, observing the energy and passion of the surrounding crew. "I was curious if you had a minute. Sam had routine questions, and I offered to talk to the employees. It was very upsetting for Alan to be questioned by law enforcement." She fabricated a story that seemed reasonable and that would hopefully yield a favorable response.

"Um, sure," Lauren said, glancing down the line to determine what needed to be completed. She casually walked to the back door as a bell rang and took the electronic reader from the muscle-bound delivery driver. She did a quick count of boxes, opening each one to inspect the quality before signing off on the order. The driver gave her a nod and a gratuitous flex of his muscles as he wheeled his handcart back out the door.

"I promise we'll be quick." Shelby turned to Stella and gave her a wink. "I must admit, I'm feeling a little off today. I'll be glad when these treatments are over."

"You really are an inspiration," Lauren said, directing her to a stool at the counter. "You don't mind if I continue to work, do you? I have a new risotto on the menu with squash blossoms, and it requires a lot of prep." She skillfully minced a shallot while she spoke. "I thought they classified Kristen's death as an accident. What does Sam need to pursue?"

Shelby thumbed through her notebook, trying to recall the specific questions she had for Lauren. "Ah, the cameras. He wondered why you had those installed."

Lauren paused mid cut and sighed. "That was a catastrophe! A few months back, I noticed things were missing. Liquor from the bar and tips from the waiter's station. When Lia started consistently failing with her deposits every night, I suspected an employee had sticky fingers. I hoped that seeing cameras around might make them rethink their choices."

"But the surveillance in the office was concealed. Wasn't that counterproductive?" Shelby asked.

Lauren pointed to a globe on the ceiling over the pastry station. "I asked Shane to install them where they could be seen. I wasn't worried about the office because that's used by managers." She looked over her shoulder at a cluster of young men gathering at the dish station. "Can you put away the produce order? I don't need the lettuce wilting."

Shelby watched the men scramble to obey and sensed Lauren ran a tight ship. "Is that why Shane installed smaller cameras in there?"

"I have no idea. Kristen asked him to do it when he completed these. I told Casi the same thing when she freaked out. I'm only concerned with my inventory and the money that comes through here." She rolled her eyes. "I included the coffee shop because Lia lives in an alternate universe where she believes everyone is good and kind. It became a running joke. She couldn't balance a deposit to save her life. Shane was there every night ensuring it was correct, and yet she still came up short when Jocelyn made the deposits." She gestured toward a small room off the kitchen. "Tell Sam he can check the video feed. Both Lia and Shane knew there were cameras and counted the money in direct view. No one came in after the envelopes were sealed."

Stella and Shelby exchanged looks, acknowledging that Lauren appeared to be legitimate. "Are all the videos are collected on your office computer?"

"Only from the cameras I had installed. Those in the main office were a different system," Lauren said.

Shelby noted Lauren checking the clock, and tiredness was edging up her own spine, indicating it was time to end the conversation. "I just have one last question. Perhaps it's of a more personal nature."

Lauren lifted her gaze from grinding saffron in a mortar and pestle. "Ok, is this for Sam or your own interest?"

Shelby regarded the pile of boxes stacked at the back door. "Both really. I'm curious why there was a conflict between you and Kristen over the produce vendor? When I was the event coordinator, my responsibility was to collaborate with the clients to choose the menus you designed. Unless they had a specific dietary request, I didn't get involved in the culinary aspect."

Lauren nodded. "And that's where Kristen and I had a problem. We always worked well together, but after she moved into your position, she suddenly gained an interest in sustainability and took on the task of sourcing alternative vendors for events. I couldn't understand why she was determined to cancel the contract we had with Honeybee farm in Mount Vernon. Their produce is excellent, and they have fair prices."

Shelby noticed the blush rise on Lauren's cheeks. "Are you dating the owner of the company?"

Lauren briefly checked behind her. "Shelby, I want this to stay private. It's not considered unprofessional for me to date a vendor with an existing account."

"Then why keep it a secret?" Shelby asked.

"I have a three-year-old daughter who I'm raising by myself because my ex is in jail. The last thing I want is to highlight my love life. Both Kyle and Casi know and have assured me it's not a compromising situation, but they have honored my request to keep it private." Lauren stated.

"I completely understand," Shelby said. "Did Kristen know? It could be the reason she felt you should use a different vendor?"

"When she applied for the promotion to fill in for you, Lia

pushed for her to get the position. Kristen struggled after her mother died, and she didn't seem to have a lot of friends. Lia suggested it would be good for her to gain experience and be in a role dealing directly with the public. She had often worked from home while she was caring for her mother. She didn't have acceptable social skills when she returned to the workplace. I tried to be professional, but when I brought it up to her, she became irate, and that's when I found out that Ryan, the owner of Honeybee Farms, was her brother. They are estranged because she felt he wasn't supportive while their mother was sick."

"Interesting. They grew up in Blackberry Falls. You didn't know either of them from high school?" Shelby asked.

"Kristen was already in college when I got into the upper grades, and Ryan was a year above me. I was completely infatuated with my boyfriend at the time." Lauren sighed. "Are you aware that I used to date Brian?"

"The accountant?" Shelby tilted her head. "He's Dylan's partner."

"Yup, and then I dated Kyle for quite some time before he fell head over heels for Casi." She regarded her cutting board with the neat piles of minced herbs. "I haven't been lucky in love."

"Maybe Ryan will be the special one," Shelby declared, willing it to be true. "It seems like a delightful combination, a farmer and a chef."

"It would be nice," Lauren said. "He's been weird since Kristen died. I mean, I literally just discovered she was his sister last week because she had cut him out of her life. Now he's busy taking care of his mom's estate and planning a funeral for his sister."

"Speaking of romance," Stella interjected. "Was Kristen dating anyone, perhaps someone with the initial S?"

"There were rumors, of course, that she put a tremendous amount of effort into losing weight, having cosmetic surgery, and a revived enthusiasm for her appearance." Lauren cast a quick glance down at her stained chef jacket and checkered pants. "Between working twelve-hour shifts and raising a kid, I'm lucky if I get a shower."

"I know how that feels," Shelby laughed. "Of course, my regimen is treatment and taking naps."

Lauren smiled. "Hey, you might want to have Sam talk to that delivery driver who was just here. Kristen spent a substantial amount of time flirting with him. His name is Simon or something. Shane knows him from the gym."

23

ESPRESSO AND EXCUSES

"Wait. Slow down," Sam laughed as he jotted notes on a pad while he clutched his phone to his ear. "I can't discuss the facts of the case, Shelby, other than to say the authorities have set it aside until they find there is sufficient evidence to pursue it." He smiled at her exuberance. "Yes, they are great clues. I promise to follow up. If it produces anything substantial, I'll share it with the police."

He regarded his notes when he hung up, unclear how cosmetic surgery, a guy from the gym, and a mysterious brother were connected. What he knew was Shelby Kincaid had put in more effort recently, while doing radiation and chemo, than the energy expended by the county sheriff's office. He acknowledged it was his own fault because he came down on them for their treatment of Alan during the questioning. He believed it was a waste of resources and a scare tactic to shake the gossip tree, and he hadn't held back when he addressed their superiors. Since then, the Kristen Martin case had been put on the back burner, destined to be ignored unless he could bring significant evidence, using his own budget.

The Blackberry Falls Police Department operated on a shoestring budget, its resources stretched thin even before his sergeant quietly retired a few months back. With no funds to hire a replacement, the small team had been making do. Carla, the night-shift patrol officer, had chased leads in her spare time but turned up nothing useful. Ben, eager but green, struggled with resident interviews, though Sam held out hope he would uncover something from the growing pile of surveillance footage. At the front desk, Doris managed phones and case files with the same no-nonsense efficiency she used to juggle the town's parking disputes. With such a skeleton crew, it was no wonder why he had to do much of the work. In a place like Blackberry Falls, where the biggest drama was usually a missing kayak or a disputed property line, no one was prepared for this.

Sam had contacted the medical examiner and asked her to meet for coffee. Her obvious disdain for Detective Sanchez would hopefully benefit him when she reviewed the results from the blood tests again. As luck would have it, Dana was in the market for a condo and happened to find out Sam's wife was a realtor, and she had been eager to meet him and exchange information. He parked on a side street and walked a block to the cafe, preferring not to draw attention to his squad car. He greeted the hostess with a smile and chose a table on the patio away from the gathering of ladies having brunch. The decibels of their laughter suggested they were several mimosas in, and he wanted to have a quiet discussion with the medical examiner. He stood when Dana arrived, uncertain if he should pull out her chair. He found modern society confusing, especially when his daughter always corrected the behavior that he deemed chivalrous. Dana looped the strap of her monstrously large purse over the back of the chair and sat like it had been an effort to stand.

"Long day?" Sam asked.

"Monumental," she said. "A murder over in Belltown."

"Will the autopsy determine what caused the death?" Sam asked, not adding that the possible murder in his town didn't seem to warrant as much attention.

"Let's just say the victim was delivered in pieces," Dana said. "Therefore, it's not really determining what brought about their death, but rather which atrocity dealt the final blow."

"Ugh, that's rough," Sam said as bile climbed up his throat at the mere suggestion of the brutal crime. Wanting to change the subject quickly, he slid a card across the table. "My wife, Heather, says she has a nice inventory of what you're looking for. I'll let you gals discuss it from here." He winced when Dana raised an eyebrow at his old-fashioned language.

She smiled, acknowledging his intent was better than his delivery. "Thanks for checking with her." She picked up the card and tucked it into her purse. "I've been inundated at work, and I don't have time to go to an endless number of open houses. I've been outbid on the last three, and if I didn't hate where I'm renting, I would give up on the house hunting. It's challenging to handle all of this as a single woman. This is one time that a man might be useful." She laughed at his shocked expression. "Sorry, a few poor relationships have left me a bit sour." She clicked on her phone and angled the screen toward him.

"What am I looking at?" Sam squinted at the tiny screen.

Dana placed her napkin over the phone when the server came to their table. "I'm starving. I know you said coffee, but I've got to eat a proper meal."

"No apologies, but please let me pay," Sam insisted. "I appreciate your taking time to meet me. I know you're exhausted and probably need to return to work soon." He pointed to an item on the menu. "I'll have the omelet with bacon and peppers. Hash browns and whole wheat toast. And coffee," he said, tapping the cup out of habit, like it wasn't obvious what the vessel was used for.

"I accept your offer," Dana said. "It's pleasant to be out with a man who is only looking for information after buying a meal." The server nodded, without being aware of the particulars but evidently sharing the same experiences in the dating world. "I'll have the French toast, sausage on the side, and I'll start with coffee, but also bring me a latte." She smiled as the server gathered their menus and signaled to the busboy to fill their coffee cups.

"I'm concerned about my daughter in this new culture. Men are apparently not behaving well," Sam said.

"Be glad you're not raising a son," Dana said, halting when Sam recoiled like she had slapped him. "I didn't intend to man bash."

Sam gulped his coffee to ease his tension, choking on the hot liquid. "I lost my son when he was fifteen. It's been a few years, but it still hits me like a freight train."

Dana reached over and grasped his hand, surprising him when tears rimmed her eyes. "I apologize for my offensive comment. I understand the pain of losing someone, and maybe that's part of what has jaded me. I see many young people on my table who should have had full lives. Whether it was their own doing or unfortunate circumstances, it's not fair when they never get a chance to live up to their potential."

"I appreciate your insight," Sam said. "That's why I wanted to meet with you today. Kristen Martin was part of Blackberry Falls, and she deserves our utmost commitment to unraveling the mystery."

Dana reached for her latte as the server placed it on the table and sipped it as if it rejuvenated her soul. "I absolutely adore caffeine," she said, looking suddenly younger than a woman in her mid-forties. She moved her napkin from the phone and enlarged the image. "This is Kristen's blood test results. We already knew about the semaglutide, and there aren't any other substances or poisons present."

"If she wasn't poisoned, could she have had a stroke from using the drugs?" Sam asked.

"All her organs were healthy." Her expression darkened, and she shook her head. "She appeared to have had her nails and hair freshly done. She had several cosmetic enhancements..." she stopped herself from revealing information that should be private.

"That's what's odd," Sam said. "By all accounts, she was living a content life. It hadn't gone unnoticed that she had lost weight or had cosmetic work done. Once her mother passed away, Kristen was independent. It seems she came into a bit of money from the estate and perhaps used it to spiff herself up."

Dana smiled and relaxed in her chair. "I find your small-town charm comforting."

Sam frowned, unsure what he had said that warranted that reaction. "Like a redneck?"

"Gosh, no. It's a genuine compliment," she said, moving her phone aside for the steaming plate of food being delivered. She drenched a lavish amount of maple syrup over the French toast and watched as it mixed with the butter to create a delectable landslide. "I grew up in Texas," she said. "I don't miss the heat, but I yearn for the kind of community where people care enough about each other to do what is right, not easy. It seems like Blackberry Falls is that kind of place."

"We don't have fancy condos, but you could find a nice townhouse at half the cost, and it's only twenty minutes from the outskirts of Seattle," Sam said.

"How's the dating scene?" Dana asked as she took a bite.

"Kristen's efforts didn't pan out," Sam said and then cringed. "Gosh, that was a dreadful thing to say."

"It really was," Dana laughed. "But that's what I like about you. These things just come out of your mouth." She lifted her mug to her lips. "Which is why I feel I can trust you."

"Absolutely," Sam promised. "Any information you give me will be kept confidential."

Dana picked up her phone again. "When you called me and asked about the blood work, I didn't think there was anything new. Then I realized I might have missed something by only testing the blood. You were passionate about accounts of the victim behaving oddly, according to witnesses. She didn't have defensive wounds that would indicate she tried to stop from falling, which is odd. Glucose levels aren't accurately detected in blood after death. I checked her vitriol and cerebrospinal fluids."

Sam stopped mid bite. "And what did they say?"

"Bingo." Dana slapped the table, drawing attention from diners around them. She lowered her voice and leaned in. "Her blood glucose was dangerously low, and she probably blacked out before she fell. The impact of her head hitting a rock is what killed her, but hypoglycemia made her pass out."

"Wow!" Sam said. "But is there still uncertainty about whether it was natural causes? She was dieting and taking medication. Is that a side effect?"

Dana gave him a sly smile "You will owe me dinner for this one."

"I'll invite you to my next barbeque. I make an incredible brisket," Sam said, eager to hear more.

"I returned and tested her plasma. It had been refrigerated, and I managed to get an adequate reading." She narrowed her eyes. "Her insulin levels were off the charts high. It wouldn't be possible for the body to produce that much, even after a heavy meal." She pointed to her breakfast. "Her stomach contents barely had a few ounces of coffee."

"How would you interpret that?" Sam attempted to comprehend all the information she was providing him.

"Irreversible neurological injury occurs when glycogen stores are depleted, since the brain depends totally on glucose for metabolism. Which indicates she must have injected insulin into her system. Or someone did. I found a slight welt on her stomach, and I assumed it was from the medication. It's not possible to determine how it was administered post mortem," she said.

"Could it have been slipped it into her coffee?" Sam asked.

"No, the stomach is too acidic. It would have broken down before it entered her bloodstream. It was definitely injected," she said.

"Can we prove it was murder?" Sam said.

"Not so fast. There are several issues," Dana said. "First, it's unknown whether she injected it herself. These days, there are an abundance of fad diets. You wouldn't believe the young women I see who have died from a random tip they found on Instagram."

"Great, a new level of fear has been unlocked for my daughter," Sam said. "If Kristen injected herself, can we at least confirm the high levels of insulin preceded her fall?"

"Another issue," Dana said. "My samples are now degraded. My evidence won't hold up in court, and this meeting is off the record."

Sam slouched. "Where do I go from here?"

"You're a detective," Dana smiled. "I've given you the lead. The insulin must have been injected within thirty minutes of passing out. Backtrack from where she fell from the trail, and you will have the approximate area where it was administered. The level of semaglutide was low. Either she stopped using it in favor of trying insulin or she made a mistake and injected the wrong drug. Either way, look for a pen-style injector. You find that and you'll have your smoking gun."

24

TOXIC SECRETS

"How do we find a discarded dispenser?" Shelby asked.

"We aren't doing anything," Sam stated as he leaned back on the sofa. "I promised to share information with you, and most of what I've told you is inadmissible in court."

"Who gave you these details?" Shelby asked.

"I can't tell you that," Sam grinned. "As I already said, it has come to my attention the victim may have experienced low blood glucose levels prior to falling over the embankment."

Shelby frowned. "I freely shared my sources."

"You're an amateur sleuth and not the head of the police department," Sam explained. "Your investigation is basically following a chain of gossip."

"I invested a great deal of effort into those questions. I feel I was quite crafty about getting people to talk," Shelby said.

"I agree," Sam said. "I appreciate you bringing these details to my attention. They may not prove to be related to the case, but it got us thinking in a new way."

As Alan and Sam slipped into a conversation about sports, Shelby turned her attention to the window. A hummingbird hovered near the feeder, its wings beating so rapidly they blurred into invisibility. Brilliant green feathers flashed in the sunlight, dazzling and fragile all at once. It dipped its beak, drank hurriedly, then darted away when another bird swooped in aggressively. The moment unsettled her more than it should have. It was too fast and frantic. Burning energy with nothing left to spare.

Alan had hung the feeder a couple of months back to give her something pleasant to focus on while she was attached to Joey Kangaroo and the steady mechanical rhythm of her feedings. She had added it to her gratitude list, noting his attention to details others overlooked. The small kindnesses. The quiet acts of devotion filled the space between crises.

She reached for her notebook, flipping through pages covered in uneven handwriting, short observations, and reminders for the home nurse. She paused, uncertain what to add this time. She hated repeating daily affirmations. They felt hollow when repeated too often. Instead, she searched for something new. Something useful.

Her eyes landed on an entry from the previous week. *Readings stable. Feeling clear-headed.*

She nodded to herself. Stability was not something she took for granted anymore.

Poor Kristen must have been completely disoriented if she had never experienced hypoglycemia before. The confusion. The dizziness. The sudden, terrifying sense that nothing quite made sense.

"Hey," Shelby said suddenly, lifting her head. "Why would Kristen inject herself with insulin? That seems counterproductive, especially if she was headed out for a walk."

Sam blinked, pulled abruptly from his conversation with Alan. "Maybe she mixed up her prescriptions or didn't realize how much she was taking."

"That's not possible," Alan said, already rising from his seat.

He crossed to the refrigerator and opened the door, instinctively reaching for the compartment where medical supplies had slowly overtaken what once held butter. "If she used an insulin pen, which I've been told is now the standard, the units are clearly marked. You must deliberately turn the dial and click it into place."

He brought the pen over, demonstrating the motion for Sam with practiced ease.

"Maybe she was buying it off market like the diet drugs," Sam said thoughtfully. "If it came in a vial, she might have added too much to the syringe."

"Then she did it willingly," Alan replied. "Or someone else injected her. And that would be very difficult not to notice."

"I could see how she might be confused if her sugar was already low," Shelby said slowly. "I get disoriented. But insulin is the last thing you should use in that situation. It would only make things worse. I can barely read the glucose monitor when I'm having an episode."

"Is that common knowledge?" Sam asked.

"Anyone using insulin would know," Alan said. "Shelby went through hours of training with a diabetic counselor in the hospital. When she came home, she insisted she could handle it herself."

"I was trying to be independent," Shelby said. "So, you wouldn't feel obligated to stay home and babysit me all day."

Alan chuckled. "Except she didn't realize you had to insert a needle."

Shelby rolled her eyes. "They demonstrated it with a dummy pen. I assumed it worked the same way."

"Good thing I checked," Alan said. "Otherwise, she wasn't getting any insulin at all."

Sam shook his head. "You didn't wonder why it didn't hurt?"

Shelby shrugged. "I can't feel my stomach anymore. After

four chest tubes and this," she gestured toward the feed tube beneath her blanket, "pain has lost its meaning."

"You needed a prescription for the medication?" Sam said, steering them back on course.

"It's highly regulated," Alan said. "We ran around to three pharmacies just to fill it. Now they're saying Shelby isn't considered diabetic anymore, so I've got a stockpile. I was planning to donate it before it expires."

"Can I see it again?" Sam asked.

Shelby handed over her reading glasses as he squinted to read the information.

Alan carefully explained each component. The reservoir. The dose selector. The injection button. The expiration date.

"It's hard to believe Kristen could overdose accidentally," Sam said.

Alan frowned. "You can inject up to sixty units at a time. But not by mistake. You must actively dial it in. Even Shelby couldn't manage that by accident."

"How many units per pen?" Sam asked.

"Three hundred," Alan replied. "Shelby takes ten units when her blood glucose is high."

Sam leaned forward. "Are the pens refillable?"

"No," Alan said. "Once it's empty, you discard it. Needle goes in the Sharps container. Cartridge gets recycled at the pharmacy."

"And leftover insulin isn't toxic?" Sam pressed.

"You wouldn't discard a pen until it was empty," Alan said. "But residue breaks down quickly if it's unrefrigerated."

"How many pens came in the prescription?"

"Five." Alan paused. He shook the box once. Then again. His brows knit together. "Shelby, you didn't throw one away, did you?"

Shelby scoffed. "Why would I? We barely used the first one. You teased me for not attaching the needle."

Alan tipped the box, peering inside. His face drained of color. "There are only four." He shook the box making sure one hadn't slipped down. "There's one missing."

Sam jumped up and rushed to Alan's side. "How is that possible?"

"I don't know," Alan said. "I'm the only one who administers it. The home nurse only checks Shelby's vitals and works with her on positivity." He looked at Shelby and asked, "No one else has been giving you insulin, right?" He closed the fridge and walked toward her chair when she didn't turn around. "Shell, did you hear me? Stella's not giving you insulin, is she?"

"No, I..." Shelby started to sputter, breathing rapidly, and clasping her chest. "Alan!"

"Shell, what's wrong?" He grabbed the bucket and held it under her chin as she began to cough and gag. "It's ok, I'm here."

"What do you need me to do?" Sam asked frantically.

Alan's eyes widened as he caught sight of the clots of blood Shelby was spitting into the bucket. "Call 911," he said, his voice sharp with fear.

Shelby sagged back in her chair as the room spun, the hummingbird forgotten, the missing pen bringing more questions than answers.

25

———

SILENT WARNING

"She will be fine," Sam said, hoping the fear in his voice wasn't noticeable.

"We don't know for sure," Alan gasped. "What if the tumor broke through her esophagus? There could be internal damage or worse, the cancer might have gone to her other organs. They warned us that if it went into her liver, it wouldn't be treatable."

"Let's not jump the gun." Sam placed his hand over the screen on Alan's phone. "Stop looking up symptoms on the internet. The oncologist advised you that it was unwise to do your own research."

"I know, but I'm worried I did something wrong," Alan lamented. "Shelby has been optimistic and tried hard to get better. What did I miss? Maybe I messed up her medication. I can't believe her insulin is gone..."

"Ok, let's occupy our time with that question," Sam urged. "When was the last time you checked the package in the fridge? Stella has been cooking, right? Maybe she moved it?"

"Why would she take it?" Alan asked.

"Not took it, but maybe it fell out of the fridge, and she put it in a different location?" Sam suggested.

"Maybe. She's had to be the caregiver for her mom off and on from an early age. She's careful about medication. I know she would never cause any harm to Shelby," Alan said.

"Definitely not," Sam agreed. "The missing pen may not even be connected to Kristen's death. It seems farfetched to use low blood glucose as a murder weapon. How would anyone even know how to do that?"

Alan's eyes widened. "You're not implicating Stella, are you? Did the detectives tell you how she reacted when Shelby had hypoglycemia while they were questioning me?"

"Yes, but I'm not suggesting it was Stella," Sam rested his hand on Alan's shoulder. "Shelby has been open about her journey. Maybe she shared how she felt when her sugar dropped?"

"Except she only came back to the coffee shop the day Kristen died. That's too tight of a timeline," Alan said.

"True, but pretty much everyone came to visit her, right? They would have noticed your medication list displayed on the whiteboard and maybe even seen you administer the medication. Can you recall anyone who asked questions or showed particular interest?" Sam asked,

"I'm barely hanging on by a thread," Alan sighed. "Shelby means the world to me, and we don't need the added stress of this murder investigation."

Sam shrugged. "Think of it from Shelby's perspective. All she's done over the past few months is battle cancer, while everyone tells her to be strong. This sad turn of events has given her the opportunity to focus her energy on something other than her illness. She has a knack for crime solving. I'm shocked by clues I overlooked."

"The State PD should investigate the case," Alan said. "It

appears as though they are indifferent to the fact that a woman from a small town was most likely murdered."

"They have a multitude of crimes that require their immediate attention. They don't have the manpower or resources to chase leads that may not turn into anything substantial. The cause of death has been ruled as blunt force trauma because ultimately what killed her was striking her head against a boulder." Sam tousled his hair with his fingers. "Personally, I feel committed to uncovering what led to her fall in the first place, and if Shelby can assist me in identifying who may have had a motive, then it's advantageous to everyone in Blackberry Falls."

"You're right, but..." Alan turned when the doctor strolled into the waiting room. He quickly assessed the surgeon's demeanor to prepare himself for the news. "Is Shelby okay?"

The doctor smiled. "She's in recovery."

"Will you move her to the ICU?" Alan asked.

"No, we want to monitor her for a few hours, but she did great with the surgery." He took a sheet of paper from the receptionist's desk and drew a primitive picture of tubes, scribbling in an area halfway down. "Think of it like your kitchen sink. Her tumor was blocking the flow to the stomach. Our fear was that she would aspirate again, even on her own saliva, and her lung hasn't healed enough to handle that." He added a thick line down the center. "The stent opened up the esophagus to allow passage."

"The oncologist said she could eat. I made her shrimp and mashed potatoes. Is that what caused this?" Alan asked.

"Eating is important for her mental health, but we don't consider all the muscles involved in swallowing. A liquid diet is not a viable long-term solution. The feed tube is ensuring she's getting proper nutrients, which are essential for healing. A small amount of food every day is beneficial and did not cause the issue." He circled the heavy line in the center and drew an arrow. "Shelby is responding well to the chemotherapy and radiation treatment. The tumor has already shrunk by half. That caused the stent to slip down into her stomach and resulted in her spitting up blood. It seemed violent, but it was more painful than dangerous."

"She only told me about it today." Alan turned to Sam for support. "She was upset about the woman who died on the trail by the lake, and then she had a spasm."

"Agitation will make the muscles cramp, and that's most likely what caused the pain," the doctor said.

"How can we prevent that in the future? I try to keep her calm, but she's taken the initiative to find out what happened to that woman. Should we encourage her to stop?" Alan asked.

The doctor smiled. "I don't know your wife very well, but from what I see in her chart about how she's handled her treatment, she does not respond well to being told no. She knows her limits, and this case is good mental exercise for her to get out of her own illness and focus on something else."

"You said she's responding well to treatment. Won't the stent continue to move?" Alan asked.

"We removed the stent," the doctor said. "Shelby is doing well, and her swallowing is almost normal. She can continue to eat soft foods in small amounts."

"Does that mean she won't have to undergo the esophagectomy?" Alan asked.

"The goal is to remove the cancer from her body for good. I'm sure the cardiothoracic surgeon will still want to perform the surgery to ensure your wife has the best outcome. The nurse will come and get you when Shelby is awake." The doctor nodded and handed Alan the crude drawing.

Alan walked to the window and stared out at the parking lot as he processed his thoughts. He watched a man helping his pregnant wife from the car as a truck skidded to a stop in front of them. Two people leaped from the vehicle, barely clothed, as one of the young men clutched his arm, which was bent at an unbelievable angle. Alan winced at the pain he must be experiencing. A security guard sternly warned the driver to move the vehicle immediately out of the red zone.

"I'm questioning if he tripped on his pants?" Sam joked as he stood by Alan's side, taking in the scene below.

Alan smiled at the remark, noting the jeans hanging below the young man's hips, making it almost impossible for him to walk in a straight line. The man with the pregnant wife hurried past them while they argued with the security officer. A buzzing sound interrupted his thoughts, and he shifted his focus to a tan leather bag on the table. "That's Shelby's phone," he said, noticing the frown on the woman's face, who had a ponytail so tight it drew her face into a scowl. She turned her head toward a sign with an x through an image of a cell phone. "Sorry," Alan said quickly, retrieving the phone from the bag.

"Why did you bring Shelby's purse?" Sam chuckled.

"Out of habit," Alan said. "Shelby calls it her magic bag. It's full of everything she needs in case of an emergency. I knew she would want it when she woke up," he choked on his words.

"She'll be alright. Look, she even has her list of culprits and their motives." Sam pointed to the notepaper escaping from the bag. "What's the matter?" he inquired as Alan's face lost all color.

Alan turned the screen of the phone toward him to show a series of text messages. "I was turning it off, and these came up."

"Who is sending these?" Sam quickly read through several that warned Shelby to back off the investigation, escalating to threatening to expose secrets if she continued. When he read the last one, his eyes widened. "See what you get when you don't listen? I'm not playing games anymore."

"It doesn't have contact information," Alan said. "The first one came a few days ago." He narrowed his eyes. "The day I was questioned."

Sam chewed his cheek. "Someone is getting worried Shelby might uncover the truth."

"I'm not letting my wife be used for bait!" Alan roared, drawing attention from the patrons of the waiting room.

"Certainly not," Sam whispered. "Think about it, though. The person is threatening things they have no control over. Sure, they probably gave information to the police to prompt them to investigate you, but obviously that proved to be false. Shelby being rushed to emergency was because of the stent, not poisoning."

"This isn't making me feel better," Alan said.

"My point is, the person who is sending the text messages has access to detailed information about Shelby that they can obtain quickly," Sam stated. "They are using that to threaten her."

"Well, information in the coffee circle travels faster than the speed of light..." Alan raised an eyebrow. "Do you think this is one of her friends? Why would they do this? Everyone loves Shelby."

Sam nodded. "It's likely the murder was accidental, and now they are afraid Shelby is discovering the truth."

Alan shoved the phone back in Shelby's bag and clutched the straps as the nurse waved him over to the door. "Sam, you're my friend, and I appreciate the support you've given us through this ordeal. You know I'm not an assertive man, but I won't allow Shelby to be in danger. I don't care if these are idle threats. My wife's health is our priority. I realize I'm selfish, but we must create a calm atmosphere for Shelby to center on healing. I'm sorry, but you, Carla, and Ben are the ones in charge of solving this case." He turned when he reached the door. "And that includes Stella. She needs to be with her aunt, not running around town stirring up controversy that will ultimately tear our family apart."

26

———

BLURRED LINES

Stella yawned while she made her way to the kitchen and poured herself a cup of coffee. She reached for the half and half, chatting about the event she had worked on the night before. When no one responded, she peered into the living room and noted her aunt sitting in the recliner as usual, and her uncle on the sofa reading the newspaper. "Why is she wearing headphones?" she asked, hearing the throng of a pop tune.

"She's isolating herself," Alan responded, savoring his coffee.

"What does that mean?" Stella asked, sitting beside him.

"She's annoyed that I asked her to stop putting herself in danger by running around town trying to solve a crime that is police business," Alan said loudly.

"So basically, she's ignoring you," Stella laughed.

"When we came home from the hospital, I advised her that avoiding the coffee shop gathering for a while would be the wisest course of action." Alan asked. "She said I was forcing her to reside in a bubble. She announced she was going on a mental retreat for a while to think things through."

"Is that the grown-up version of running away?" Stella asked.

"Apparently," Alan sighed. "Did you know she was receiving threatening text messages?"

"No, from whom?" Stella asked.

"They don't have contact information. Just a reference to spilling secrets and making her pay. They knew she was admitted to the hospital and said that's what she gets for putting her nose in other people's business," Alan said.

"Can I see her phone?" Stella asked.

"It's on the nightstand," Alan said. "I kept it there last night because I wanted her to rest."

"Ah, you monitored her access to the outside world. You should get her an ankle monitor in case she tries to wander away," Stella said.

Shelby laughed and slipped the headphones from her ears. "He thinks he's protecting me, but I'm not safe if I'm cut off from the world."

"I see you have returned from your isolation. Did you have an enjoyable trip?" Alan joked.

"It gave me time to think," Shelby said.

"Hopefully, to come to your senses and see that you've given it your best shot to help with Kristen's situation," Alan said, stopping to kiss her cheek as he walked by to refill his coffee.

Stella scrolled through the messages on Shelby's phone. "This person knows your routine and enough about your life to use it against you. They are afraid you are close to finding the truth."

"Exactly!" Shelby said. "Can you hand me my purse?" She took the bag from Stella and rustled through to find a paper and pen. "What is this drawing?"

"That's your esophagus," Alan said. "The surgeon was showing me how the stent slid down."

Shelby turned the paper in a different direction. "It looks

like a pipe with a clog. I hope he's a better surgeon than he is an artist."

Alan laughed. "It got the point across."

Shelby found the paper she was looking for and set it on the table beside her. She dug through a basket and retrieved a set of colored pencils. "We know Kristen died because she bonked her head. What is unclear is whether she took the insulin willingly or if was given without her knowledge. Also, if it was from my prescription, how would she not notice the label?"

"And just like that, we're back in the crime solving business," Alan sighed.

"Honestly, Alan, if you want me to be out of harm's way, we need to find out who did this. I'm implicated if my medication was used to commit the crime and that puts me at risk because I'm sure the next thing the police will ask me for is a compilation of people who had access to our fridge," Shelby said, holding up a list of names. She extracted a pink pencil and crossed out the first three. "We can safely say that the individuals present in this room didn't do it. Although we all could have taken the pen, how would we get Kristen to use it? We didn't have contact with her that day." Shelby turned her head toward Alan. "Actually, you did, Alan, but it was well after she seemed to be reacting from the injection."

Alan took the sheet of paper. "When did you write this?"

"In the hospital. The nurses were very helpful. They said insulin works quickly, and if a person injected it without having high blood sugar, they could be at risk of slipping into a coma within an hour. Since Kristen was exercising, that would expedite things."

"I hope she didn't take it willingly, and it backfired. It seems people are eager to do anything these days to lose weight." Alan regarded the packaging of Shelby's supplement bag. "As a former athlete, I always thought of food as fuel. When you don't get enough, your performance declines."

"You should explain that to the models in LA. They are desperate to try anything to keep their weight down. Some of the girls get severely ill, but the agencies bully them with unrealistic expectations," Stella agreed.

Alan winced as he watched Stella talking with matter-of-fact confidence. "Sweetie, please assure me you aren't doing anything unhealthy to maintain your weight. Remember, we promised to support the opportunity for you to model, but if the pressure is too much, there are countless other jobs you can do."

Stella smiled. "I promise I'm not doing drugs, legal or otherwise."

"You've always made good choices," Shelby praised.

Stella exhaled. "It makes it easier when you've had to pick your mom up a gazillion times after a bender. I vowed I would never live that life. I've learned to make a cocktail last all night at the club while looking like I fit in with the other girls."

"Never leave your drink unattended," Shelby warned. "I remember a girl in college who had an unfortunate outcome when a creep slipped something into her drink without her knowing." Shelby's hand instinctively covered her mouth. "Oh my, do you think that's what transpired with Kristen?"

Alan tilted his head. "You think drugs were put in her coffee?"

"It could have occurred at the espresso bar that morning," Shelby said. "I believe I recollect Kristen interacting with that delivery man. What was his name? He works for the farmer."

"Is this chemo brain? You're usually quite good with names," Stella asked, leafing through Shelby's notebook to find the names they were given by Lauren.

"My head is foggy lately," Shelby sighed. "Alan, have I had my water? Maybe I'm dehydrated."

"For goodness' sakes," Alan leaped up and rushed to the kitchen. He came back with a syringe and began the process of disconnecting the food pump before meticulously cleaning the tube. "I really wish you and Casi hadn't tinkered with my whiteboard. Between my notes all being erased, your trip to the hospital, and the fear of a blackmailer, things have been rather chaotic."

Shelby smiled and brushed her fingers through his mop of chestnut hair with swirls of cowlicks, making him appear much younger than fifty-two. She waited to speak until he had secured the syringe and slowly released the water into the tube. "I feel better already," she lied.

"Hilarious," Alan said. "Give it about twenty minutes, and I'm sure you'll bounce right back. We're a day behind with radiation, but the oncologist said we'll move it to the end. It will fit in perfectly because of the delayed chemo when your numbers were down." He sat back on his heels and watched the emotions play out across Shelby's face. "Since you refuse to give up the chase, why don't I take you to the coffee shop later and you can interrogate a few more people? You could use the health crisis strategy to get folks to talk. There must be new gossip churning while you were away."

Shelby leaned forward and brought her lips to his, lingering to feel the deep connection between them. "I love how you say our treatment and we will fight this. It makes me feel like we are a team."

"Alby," Stella giggled. "That's your celebrity couple's name."

Alan chuckled. "Well, team Alby needs to get dressed if we aim to make it to our appointment on time."

SHELBY RELAXED IN THE CHAIR, letting the medication ease her into a gentle sleep. The lilt of light rock music eased her mind and freed her from the details of daily life. As she drifted away, she was aware of Alan cautiously tugging on her ice slippers. He moved the tablet from her lap and slid the insulated gloves on her hands, trying his best not to wake her. She smiled and let her eyelids drop fully to obscure the sight of the IV drip. The clank of the pole against the stool as the nurse switched the medications roused Shelby enough to glance at the bag filled with liquid and the plastic tubing running down to the mid-line in her upper arm. With a yawn, she recalled how she had been scheduled to get a port before chemo, but the unexpected lung collapse had set off a series of chaotic events. It had been decided it wasn't worth the risk of placing a port after several infections scarred her veins. She generally avoided looking at the mid-line, not liking to think about the part threaded through her body. Warmth rode up her arm, heating her veins with a sensation. Shelby's eyes flew open, and she searched the room for Alan, who was nowhere to be found. The nurse who had started the IV was a temp filling in for Nancy, who usually assisted. Her regular nurse had been a source of comfort, always encouraging Shelby and explaining each step of the treatment. Shelby tried to focus on the label of the drip bag, but her vision was blurred. As she moved her hand forward to grab the pole, her ice glove slipped off, knocking the contents of the table to the floor in a domino effect. Fear rose in Shelby's chest as the acrid flavor of bile made her nauseous. She felt trapped in the armchair as the anxiety escalated, and her legs refused to cooperate as they twitched.

"Alan!" she called out, needing his assistance to stop the nightmare that was unfolding.

"I'm right here," Alan soothed, appearing like an apparition.

"They're poisoning me. I can feel it burning my veins," she grabbed his arm to make him listen. "They know I'm still finding clues, and they are trying to make me stop." Tears streamed down her cheeks, burning her sensitive skin.

"Can you come help us?" Alan asked as the nurses chatted at the desk, sharing the details from a night out.

The nurse huffed and eyed the IV drip. "She still has twenty minutes and then the flush."

"We know the schedule," Alan snapped in an uncharacteristic tone. "You can see my wife is in distress. Did you give her the pre-meds?"

The woman looked like she had been slapped. "I followed the protocol."

"Please get the oncologist," Alan demanded. He regarded the room of patients looking on in horror, not knowing if Shelby was hallucinating or if she had accidentally received the wrong medication.

"What's happening, Shelby?" the oncologist soothed as she drew the curtain around the chair to offer privacy. She perched on the stool and grasped Shelby's hand. "Are you in pain?"

"It just feels different," Shelby whimpered. "I feel like I'm being poisoned."

The oncologist smiled. "You've been through a lot recently. It's normal to be afraid. You were under anesthesia recently, and it takes time to fully leave your body." She pointed to the label on the bag. "This is the same brand you've been getting, but your body is adjusting." She rubbed Shelby's leg as she twisted under the blanket. "You're reacting to the antihistamine, which can cause anxiety and restless legs. We'll cut you back next week. This is normal, okay? I promise we won't cause any harm to you."

"Thank you," Alan exhaled.

The oncologist nodded and typed on her tablet. "I'm prescribing a mild anti-anxiety pill. It dissolves under her tongue. It's non-habit forming, and she can take it if she's feeling overwhelmed, especially before eating, to help her remain calm." She smiled at his expression. "It would be like having a glass of wine. It's just enough to relax her, and only if she needs it." She opened the curtain and indicated the nurse should follow her to the corridor.

Alan watched the interaction and guessed the doctor was not happy about the lax treatment of the patients. He faced Shelby and sat on the stool as he slipped her glove back on. "You okay, Shelby Bean?"

"I freaked out a bit," she blushed.

"Hey, you're doing great. I know it can feel claustrophobic to have all those tubes sticking out of you and everyone wants to jab you constantly," he said.

"I feel separate from my body. I try to put it out of my mind; however, I suppose it bubbled up today," she regarded the drip, glad it was almost empty. "Alan..."

"What's the matter?" he inquired.

"Can you look up if insulin can be ingested?" she asked.

"What? Why?" He frowned as he typed the question into his phone. "Huh, it says the acid in the stomach would break it down before it could be absorbed."

Shelby nodded. "I thought the diabetic nurse mentioned that when she was demonstrating how to use the pen. I had asked why I couldn't take it as a pill." She tilted her head toward the pole. "If Kristen took it without knowing it, maybe someone swapped it out with her weight loss medication?"

27

CATS AND CHAOS

Stella paused in the driveway and glanced at Shelby. "Are you certain that you're up to a visit to the coffee shop? Uncle Alan reported there was an incident at chemo this morning."

Shelby gently touched Stella's hand. "I had a meltdown and accused them of poisoning me."

"Oh no! Why did you think that?" Stella asked, easing the car into the street.

"The nurse had a peculiar vibe, and I didn't feel she was paying attention to my medication. Nancy never rushes me and explains each step, even though I know the routine. This young girl was more concerned about chatting with the other nurses about her upcoming wedding and the ten pounds she's trying to lose to look good in her dress," Shelby explained. "I'm sure I looked like a hysterical old lady, but they don't know about the text messages threatening my life."

Stella shivered. "Maybe Uncle Alan is right, and it's better if we leave this case to the police."

"I believe I'll be safer if the killer is caught," Shelby asserted. "I would like to make a quick stop on the way to the coffee shop. Turn on Elm Street." She gestured towards a street with quaint bungalows painted in soft pastels.

"Who are we visiting on this side of town?" Stella asked, pulling to the curb.

"I need to pick something up," Shelby said, climbing out of the car and ensuring her legs were steady before proceeding up the alley behind the homes. She kept her head down as a man walked by with a border collie, then made a swift right turn up a driveway. "Stella, hurry," she urged.

"Why do I get the impression we're involved in mischievous acts that are probably against the law?" Stella asked.

"I'm just visiting a friend. There are no laws against that," Shelby assured her. She moved a potted plant to the side and extracted a key.

"Except this friend is in the morgue and you're entering her premises to snoop for clues," Stella guessed. "How did you know the key was there?"

"I gave Kristen a lift one night after work. You know how I always emphasized the importance of waiting until the person is safely inside before you leave. I noticed she kept the key there, which isn't out of the ordinary in this tiny community. Many people don't even lock their homes," Shelby said, before easing the door open. She took latex gloves from her purse and handed a set to Stella.

"Where did these come from?" she asked.

Shelby smiled. "I liberated them from the nurse's station. It was proof no one was paying attention."

"Basically, you're a thief and a burglar," Stella giggled.

"I'm resourceful," Shelby said, snapping the gloves with professional flair.

They walked into the small living area, which was exceptionally tidy. The cats Casi had seen appeared to have been removed, and only a few remnants of hair remained adhered to the pillows of the slate gray sofa.

"What are we looking for?" Stella whispered.

"I'm not sure. I'll know when I find it," Shelby answered. She stopped at the center of the room and surveyed the scene. "The police have already been here and have removed her laptop and probably any medication that might be associated with her demise. They recovered her phone at the scene and towed her car to the impound. My guess would be that her brother inherited the house and relocated the cats, hopefully, to a suitable home."

Stella looked at photos on a shelf, mostly of Kristen and her mother. A prominent display of two long-haired gray cats took center stage. "She lived here with her mom?"

"Yes, she was her caregiver until she passed away. I didn't understand the huge impact it had on her," Shelby said.

"She sure changed a lot over the past year," Stella pointed to photos of a stout woman with mousy brown hair and glasses beside an older woman of a similar stature.

They made their way to the kitchen and noted the complex display on the refrigerator with before and after photos, weights and measurements, and inspirational messages. "I'm sure she didn't realize there would be strangers poking around in her home," Shelby lamented.

"Like us?" Stella asked.

"We're here to solve the mystery of what happened to her," Shelby stated. "I meant the police and whoever removed the cats. These charts should be private." She sighed at the photos of Kristen in a bikini that was too small, evidently intended to inspire her to reach her goal weight. "Do you store the weight loss medication in the fridge?"

Stella did a quick internet search on her phone. "Yes, it seems to be similar to your insulin."

Shelby opened the fridge and perused the sparse contents neatly displayed on the shelves. She opened the vegetable drawer and reached behind a wilted head of celery. She smiled as she pulled out a package wrapped in foil. "I bet this is the medication."

"Shouldn't we leave it here for the police?" Stella asked.

"They should have been smarter to look for it," Shelby said. "Anyone who has been on a diet knows you hide the contraband behind the healthy foods." Shelby glanced around the room with very few personalized decorating choices. "Although she lived alone, it's likely some habits remained from her youth."

Stella laughed. "I didn't think you hid anything from Uncle Alan."

"He's supportive of my efforts, but when I fell off the wagon and eat cookies, he didn't understand why I would sabotage myself." Shelby shrugged. "I was slender in high school and then I suddenly gained weight at an alarming rate after college. It's really been such a struggle. Maybe I got cancer so I could finally break the cycle."

"That's sad, don't say that." Stella embraced her.

Shelby carefully unwrapped the package and peered inside. As expected, it contained vials of weight loss medication in single use doses. She took several pictures and pressed the edges of the foil securely around the medication before placing it back in the fridge, barely covered by the celery. "I'll alert Sam that the State PD might have missed a clue in the house. Maybe he can get it tested and see if they are all contaminated or if only the pen she used contained insulin."

"We are still unclear if that's what happened," Stella said.

"True, but at least we know what the empty cartridge would look like," Shelby said, closing the door. A slip of paper fluttered to the ground, followed by a photo that had been tucked behind the weight chart. Shelby studied the image of the grand opening of the luxurious lakeside resort on the front steps. She recalled that day two summers ago when they were eager to begin working at the beautiful location. She had worried about leaving a good-paying job in Seattle at a hotel, but Alan had assured her his income could support her if things didn't pan out. Not having children beyond her nieces and nephews, Shelby prioritized her career, and the move excited and terrified her simultaneously. Upon reflection, it had placed her in a supportive environment for going through cancer treatments, because everyone had rallied around her. Her old employer barely acknowledged her absence when she left. She ran a finger over the faces of the women on the list Kristen had created. They all had their arms wrapped around each other, happy to be in the moment. Kristen stood to the side, clasping her arm with her other hand, physically separating herself from the group. The sunlight bounced back from her thick glasses, obliterating her expression. Shelby sighed with the realization she had never noticed how Kristen might have felt left out of the tightly woven social circle.

"Interesting," Stella said, bringing Shelby's attention back to the present. "Check out all these nutritional supplements. It has a card with an address in Renton and a number for a guy named Simon."

"Lover or drug dealer?" Shelby raised an eyebrow. "Either way, it was hidden behind something that ties it all together. I wonder if she felt losing weight would make her fit in, and maybe this Simon guy helped with that?" She used her phone to take pictures and tucked the photo back in place on the fridge, leaving it partially exposed. They separated and quickly searched through drawers in every room of the house, scanning for items of interest. Shelby kneeled, cautious of her feed tube as she reached behind a Crockpot that looked like it was rarely used. Her fingertips brushed the top of a paper bag, and she eased it forward carefully to avoid spilling the contents.

They heard a key in the lock of the front door, and Stella grabbed Shelby's arm. "Should we run?"

"Let's slip out the back," Shelby whispered. They successfully reached the stairs, closing the door just in time before they heard heavy footsteps coming toward them. "Don't move," Shelby said, knowing they couldn't make it to the vehicle without being seen. She braced herself on the top step as the door flew open. "Oh goodness, that was fast! I just barely knocked."

The man with brown hair and a neatly trimmed beard looked them over. "Why are you here?"

"I'm Shelby, and this is my niece Stella," she extended her hand, cringing when she realized she still had her gloves on. "I was coming home from my chemo appointment, and I was concerned about Kristen's cats. I asked Stella if we could stop by and make sure someone was coming around to feed them."

The man directed his gaze to Shelby's tufts of hair, and his shoulders slumped. "That was thoughtful," he sighed. "We met when the resort first opened. I'm Ryan, Kristen's brother." He held out his hand. "I supply the produce for the restaurant."

Shelby bit her cheek to stop herself from asking about his relationship with Lauren, dying to know if they had patched things up. "I wasn't aware you were Kristen's brother."

"We weren't close," he said. "If she had gotten her way, my company would have lost the account."

Shelby pinched Stella's arm to warn her to go along with the story. "I understand. I have a sister like that. We don't see eye to eye on many things. Every family has challenges."

"Kristen wasn't happy I left her to deal with my mother. I couldn't handle all the drama. I wanted a simple life on my farm away from their constant issues," Ryan said.

"Is Simon your delivery driver? I saw him the other day," Shelby said. "I believe he said he lived in Renton." She hoped he wouldn't ask why that piece of information was necessary.

Ryan scoffed. "He does business over there..." He glanced at Stella and sighed. "During the initial stages of starting my farm years ago, my mother refused to give me the inheritance from my father. She said I would squander it, and she couldn't understand my vision for an organic farm. To raise capital, I cultivated marijuana in a field. It brought in a good profit, and I kept it going until the beehives and produce could sustain the business. My mother referred to me as a drug dealer even though my clients were suppliers who turned it into gummies and salves for medicinal purposes."

"I use a salve for pain management because I can't take pills anymore," Shelby asserted.

"Exactly!" Ryan said, pleased she understood. "Anyway, Simon was a friend from school, and I brought him on to make deliveries. Once I secured the account for the Blackberry Falls Resort, I focused my efforts on honey and produce. I grow over 12 varieties of mushrooms. The chef there, Lauren, is brilliant at coming up with recipes, and it has inspired me to expand my offerings." He blushed when he said her name, and Shelby hoped that meant he still had feelings for her.

"Can I ask why Kristen wanted you to lose the account? Was she jealous you were doing well?" Shelby asked.

"It was because of Simon. Apparently, he was making deliveries beyond produce. I already knew he was still working for the medical marijuana places, and I didn't care, but I heard he was getting mixed up in diet drugs and supplements," Ryan said.

"Why was that an issue for Kristen?" Shelby asked.

"Oh, it didn't bother her. I heard she was one of his best customers!" Ryan said. "You saw the transformation my sister went through this last year. Everyone figured out she took that crap." He noted the confused expression on Shelby's face. "She sunk a fortune into those drugs, and he threatened to cut her off recently because she was running short on cash."

"I thought she inherited everything from your mother. How much did those drugs cost?" Shelby asked.

Ryan looked at his hands. "Look, I'm uncertain about how

much of this information I'm supposed to share. The authorities have ruled Kristen's death an accident, and I honestly just want to clean this place up and sell it." He chewed his bottom lip. "I discovered Kristen had put a second mortgage on the house and gone through all her savings. I couldn't believe she had been so foolish, especially when she's the one my mother trusted with the money. I uncovered she was having an online relationship with a guy in another state. She was sending him pictures that were ridiculously touched up, and I assume she was desperate to look like that before she met him in real life."

"Was she sending him money?" Stella asked. "My mom got caught up with one of those online scams."

"Yup, it was temporary until his funds were released." Ryan made air quotes around the last word. "Lauren showed me posts on Facebook where Kristen was blaming a bunch of people for meddling in her life and holding her back from achieving her goals. I'm not on social media, and I kinda had to back off from things with Lauren for a bit." He blushed again at the realization that he had revealed the relationship. "Lauren is amazing, but I need to handle all this crap right now."

"Lauren is lovely," Shelby said. "I hope you're able to work it out."

Ryan smiled. "To be honest, it's not Lauren that I had a problem with. It's her sister Lia who has a weird dynamic with Kristen, and I wanted to stay as far away from that as possible."

"Do you think Lia is involved in the drug business?" Shelby asked, recalling the incidents with the missing money.

"I can't say one way or another," Ryan held his hands up. "I hope to have this house listed for sale by the end of the month, and then I can redirect my energy to my business again."

"What about the guy she met online? Do you have his information?" Stella asked. "Or did you give it to the police?"

Ryan cocked his head. "I gave the information to the state

law enforcement agency. They didn't believe it was connected to Kristen's death."

"Do they have Kristen's computer?" Shelby asked.

"No, they returned it. Lauren suggested I give it to Casi and have her verify whether there were any work documents on there before she wiped it clean. She's some kind of tech expert. I plan to sell it along with everything else so I can pay off the debts Kristen left," Ryan said as he turned to go inside.

"Thank you for talking to us," Shelby said.

"The cats are fine," Ryan smirked as Shelby and Stella exchanged confused glances, trying to decipher what that meant. "You said you came to check on the cats."

"Oh, right..." Shelby grimaced.

"I took them to the farm, and they love being outside. Kristen never let them out." Ryan smiled. "Casi mentioned you were trying to unravel the mystery of what could have transpired with Kristen. My mom made Kristen the person she became by always belittling her and forcing her to be a caregiver for years. I understand why Kristen hated me for bailing on her. I didn't get along with my sister, but if her death was not an accident, I hope you figure it out. I want the person responsible to pay."

28

DELIVERIES AND DEALS

Sam looked up from his desk as Alan entered the police station. "Did Shelby send you to dig for information? Help yourself to coffee. It's not fresh, but it's hot. Unfortunately, Doris is out all week tending to a sick relative. I'm alone here while Ben is on traffic duty." He strolled over to look inside the bag set on the counter. "Lia makes the best pastries. That woman may have her head in the clouds, but she sure can bake." He selected a blackberry Danish and took a bite.

"Was the information Shelby sent you yesterday helpful?" Alan asked, frowning at the coffee grounds floating in the pot. "Did Ben make this?"

"I can only teach him one thing a day," Sam chuckled. "As for your wife's sleuthing skills, the woman has a gift."

"Did she crack the case?" Alan asked.

"She discovered unique clues that authorities overlooked." Sam settled into his chair and brushed crumbs from his shirt. "Unfortunately, the county feels there's not enough evidence to keep the case open. I bought us until early next week, but they're firm in their decision to categorize it as an accidental fall and release the body to her brother for cremation."

"Shelby said there was a likelihood of an online romance. Can they at least investigate that?" Alan asked.

"The victim is dead, and it's unlikely that is what lead to her demise, at least directly. Although, who knows, maybe she was distraught if it ended, and it prompted her to throw herself over the edge," Sam said. He reached into the bag for another pastry, taking his time to select a caramelized apple tart. "The issue with these gals and their amateur sleuthing is they're technically committing crimes to dig up information."

"It's perfectly legal to converse with people around town," Alan said.

"True, but how about breaking and entering?" Sam asked. "Shelby and Stella were seen entering Kristen's house, and then when Ben and I went back to the scene, it was obvious items had been planted or at least moved to be in plain sight. That's tampering with evidence, which makes it inadmissible in court."

Alan sighed. "Shelby just wants to uncover who had a motive. You confirmed Kristen had insulin in her system. As a person who isn't diabetic, how does that happen?"

"You're right, the State PD wants to disregard that fact. We have confirmed Kristen was using weight loss medication, which was conveniently discovered in her fridge the second time we checked her house," Sam said.

"You think Shelby moved it? What happens if her fingerprints are found on it? I don't want this coming back on her. You know she was not involved in killing Kristen," Alan asserted.

"Shelby is savvy enough to wear gloves. She's watched a lot of crime shows. The medication was wrapped in foil, which I discarded just in case," Sam said. "We went from five women that Kristen wrote on a list of what appears to be blackmail. Now, with Shelby investigating, we've discovered Shane might be involved in the illegal drug compounding trade. He has a record and shouldn't be associated with felons. I have assured him I will keep it under wraps if it turns out it is unrelated to the case."

"Will that compromise your job?" Alan winced.

"Right now, all we have is that he gave Kristen the name of someone in the business. If he didn't buy or sell the product and had no incentive, it would be tough to say it was illegal. I have given the State PD the name and address of the facility because it's in their jurisdiction. There was no need to mention Shane."

"Thank you. I know he's already had a rough patch already. From what I know about him in the last few years, he's a good guy and an asset to the community," Alan said. "Who else has been exposed?"

"Kristen had a brother named Ryan, and he has admitted to growing marijuana in the past, over the legal limit. Again, since I believe it has nothing to do with the case and his farm is in Mount Vernon, I didn't pass along the information. He stopped growing a year ago and only does vegetables and honey now," Sam said. "His delivery driver reportedly sells steroids and pills. I'm monitoring him closely. Ryan said he told him to stop several weeks ago, but the driver doesn't seem to be very bright."

"Probably not smart enough to be the leader of a drug operation then," Alan chuckled.

"I have Ben observing his route to determine if he's deviating from his deliveries. So far, there's nothing suspicious," Sam said.

"What should I tell Shelby about her investigation?" Alan joked, checking his watch. "I've got to go pick her up. She was eager to chat with her friends while she's feeling energetic. Fridays, we usually spend with the bucket."

"She's a trooper," Sam said. He held up his finger to have Alan wait as he answered the phone. He exhaled as he hung up.

"That was Ben."

"Did the delivery driver change his route?" Alan asked.

"Not yet, but Ben went through Kristen's car again. He found the weight loss vial she probably used that morning. The ME said the insulin would be degraded by now, but it would still show up in testing. If that's the case, we know her medication was altered. Now that is a crime."

"JUST IN TIME," Shelby smiled at Stella as they pulled into the parking lot of the resort. She pointed to the delivery driver headed to the back of the restaurant with a hand truck full of crates billowing with colorful vegetables. "Park beside him and wait for him to come out."

They waited patiently, playing a guessing game as people came and went from the sprawling hotel. "Those two are having an affair." Shelby pointed at a couple who walked out of the building a few minutes apart but kept glancing at each other as they strolled to their cars at separate ends of the lot.

"Creeps," Stella laughed. "The woman in scrubs looks anxious."

"That's Jocelyn's daughter. She's a receptionist at the senior home. She appears to be a little troublesome," Shelby said.

Stella noted the agitation in the woman's expression and assumed she was waiting for her mother. "Are they close?"

"I assumed she was significantly younger the way Jocelyn fusses over her. She's almost thirty, and it appears her mother pays for everything and jumps in to fix problems at work," Shelby said.

"I don't like the look of her," Stella said. "I can see why Jocelyn drinks on the sly."

"My goodness, you've turned into an old lady judgy pants," Shelby laughed. "I agree, though. It's impossible to have a conversation with Jocelyn without that one calling to interrupt. We were out for Happy Hour once and, I think her name is Becca, phoned her three times to tell her about the drama she was having with a coworker. Finally, Jocelyn had to leave because her daughter was becoming hysterical."

"That's sad," Stella agreed. "Here comes the driver."

They watched the driver stroll to his truck, clanking the empty hand truck across the parking lot while he chatted on the phone. His muscles bulged with tattoos in a t-shirt that gave the impression of being a size too small. Shelby grabbed Stella's arm and paused beside a redwood tree to avoid being seen. "Hold on, Becca is saying something to him."

The driver picked up his pace as the large woman clad in burgundy scrubs stomped toward. "You don't just stop after a year, Simon," she yelled. "You know what that messes up. Don't think you can walk away without consequences."

Shelby contemplated giving up the attempt to speak to Simon to avoid the scene, but Jocelyn stepped out from the kitchen and became the target of Becca's wrath instead. Shelby quickly made her way to the driver's side door before Simon could escape. "Oh hello," she said pleasantly.

Simon furrowed his brow, probably expecting another verbal attack. "I gotta get back to the farm."

"This will just require a minute," Shelby said. "I have a quick question about..." she glanced around the vicinity and lowered her voice. "My niece over there was quite heavy, but she's been using a diet drug, and look at her now." She pointed at Stella beside the tree.

Simon gave her an admiring grin. "She looks good."

"Yes, well, she had gotten it in LA, but I'm uncertain of the method of getting it here. I don't want to go through the entire waiting period thing with my insurance. I'm attending a wedding in a few months and really want to look my best," Shelby said.

Simon looked her up and down and pursed his lips. "Why are you asking me about drugs?"

"I apologize if I got the wrong person," Shelby leaned closer. "My friend Kristen had recommended you as a supplier."

"Kristen's dead," he snapped.

"Of course, but not from the drugs, right?" Shelby said.

He surprised her when he chuckled, exposing a few missing teeth. "I heard she took a nasty fall. She probably worked out too much. I tell people they need to watch their hydration and take vitamins." He flexed a muscle. "Gotta stay strong."

"That's a valid point," Shelby remarked. "How would I go about getting a prescription or supply, whatever you call it?"

He shrugged. "I only handled drop offs." He shifted his attention to the voices escalating into a full-blown argument. "I gotta go. My boss doesn't want me to mess with that stuff anymore. He said I need to stick to deliveries from his farm."

Shelby smiled, comprehending that the man's mental capacity was limited to working out and making deliveries. "I appreciate your time," she said as she walked back to Stella.

"I can't believe you said I used to be fat," Stella said.

Shelby laughed. "It was for the greater good." She noticed Becca pointing at her while Jocelyn expressed her disapproval. "I wonder what that's all about."

"One way to find out," Stella said, walking toward them. "Hey Jocelyn, what time is the event tonight?"

"You have your schedule on the app. I'm not your personal assistant," Jocelyn snapped.

"Ugh, ok," Stella said, looking at Shelby.

"Is everything alright?" Shelby asked, feeling protective of Stella and disapproving of the way she was spoken to.

"Sorry," Jocelyn replied. "Becca needed to borrow my car, and I'm just a bit overwhelmed right now."

Becca extended her hand and waited for Jocelyn to transfer the keys before storming off without another word. Shelby waited for Jocelyn to explain the rude behavior but was surprised when she said, "Poor Becca has so much on her agenda trying to help everyone at the nursing home. The least I can do is lend her my car."

"What about her boyfriend? I recall they live near Seattle. Couldn't one of them use the light rail while her car is in the shop?" Shelby suggested.

"Becca likes to be independent," Jocelyn praised, not seeing the contradiction. "It's easy for me to stroll in this small town."

"I can give you a ride after the event," Stella said.

"Good idea. Remember, there might be a killer roaming around town," Shelby said. Jocelyn blanched and held on to the wall for support, and Shelby quickly corrected herself. "Sorry, that was a tasteless joke. Stella drives right by your place on the way home. She would be delighted to drop you off." She glimpsed blonde hair shimmering in the sunlight and moved toward the door. "We'll just pop in and say hello. I get lonely being at home all the time. I miss the hustle and bustle at work." She pulled Stella behind her, zigzagging around the half empty produce boxes. She heard Lauren giving orders like a drill sergeant, not pleased the crew was taking their time with the task.

"We didn't get much from that delivery driver," Stella said, matching her pace to Shelby, surprised by her speed.

"Actually, we can rule him out as a suspect," Shelby said, taking a hard left when they entered the foyer. "He's nice to look at, but there's not much going on under the hood."

Stella laughed. "He's not my type. I'm not into guys who use steroids."

"Do you believe he does?" Shelby asked.

"Absolutely. Didn't you notice the veins bulging in his neck?" Stella said.

"I was distracted by a misspelled tattoo on his biceps," Shelby replied as she knocked on a door, then opened it without pausing for a response. "Hi Casi, I noticed you walking in. Is that Kristen's computer?" She gestured towards a laptop on the desk.

"Yes, I was just about to call you. I'm glad you're here." She set down the phone, and Shelby was thrilled to observe her name lit up on the screen. Her trust in people was waning, and it hurt to doubt her coworkers' intentions. Casi smiled. "The police aren't pursuing this as a murder. Unless we have solid evidence before the week is over, Sam said the State PD is releasing her body to her brother, who wants her cremated."

"Then our evidence will literally go up in smoke," Shelby gasped. She opened the photos on her phone and turned the screen to Casi. "Remember the grand opening? I didn't realize Kristen was somewhat of an outcast."

Casi pursed her lips. "I honestly didn't remember her being there. Until I began having issues with her recently, I couldn't have picked her out from a lineup. Anna and I oversaw the spa, a member of the investment team who has a background in hospitality staffed the hotel, and Lauren handpicked the restaurant and kitchen crew." Casi redirected her attention to the laptop. "Anyway, I took her computer to a friend of mine, who is a hardcore tech genius. He removed the password, which was Maine Coon, whatever that means."

"That's a type of cat," Shelby said. "I'm pretty sure that's the breed Kristen had. Ryan has them on the farm now. I hope they've adjusted to being field cats."

"I'm sure it's a better life than being stuck inside all day,"

Casi said as her fingers flew across the keyboard at an impressive speed. "My little Jezebel was a barn kitten on Kyle's parents' farm. He gave her to me when he proposed." She beamed at the remembrance of the romantic gesture.

"You sure are skilled on the computer," Stella said in awe as several windows popped up and Casi organized them in layers.

"I'm more than just a pretty face," Casi teased. She paused and turned in her chair to Stella. "I was fortunate to have a mentor to guide me in my career. She made sure I got an education and gained the skills I needed later in life. We should have a conversation about your plans once you head back to LA. Being a server for now is great money. Save up and have a nice little cushion in the bank." Casi directed attention to the screen. "Look. About 6 months before her mom died, Kristen seems to have gotten involved with a man online. They started with the standard Meet and Greet in a group on Facebook. Their shared interest is cats."

"I'm glad she found someone with similar hobbies," Shelby said.

"Things escalated from there," Casi said. "He talked her into investing in a cat rescue foundation and sent her a bunch of pictures of abused animals."

"That's traumatic," Stella said, wincing at the photos.

"Fast forward a few months. Suddenly she's talking to him about moving to California and joining him in building a sanctuary."

"She probably wanted a change after her mom died," Shelby said.

"Except she wasn't dead. Not even very ill," Casi said, indicating a medical report. "She was a hypochondriac who had a bunch of aches and pains but nothing life threatening. She took too many pain pills and passed out in the bathtub while Kristen was at work."

"That's convenient," Shelby said. "But what about the grief

group she joined? I thought her mom died of cancer. Was she possibly working through the guilt?"

"It was court ordered," Casi said as she opened another document. "Her brother challenged the will because he had been written out of it. He accused Kristen of mishandling her mother's accounts. They had to go to mediation, and they each had to find appropriate therapy. Ryan went to anger management, and she did grief counseling."

"Oh no, do you think Ryan is responsible for pushing her off the trail?" Shelby covered her mouth with her hand.

"Questionable," Casi said, opening the emails. "It seems his issues were as a victim of a verbally abusive mother. He wrote this email to Kristen about their dysfunctional upbringing and asked her to forgive him for leaving her alone with their mother. I just skimmed it out of respect for their privacy," Casi giggled.

"Very thoughtful," Shelby laughed.

"While she was participating in her grief group, she began to lose weight and get plastic surgery?" Stella asked.

"It seems the online guy was pressuring her for money. She refinanced the house and used up most of her savings for her procedures. Sadly, it would appear she felt that if she could get herself to California and be with him, he would be excited to meet her in person. The problem was, she photoshopped all her pictures, and she had to strive harder to match the image she projected for him."

"He's probably bald and chubby," Stella said.

"Actually," Casi reclined in the chair. "He doesn't exist."

"What?" Stella and Shelby spoke simultaneously.

"His IP address isn't in California. It's Seattle, specifically Renton. Are you aware of who lives there?" Casi asked.

"Simon?" Shelby said.

"Shane works there," Stella said.

"Yes, to both," Casi said. "I don't feel Simon has the brain-power to pull this off, though."

"We just talked to him. He's rather dim," Shelby agreed.

"I can't believe Shane would involve himself in something cruel like that," Casi said. "I've known him for years, and he's a truly nice guy."

"So, we are at a dead end again," Shelby said.

29

DARK DISCOVERY

Shelby waited for Alan's light to go off in the bedroom before she eased the bag on her lap. Gus stirred on his bed, turning three times before curling up in the middle and using the blanket as a pillow. He grunted, and she watched his body relax as he drifted off to sleep. She sat alone in the dim glow of the living room, listening to Alan's soft snoring across the hall and the ticking of a clock in the kitchen. She glanced at the time, guessing she had several hours before Stella would return from work, tiptoeing to the guest room to avoid waking Shelby, who should be asleep in the recliner. She wasn't sure if it was the steroids that made her feel anxious or the discovery of what they had found on the computer. She clutched the bag to her chest, wondering for the millionth time if she should be honest about finding it at Kristen's house. She knew Casi was holding back information, deleting a file as she distracted them with videos. The intention wasn't clear and could simply be that she aimed to spare Shelby's feelings if it contained negative emails, like they had already uncovered. She suspected it might be more self-serving, perhaps a link to the drug operation that Casi claimed she didn't know about.

Something didn't ring true, especially since Casi had lived in LA for years and was known to be very savvy.

Shelby pushed the thoughts from her mind and focused on what was inside the bag. She had discovered it behind a crockpot, which had caught her eye because of how it was shoved haphazardly on a shelf in contrast to the pristine order of everything else in the kitchen. When Ryan had entered the front door, she hadn't had time to alert Stella as they hurried out the back. In a typical chemo haze, she had forgotten about it stashed in her handbag until Casi showed them the documents on the computer. As doubt crept up her spine while they were in the office, she decided it would be best to keep the evidence to herself unless it proved to be useful for the case. She realized Casi might be thinking the same thing about the data on the computer. Ultimately, they both needed to come clean.

She extracted the papers from the bag and noted that they were mostly stacks of prescription forms and folded prescription boxes. There was a typed list detailing the names of people who had been receiving the drugs and were paying a hefty sum for Kristen's services. Beneath the list, a series of notes, scribbled hastily on scraps of paper, showing payments to certain doctors willing to falsify prescriptions for the right price. Shelby's breath caught as she realized the scope of what Kristen had been involved in. This wasn't just a side hustle; it was a full-blown operation. And Kristen had been at the center of it all, orchestrating the illegal distribution of drugs to those desperate enough to pay. But there was something else that was more disturbing. Among the documents, she found references to two names she recognized: Shane and Lia. Both were mentioned in various places, suggesting they might have been involved, though it was unclear to what extent.

Shelby felt a knot form in her stomach as she considered what this could mean for the investigation and for her friends.

But before she could process it fully, her cell phone lit up, thankfully on vibrate so it didn't disturb Alan. A cold shudder went down her spine as she saw Casi's name, almost as if she had sensed Shelby was holding hidden clues. "Hello," she said in a whisper.

"Oh sorry, did I wake you?" Casi asked.

"No, I'm up, but Alan's in bed. He gets up early to work on reports before I go to my appointment," Shelby explained.

"I can talk to you tomorrow if that's better," Casi said.

"No, I wanted to share information with you, too," Shelby bit her lip. "There might be more evidence than what's on the computer."

"Actually, that's why I'm calling," Casi sighed. "There were files I was reluctant to open when we were in the office together. I needed to understand the situation before we give it to the police."

"You don't trust Stella?" Shelby asked.

"Of course I do!" Casi said. "It's just that...." Shelby could hear her voice breaking. "Shane and Lia might be more involved than we thought. I wanted to find out exactly how. If Shane gets caught selling drugs, he's back in jail. That will devastate his girls. I can't risk messing up his life unless there is concrete evidence proving he's involved. After that debacle with the cameras, I feel insecure in the office."

Shelby exhaled, realizing she had been holding her breath. "I understand. I found things at Kristen's that no one knows I have. It suggests Lia and Shane were part of the distribution process." She heard Alan shifting positions in the bedroom and waited until he started snoring again. "It appears Kristen was running a drug trafficking ring with more than just weight loss drugs. She was making a bunch of money."

"How is it even possible? Her brother said she had a huge amount of debt. This doesn't add up," Casi said.

Shelby heard a car idling out front as the headlights filtered through the blinds. "Are you at the resort?" she asked.

"Yes, I'm about to leave." Casi muttered clearly exhausted. "I can't say I'm eagerly anticipating the weekend, because we have the Hanson wedding."

"Would you like me to come help?" Shelby asked.

"Of course, I want you, but Alan will kill me for asking," Casi said. "Kyle is already irritated that I've taken on so much, and I'm sure I'll be the topic of contention at Monday's sports night."

"Perhaps I can review the contract and make sure all the tasks have been handled. I know the bride has been difficult, and I wouldn't want anything to fall through the cracks," Shelby said.

"That would be awesome. I'll make a duplicate and give it to Stella. She should be headed home soon. They're almost finished breaking down from the event," Casi said.

Shelby smiled as she hung up, feeling excited about being included in the upcoming event, even if it was only a minor role. She realized part of her dissatisfaction lately arose from not having anything outside of her cancer treatment to talk about. She recognized that finding who was responsible for Kristen's death had become an obsession to replace the feeling of accomplishment she gained from her career, and being at home, away from the excitement at work, was leaving her at a loss. Sam's insistence that she drop the case felt like another blow on top of everything she had faced recently. Her mind wandered to the complexities of her situation, and she was uncertain about the passage of time until Gus let out a deep growl and walked to the back sliding glass door to stare into the pitch black of the backyard. The hair across his spine bristled as he hunched and barked. Shelby slid from her chair and flicked on the light, hoping she wouldn't see anyone on the patio. The trees rustled with movement and made her shiver.

She held Gus's collar and slid open the door, verifying the area was clear before releasing him. He ran in circles, then sniffed the perimeter of the grass before putting his front legs up on the tree to growl at the branches above.

"Gus, come," Shelby called, worried the light and barking would wake Alan.

The dog gave a final gruff warning before trotting back to Shelby. She gave him a pat and handed him a biscuit before locking the door and checking it twice. She scrutinized the redwood one last time and turned off the light. The click of a door at the front startled her, and she quickly noted that Gus was wagging his cropped tail and wiggling up to the person entering.

"Stella, I didn't hear you pull into the driveway," Shelby said. Her eyes widened when she noticed the tears staining Stella's cheeks. "What happened?"

Casi stepped in behind her. "She had a bit of car trouble, so I gave her a ride home." She handed Shelby a folder with papers.

"Oh, honey, don't worry about the car. It's just a hunk of metal. Anything can be fixed," Shelby said.

Casi and Stella exchanged glances. "Actually, Shelby, the tires were slashed and a message was keyed across the side." Casi held up her phone to display the crude sentence, "back off before you get hurt."

Shelby pulled Stella into her arms. "Are you okay?"

"I'm fine," Stella sobbed, clinging to her aunt. "It just scared me."

Casi exhaled and tapped the folder in Shelby's hand. "I made copies of the event for tomorrow. If you have time, can you make sure we have everything covered? I know Fridays aren't your best day, so no pressure."

"It'll take my mind off the nausea," Shelby said. She eyed the folder, which seemed unusually thick. "Did Kristen add instructions? I thought we had everything finalized months ago."

Casi stepped toward Shelby and whispered. "I downloaded files from Kristen's computer. It seems to align with what you discovered regarding Shane and Lia working with Kristen to sell drugs at the resort. Essentially, it could ruin our entire business if this got out."

"How did we miss this?" Shelby asked. "Why would they do this to the investors?"

"That's the thing," Casi whispered. "I don't have proof, but I believe the information might be fake. I know Kristen was highly organized, but seriously, who documents every drug deal with a time and date? Lia is a bit scatterbrained, and I cannot imagine her coordinating drop-offs and recruiting customers. For goodness' sakes, she can barely get a coffee order correct!"

Shelby stifled a laugh at the thought of Lia being a drug kingpin. "And why would Shane risk his career and the welfare of his children?"

"Exactly," Casi said. "Which creates a bigger problem."

"Isn't it a good thing if it's been fabricated?" Shelby asked.

"Not if someone is willing to kill to keep the truth hidden," Casi said. "We should let Sam know we discovered nothing new. These threats might be fake, but I'm not willing to sacrifice our safety or livelihood to figure this out."

Shelby frowned at the folder. "Then why did you divulge the information to me if you're suggesting we don't continue to figure out the clues?"

"By all appearances, we should create the illusion that this last threat scared us off. I've transferred the digital files to a flash drive and deleted them off the computer. I'm sure I was followed. Kyle will take care of your car tomorrow and return it to you next week." Casi nodded. "In private, I'm hoping we can read through the files and figure out who is behind this without letting them know what we are doing. Paper copies will be safer than having an online presence." She twisted her hands together. "I've dealt with a lot of shady characters in LA, and it was a rough ride for me at the end. The people of Blackberry Falls welcomed me and made me feel safe. I won't turn my back on Lia or Shane. If they're involved in this, then that's on them, but I want concrete evidence before I release any of this to the police."

Shelby hugged her. "We're in this together."

"I'm grateful," Casi said, opening the door. She gave Shelby a wink as she stepped out onto the porch. "Let Sam know there was nothing on the computer worth seeing. I'll give it back to Ryan, and we can move on from this. Sadly, it was just a tragic accident."

Shelby observed her strolling to her car and noticed a truck idling a few doors down. She shivered after seeing that Casi was right to be suspicious of people lurking in the shadows.

30

______

BREAKING POINT

"Sorry I'm late," Stella said, pushing through the back entrance and quickly putting on her apron.

"This is an inconvenient time to be lagging," Jocelyn snapped. "We needed you here twenty minutes ago to help with setup."

"I'm here now," Stella said curtly. "What would you like me to do?" She observed the expansive patio with round tables, noting the tablecloths needed straightening.

Casi rushed in from the parking lot with an arm full of papers, losing half of the load while struggling to open the door. Her gigantic tangerine leather purse teetered on her arm, knocking her off balance. Stella grabbed the door to prevent it from swinging back into her. "Thanks," Casi breathed, transferring the rest of the stack to the counter while Stella bent to gather the fallen leaflets. "I had to do a last-minute print run of the menu. Apparently, there was a misspelling of the bride's name, and that is unacceptable."

"I'm glad you caught it," Stella remarked.

"Your aunt did," Casi said. "She called me this morning

before her appointment. She reminded us that one guest is gluten-free, and another has a serious peanut allergy."

"That would have been nice to know beforehand," Lauren huffed as she rearranged pots on the stove.

"It was in the file," Casi said. "I'm uncertain about Kristen's methods, but we need to cooperate to navigate through this event."

"Easy for you to say," Jocelyn said. "You can breeze in and out at your convenience. Some of us actually work here."

"That's the point!" Casi yelled. "I'm not employed here! I have no idea how any of this is supposed to go, and I had to cancel a meeting for my real job to help."

"I don't think any of us are thrilled to be working overtime and not getting paid," Lia said, balancing a tray of glasses.

"Gross, Lia. Wipe the rims with a damp cloth. Those glasses are disgusting with water spots," Lauren said, tossing a rag toward her sister.

"This isn't my job," Lia complained, setting the tray down with a thud.

"I'll do it," Stella said, efficiently polishing the glassware.

"Why don't we all pause for a moment and do a quick recap of what needs to be done before the wedding party arrives?" Shelby set her handbag on the sideboard.

"Oh, thank goodness you're here!" Casi exclaimed.

"You should put your bag in the office. Haven't you heard there are thieves around here?" Jocelyn said, eyeing Lia.

Lia's bottom lip quivered, and Shelby put her hand on her shoulder. "I'm not worried about the contents of my bag. I need my medication close by in case I don't feel well."

Casi embraced her. "If you can just help get this set up in time, feel free to head home."

"I'll be alright," Shelby smiled. "It feels good to be back in the saddle." She removed the cap from a dry-erase marker, and the aroma filled her with joy as she wrote the agenda on the whiteboard. Each stroke and squeak of the pen brought a feeling of empowerment and mastery over her illness. She stepped back and admired her work. "This will ensure that we are ready for the wedding party's arrival. Is the champagne chilled?"

Glances darted around the room, and Shelby sighed. "Stella, bring a dozen bottles from the far end of the cellar. It's good and cold down there, and we can get them into the walk-in to chill for service." She quickly checked her watch. "We have an hour. Lauren, what's the timing of the appetizers?"

"Well, I had to remove the satay chicken…" Lauren paused, realizing the complaint was unnecessary. "I've switched it to lemon chicken skewers. It will be ready on time."

"Thank you," Shelby marked the item on the agenda with a check. "Lia, what about the cake?"

Lia stared at her phone without speaking, and Lauren stormed toward her. "Do not tell me you forgot to order the cake!"

"I, um…" tears sprung to Lia's eyes. "Kristen didn't remind me to confirm the order. I was supposed to send the deposit, but it looks like they canceled it." She rotated her phone to show them an email from the bakery.

"Well, Kristen couldn't do it because she's dead," Lauren snapped. The room fell silent, and the hum of the equipment reverberated around them. Her cheeks reddened with shame, and she covered her face with her hands. "Ugh, I'm sorry. I have no idea why I said that."

Casi giggled, and all eyes turned to her. "Look, guys, we need to get through tonight. We've all been distracted, and yelling at each other isn't working." She cocked her head. "Lauren, is it possible to bake a hundred cupcakes by dessert time? We could use one of Lia's mini cakes from the freezer for the newlyweds to cut."

Lauren exhaled. "I could get the cupcakes done in time if I do a simple decoration with buttercream frosting."

"But won't the bride be upset she doesn't have the cake she wanted from the bakery?" Lia held up a photo from the file of a four-tier cake elaborately decorated with pink and purple flowers.

"We could decorate it with flowers from the garden," Shelby said. "It would be pretty for pictures."

"The bride's family will be thrilled when we comp the dessert," Casi said. "I'll clarify there was a complication with the order, but our chef made her signature cupcakes instead." She directed their attention to her phone with trending posts for wedding cupcakes. "The woman getting married posts constantly on Instagram. She'll be happy to jump on board with the cupcake theme."

A crash brought their attention to the patio, and Shelby cringed. "Please tell me that wasn't the chandelier."

"Nope, all good," Shane said, dusting himself off from his fall from the chair. "Just glasses."

"Darn, the ones I polished," Stella sighed.

"Shane, use a ladder, you lamebrain," Casi chastised. "It's crucial to have the lanterns up before we can finish the table setup. This event will end up costing us money if we keep making mistakes." She directed her attention to the group. "Where are the flowers?"

"That was Jocelyn's job," Lia volunteered.

Shelby clucked her tongue as Jocelyn looked sheepish, and Shelby put an x on the board. "Do we have enough in our garden?"

"Not really, since it's the backdrop for the ceremony," Casi lamented. "It will look weird if we strip out all the roses."

"I can call Ryan and see if he can bring some," Lauren retrieved her phone. "He's making a last-minute delivery of mushrooms because I had to change the entrée for the vegetarians."

"Awesome," Casi said, turning to Shane. "Follow me to the office and get the ladder. We've got one hour to finish the décor."

"You didn't say please," Shane teased.

Casi raised an eyebrow. "You would do well not to test my patience today." She turned quickly and saw a reflection in the mirror of Shane mimicking her, and she playfully swatted his arm. As they made their way through the grand foyer, beautifully streaming a mosaic of color from the sunlight through the stained glass above the majestic staircase, Casi stopped and grasped Shane's arm. "I have to ask you a personal question."

"Lia and I are not getting a divorce," he answered. "Things are tough right now, but we love each other and we'll figure everything out."

"Is a shortage of money the issue?" she asked.

Shane frowned. "I mean, not really. You own our house, and I know you're giving us a break on the rent. Raising five kids isn't cheap, but Jake covers most of the expenses for the boys." He sighed. "You don't believe Lia is embezzling from the coffee shop, do you? I think she's just terrible at math."

"It's illogical for Lia to be taking money from her own business," Casi agreed. "We'll investigate that further and figure out what's happening, but I must tell you I found evidence that suggests, no, blatantly states, you and Lia are selling drugs. I'm your friend, and I will erase the documents if it's true, but you can't lie to me."

"You would commit a crime to protect us?" Shane smirked.

"Yes, because if you end up back in jail, your girls won't have a father. I'm certainly not stepping up and raising your little brats," she teased.

Shane chuckled. "I appreciate your honesty. My drug days are behind me. I told Shelby I connected Kristen to a guy in Renton who does his own drug compounding. I didn't make any money from it and only did it to ensure she would leave Lia alone."

"The drug guy is Simon, the delivery driver for Ryan's farm?" Casi confirmed.

"He's the middleman, but it's another guy who makes it. I don't know his name," Shane said.

"Why would evidence be planted implicating you and Lia?" Casi asked.

"To throw the police off the trail of the killer?" Shane said. "I'm an easy victim because I have a previous conviction. Lia is naïve and gives away too much information. Maybe it's the same person who's taking money and they're trying to cover their tracks?"

31

SMOKE AND DECEPTION

Casi pushed the office door open, and a rolling chair skidded across the room as the person jumped away from the desk, hitting the exit tab. "Becca, why are you on the computer in our private office?"

"My mom wanted me to check the schedule for her. She's been ridiculously busy filling in for everyone else slacking at their jobs that she hasn't had time to make a doctor's appointment," Becca scoffed.

"Who is she filling in for? Shelby's on medical leave, Kristen's dead, and I don't even work here. I doubt anyone has asked her to go beyond her regular work tasks. She can make an appointment, and we'll cover her shift if needed," Casi said.

"Whatever." Becca pushed past her to the hallway.

Shane cringed. "Is that Jocelyn's daughter?"

"Yup, she's a prize, huh?" Casi said, pulling up the history on the desktop. "She was accessing employee files." She checked her watch. "I don't have time to go deeper, but I'll investigate after the event. The ladder is right there." She gestured toward the corner.

Shane grabbed her hand before she could leave. "Casi, that

woman is dating the drug dealer from Renton. I've seen her pick him up from the gym."

"Interesting..." Casi turned to a commotion in the foyer.

"It's unbelievable that you, of all people, are body shaming my daughter! Have you looked in a mirror, Shelby? You're not exactly slim even after your significant weight loss," Jocelyn spit the words with a slur that highlighted her red nose and flushed cheeks.

Tears streamed down Shelby's cheeks. "I just said leggings aren't appropriate attire for an event and asked if she brought a change of clothes."

Casi glanced over Becca's clothing choice, not noticing it before. She stepped closer to Jocelyn and gave her a piercing look. "Shelby is correct about the dress code, and if we weren't behind already with this event, I would send both of you home."

"Because I'm defending my daughter?" Jocelyn gasped.

"No, because you've obviously been drinking. Becca is a temporary employee who has been hired for an event. The only bully here is you," Casi snapped.

"You don't have the authority to tell me what to do. You're not my manager," Jocelyn said.

"The Board oversees the employees. Would you like to try to guess who they report to?" Casi asked. "That's right, the owners, of whom I am one. We will overlook the leggings for tonight, and you can apologize to Shelby for your rudeness." Casi turned back before she left. "I had better not hear about you taking one more sip of alcohol on these premises or I will personally call Sam to escort you out of here."

The rumble of jovial laughter signaled the entrance of the wedding party, and Casi rushed to meet them at the front gate. She directed the bride to a private suite to relax with champagne and canapes while the guests were seated. The mother of the bride held back a smile while Casi explained the issue with the cake, but when the bride clapped in excitement, the relief was palpable. A heady fragrance of fresh flowers and gourmet cuisine lingered in the air, promising an evening of elegance and celebration. The couple, blissfully unaware of the storm brewing behind the scenes, were poised to begin their journey as husband and wife. The night unfolded with happy tears and Instagram moments, complete with hashtags and blessings. Fortunately, the weather was spectacular, and the evening chill brought the older guests huddling together next to the patio heaters while the younger generation strolled along the shoreline to enjoy the beautifully landscaped grounds strung with fairy lights.

Shelby exhaled, not realizing the tension pinching a nerve in her spine. She sipped the protein drink, hoping to finish it and keep her promise to Alan. The chalky texture clumped in her throat, making it difficult to swallow. Although it claimed to be organic, there was an underlying sugar substitute flavor that caused a distasteful residue. A surge of queasiness threatened, and she stumbled toward the parking area, intent on being discreet if she couldn't fight the growing impulse to vomit. She certainly didn't want to look like a drunken partygoer, and the bushes seemed more appealing than a public bathroom stall. Shelby grasped the light post and recited the mantras in her head, trying to quell the sickness as she placed a dissolvable pill under her tongue, hoping it would absorb into her bloodstream in time. She had believed this Friday would be different, telling Alan she would be too busy to give into the nausea, but the moment she slowed down it came on like a freight train. She smiled, watching Jake skillfully maneuver his truck, which appeared to be packed with small children, hearing earlier how he had been the designated babysitter for the night. He appeared gruff at first sight, but he had a gentleness about him that was endearing. Shelby sucked in the cool night air, realizing her stomach would not give her a break tonight. She steadied herself against the fence as she managed to heave into the bushes below. A hand smoothed over her back, making her jump at first, but her body needed the solace of the warm touch.

"Too much champagne?" Jake chuckled, gently tucking her wrap away from her face.

"I wish," Shelby accepted the handkerchief he offered. "I almost made it through the entire night."

"That's wonderful," Jake said. "Do you want me to give you a ride home? I just need to take Shane's girls and Lauren's daughter upstairs."

"Where are the boys?" Shelby glanced toward the truck.

"Kyle has them. It was a party at our house tonight with all these kids. Casi will be sorry she missed out," Jake joked.

Shelby blanched and aimed for the bush again while Jake soothed her. She wiped her mouth and sighed, "You're a great dad."

"Hey, kids and drunk women are my specialty," he laughed. "Ask my sister-in-law. I've had to hold her hair back a few times over the years."

"They are lucky to have you," Shelby praised. "I believe I will accept your offer. Stella needs to assist in breaking down the event, and I don't want to rouse Alan."

"I heard your car got vandalized," Jake said. "Any word on who did it?"

"I only know someone attempted to get me to stop looking into Kristen's death. I'm stunned it could be a resident of this town." Shelby shook her head with disbelief.

Jake glanced behind him. "Don't believe the gossip about Shane and Lia. She gets manipulated easily, and it's likely she's being used as a pawn. I'm relieved I'm not on the list because if private information is being used against people to make them look guilty, they would have had a blast with my background. My guess is that it's distracting the police from the real culprit."

Shelby furrowed her brow. "How could a person go about doing that?"

"I don't know. I can barely operate my phone. Casi is a tech wizard. Now that her mind is off this event, I'm sure she can come up with ideas." Jake turned toward the truck and grabbed a small child who had woken up and was trying to climb out. He hoisted another one on his hip and directed the group toward the walkway. "I'll be right back, Shelby."

Yelling erupted through the back door of the kitchen, and Shelby and Jake exchanged worried looks, hoping the commotion couldn't be heard over the music on the dance floor.

Lauren ran outside and grabbed her daughter from Jake's arms, wrangling the children away from the kitchen. "There's a raging fire in the office!"

"Keep the kids out here," Jake said, grabbing a fire extinguisher from the wall and rushing down the hall.

He rounded the corner and collided with Casi as she stood motionless outside the office. "Move it, Monkey Brains," he shouted. He halted when he realized the source was the desktop computer, sputtering flames to the paperwork on the surrounding surface. He kicked the plug out of the socket with his boot and directed the spray of the extinguisher in an even pattern until the flames were snuffed out.

"What happened?" Jocelyn asked, poking her head through the gathering of employees in the hallway.

"There was a lit candle on the desk, and it must have caught the paperwork," Jake said.

Casi folded her arms across her chest. "That candle is from the guest tables, and electronics don't burst into flames."

Shelby exhaled. "Perhaps someone didn't want us seeing the files that were on the computer."

Casi focused her gaze and turned to the onlookers. "Whoever did this doesn't realize I've already backed everything up on the cloud." She pushed through the group and grasped

Shelby's arm, noting that she wasn't looking well. "I'll drive you home. I'm too tired to clean up this mess right now." She turned to her brother-in-law. "Jake, can you give Stella a ride when she's done? I would feel safer with you here to watch over the resort."

32

———

METADATA MAYHEM

S helby sat beside Casi at the kitchen counter, as she opened files on her laptop. The silence was penetrated by the clicking of the keys as Casi's fingers danced across the keyboard. Casi slipped on reading glasses with a sigh. "My eyes get blurry when I'm on the computer too. I'm still exhausted from last night's event."

Shelby smiled at Casi's embarrassment in needing the glasses. "They look cute on you."

"I appreciate that," Casi said. "I'm not understanding the correlation between Becca accessing the employee files and the other documents we found. After downloading them, I noticed rookie mistakes, like using different fonts to plant false information. Once I detected that, I examined the metadata and recognized repetitive language woven throughout the files."

Shelby moved closer and peered at the document. "Jake said something last night that resonated with me."

Casi laughed. "He's the last person who should give technology advice."

"He said that, too," Shelby smiled. "He pointed out that maybe private information was accessed and used to misdirect the police. He suggested that the employee files contained personal details that were being used against us. It made me think about Kristen's list and how she labeled us incorrectly for crimes she felt we committed."

"Because of what she saw on the cameras," Casi said, directing her concentration to the screen and opening several windows. "I found the files from the video feed!"

"How?" Stella asked.

"Sneaky girl," Casi scoffed. "She named it as the Cameran Event in the contract files."

"Oh, camera!" Shelby inched forward. "That's clever."

"Hidden in plain sight," Alan said, suddenly interested in what was on the screen. "Sam will be here soon. I hope you have valuable advice for him because he's really going out on a limb."

"We are helping him do his job," Casi corrected. She spun around in her chair. "Speaking of valuable...guess what happened at the function last night?"

"I heard about the fire and my wife throwing up. I hope there isn't more than that," Alan frowned.

"The cash tips went missing," Casi stated.

"How? Didn't they tip out on the final bill?" Shelby asked.

"Yes, but they added another twelve hundred dollars in cash to be split between the employees who worked the event. They were extremely pleased with how everything turned out and thought the cupcake table was gorgeous. The bride filmed it all and made a reel for Instagram," Casi said.

"I'm thrilled they were happy," Shelby beamed. "It was quite chaotic in the beginning."

"I noticed the bride hand you an envelope, Casi. I was excited at the prospect of receiving a bit of extra cash," Stella said.

"And I put it in my purse in the office after I counted it. I planned to give everyone money after the cleanup," Casi said.

"Oh no, did it burn up in the fire?" Shelby shuddered.

"That was my initial assumption," Casi said. "I figured it was my fault and planned to cover the loss myself."

"That's unnecessary," Shelby said.

"When I told Kyle about the fire, he said it was impossible for the computer to ignite from a candle. We went by there this morning to check the damage, and he noted a flammable fluid had been poured over the hard drive and lit. The papers were added after to give the impression they were the source. The desk was barely scorched."

"What about your purse?" Alan asked.

"Missing," Casi declared. "I figured it would be a charred heap, but there's not even a scrap of it there."

"Do you think someone witnessed you put it in the office?" Shelby asked.

"Kyle suggested the person responsible took liquor from the bar intending to destroy the computer. When they entered the office, they saw my purse and snatched it, assuming everything on top of the desk would burn up," Casi said.

"How did you manage to drive home without your purse?" Stella asked.

"My keys were in my pocket because I was carrying the leaflets when I came in. I left in such a hurry after the fire that I didn't realize I left it behind," Casi said.

"The mystery lingers," Sam remarked, putting a box of donuts on the counter. "Have you narrowed down the suspect list?"

Casi's expression brightened at the gleaming batch of sweets before choosing an apple fritter. "Shane and Lia's names keep popping up in every document." Shelby's eyes widened in surprise as Casi casually revealed her friends' involvement. "But that's more to do with the drugs rather than the murder."

Sam winced. "You realize I'll have to escalate this to the

federal authorities? I honestly think they're more interested in the drug ring than the murder."

"We understand," Casi replied with a sly smile. "Which is why we'll uncover the true culprits and how they're connected to Kristen. Someone went to a lot of trouble to expose Shane and Lia and make them appear guilty. It's an amateur move to drop names like that." She shrugged. "I might know drug dealers from LA, and there is no way they would use their real names or email people receipts for purchases. I'm well aware of Shane and Lia's finances, and their income can be verified."

Shelby exhaled with relief as she understood Casi's game plan. "I agree. All of us have been targeted, but none of the accusations hold up."

Sam bit into a glazed donut. "I'm listening."

"Also, Shane recognized Becca as the girlfriend of the drug dealer in Renton. That's a connection we didn't know about before." Casi stated.

"You think she was involved with Kristen?" Sam asked.

"I think this runs deeper than what we first suspected. Kristen accused me of stealing, but I was actually putting my own money into the deposit to cover shortages at the coffee shop," Casi said. "Last night, a large sum of money went missing during the event."

"Lia seems to be the person who keeps coming up short on money," Sam said. "Was she at the event?"

"Yes," Casi cringed.

"And Shane?" Sam asked.

"Sure, but how is that tied to Kristen's death?" Shelby interrupted. "Stella and I were there. Maybe we took the money."

"It's most likely whoever caused the blaze in the office," Casi said. "They didn't want us to see the search history."

"Aunt Shelby was in the parking lot throwing up, and I was serving dessert," Stella said.

"Are you okay, Shelby?" Sam asked with concern.

"Fridays are when the steroids wear off and the chemo nausea hits me. I'm just tired today," Shelby smiled.

"Who knew you would show up last night?" Sam asked. "You said Jake put the fire out. Was he working the event?"

"Casi asked me if I could double-check the contract. No one else knew I was coming in," Shelby said.

"Jake only came to drop off Lauren and Shane's kids," Casi said. "Lauren knew what time he would be there."

"And she's the one who discovered the fire?" Sam asked.

Casi leaned back in her chair. "Yes, she told me and then ran to get Jake. Shelby waited outside with the kids."

"It could be possible she wanted the files destroyed but not risk the fire advancing through the building," Sam said.

"Becca was on the computer when Shane and I entered the office to get a ladder," Casi said.

"Could they be working together?" Sam asked. "Selling drugs and covering their tracks?"

"But why would his name be so obvious throughout the files? He wasn't on Kristen's list," Shelby pondered.

"A name starting with S," Sam reminded them. "Shane and Simon." He briefly observed Stella. "You arrived the day after the murder, right?"

"Yes, and I have proof of that," Stella said.

Sam chuckled. "I'm not considering you a suspect. We have already established it's unlikely anyone knew about the list prior to Kristen's death. If she had a personal vendetta against the people on her list, and she was blackmailing them with the information, maybe they killed her to protect their secret."

33

***

FALSE FILES

Casi directed her attention to the computer and opened the video file, clicking on her own name. "Here's me placing money in the night deposit. From this angle, it looks like I'm taking it out instead since I was counting it to see how much I needed to cover." They looked at the video feed, watching Casi's careful process as she extracted an envelope from her large handbag and counted out twenty-dollar bills. The next video was Lauren entering the office with a smile, being joined by an attractive man with chestnut hair who pulled her into an embrace. Casi stopped the video and fast-forwarded. "We don't need to watch this part." She indicated the man on the screen. "Kristen was upset with Lauren because she felt her brother was given a better contract for his business, since he is in a secret relationship with Lauren." She narrowed her eyes. "Kristen had no business having cameras installed. It was not okay for her to monitor others. She has no idea how much we have all been through and the challenges we faced building the business."

Shelby put her hand on Casi's shoulder. "I remember when you bought the property, and people figured it was a money pit.

You had a vision beyond what existed. You've created an incredible business, with significant opportunities for all of us."

Casi nodded. "I did it for Kyle, mostly. He's kindhearted, and it hurt him to see Lauren defeated after her dream was destroyed by that jerk." She beamed with the recollection of Kyle's excitement when he showed her the property. "He had a passion for transforming that old building into a magnificent hotel again. Money is worthless if you don't use it to lift others."

Shelby took a marker and checked off names on the whiteboard. "What did she have on me?"

Casi frowned when she advanced to the next file. Shelby was seated in the office with Casi hugging her tightly before handing her a piece of paper. "Kristen should have sprung for cameras with audio recording. I figured she was jealous of the attention you got from having cancer."

"Oh, that's sad," Shelby said. "What's that file you handed me? I don't remember."

"That's the paperwork for the insurance company," Alan scoffed. "The Board approved your medical leave, and disability insurance covered the difference. Kristen had no right to put her nose in our business."

"Which is why I kept it private," Casi agreed. "It didn't affect Kristen's salary." She grimaced. "The Board approved bonuses from the events Shelby booked before she took leave to the monthly stipend. It was fair for you to be compensated for previous work. Kristen still got a share for completing the contract, but if she found out what I did, maybe she felt slighted."

"I appreciate your diligence in making things right. I hope it didn't compromise your position at the resort," Shelby sighed.

"It was on the up and up," Casi said. "Brian handled the financials, and everything was aboveboard. I was the representative from the company who gave you the paperwork, but I didn't disclose the information to anyone. I'm not sure how Kristen would have found out."

"Could whoever accessed the files have seen the deposits?" Alan asked.

Casi squeezed her eyes shut. "Of course! There would be a digital trail because I wasn't doing anything sneaky. My conversations with Brian were mostly by email."

"Wait, if Kristen was accessing the emails, was she the one planting evidence about Shane and Lia? That sounds counterintuitive," Stella stated.

"You're absolutely correct!" Casi said, leaning closer to the computer. "Are we thinking another person was rifling through the files and maybe giving select information to individuals?"

Sam rubbed his chin with his thumb. "It could be how the killer kept tabs on Kristen and realized she was becoming a threat."

Shelby's eyes widened. "Maybe they set Kristen up! She already suspected people didn't like her or were getting unfair advantages. If someone played on her delusion and gave her ammunition, she might have become paranoid."

"Gaslighting," Stella suggested. "By getting Kristen worked up about imaginary situations, they used her as a distraction while they were the ones actually committing the offenses."

Sam stared at the list. "Kristen had video evidence that she planned to turn over to the Board. If anything, that rules you five out as suspects because the cat was already out of the bag."

Shelby raised her hand. "What's the deal with the online scammer who was taking money from Kristen for the cat sanctuary? Maybe she discovered who it was and planned to go after them?"

"But they got to her first," Sam stated.

Shelby made a tick mark beside her name and glanced at the next two videos. "Lia was suspected of taking money from the coffee shop, and Jocelyn was consuming alcohol while working."

Sam exhaled. "We know there were several perceived crimes being committed, and Kristen intended to crack the case using video surveillance. What she didn't know was a person was pilfering employee data and apparently also involved in drug trafficking."

Casi's eyes widened. "Which might be why that person freaked out when they realized there were cameras!" Her face paled. "Oh no, am I responsible for Kristen's death because I made such a big stink about the cameras? After our argument, everyone knew."

"It's not your fault," Shelby said. "If Kristen discovered an employee was stealing personal information, she may have intended to alert the board, but she would have been fore-warned that the person couldn't be trusted."

Sam jumped as his phone vibrated in his pocket. "It's the medical examiner," he said as he put it to his ear, nodding as she spoke. "Interesting, hmm, okay, I'll follow up with them."

"What was that about?" Shelby asked.

Alan noted Sam's hesitation and said, "I know you gals didn't want to listen to me before, but I you have exhausted all your efforts to find evidence. Let's let the police take it from here."

Casi laughed. "Oh, you're serious? That won't work for us. We've invested too much time to give up now."

Shelby laughed. "I agree with Casi. You can't leave us hanging, Sam. If you have additional evidence, you should share it."

He shook his head. "You won't like it."

"Is Alan a suspect again?" Shelby giggled.

"Gosh, don't even joke about that," Alan shuddered.

Sam smiled. "Ben located Kristen's pen for the weight loss drug she was using and transferred it to the forensics team. The medical examiner confirmed it contained insulin, like we suspected."

"That proves the cause of death. That's good, right?" Shelby asked.

Sam sighed. "The packaging is not from an illegal manufacturing company. There's a supplier near Seattle, and they stamp the medication with a lot number and date."

"That rules out an illegal compounding company in Renton?" Shelby asked. "Which would eliminate Shane and Lia as dealers, therefore making all the references invalid."

"That part is good," Sam agreed. "Since the company isn't illegally manufacturing the drugs, it's obvious they were stolen."

"Great, now we need to determine who had access," Casi said.

"No, the State PD will take over from here. Kristen died in Blackberry Falls. I'm not involved in the investigation outside of that. That means you three are not permitted to pursue it either, which, technically, you shouldn't have been allowed to do at the start." He held his palm up as they all began to speak at once. "I'm sorry, but this ends here. The drug enforcement agency will investigate the drug theft, and the FBI handles cybercrimes. Unfortunately, since the person affected by the online scam is deceased, it's unlikely it will be a top priority."

"That's it? We just let them classify Kristen's death as an accidental fall?" Shelby asked.

Sam shrugged. "Unless you can find out something at a local level that contributed to her death, the case is closed."

34

HIGH STAKES

"Whiskey neat," Sam muttered while taking a seat at the slot machine in the dimly lit casino. The stench of cigarettes still permeated the carpet and vinyl upholstery, even though this section had been declared smoke free years earlier. A deep longing followed the aroma, transporting him back to his early twenties, when he wouldn't have thought twice about lighting up and taking a drag. The onset of children and a determination to live a healthier lifestyle had won out over his addiction to tobacco, and he had never gone back.

Sam indulged in the amber liquid the waitress placed in front of him. He let it glide across his tongue, welcoming the familiar bitterness. He longed to swallow the liquor and order another drink until the deep pain in his heart was numb. Instead, he positioned the glass on the table and forced himself to leave it there. It was a reminder that he was in control, a test he set for himself, a quiet victory when he didn't give in to the pull of alcohol and the relief it promised.

Heather hated it when he played this game. She declared he was tempting fate and one day he would fail. Every day of the year he believed her, except today. On the day he lost his son, he had no control over his weakness. The traces of the whiskey coated his tongue, and he contemplated taking another sip but knew it would end like it had on the rare occasions when a second sip turned into a bottle and Heather was answering a call from a friend who had found him passed out. He was fortunate to reside in a town where he knew most of the residents and invariably one of them would help him home or let him sleep it off on their couch.

A ping from his phone pulled his attention to a text, and he was surprised to see it was from Dana, the ME. He had appreciated her updates on the case and had kept his word not revealing his source to the authorities. It had been difficult to witness Shelby's disappointment that the evidence she uncovered wouldn't help identify Kristen's killer. Alan had tried to explain that real investigations weren't like her crime podcasts, wrapped up neatly in a few hours. Sam had noticed Shelby's emotional retreat, her claim that fatigue from treatment was to blame. He understood the case had given her purpose, an escape from her cancer reality, something bigger to fight for. Even Alan, despite his protests, lit up whenever Shelby recounted her investigations, her excitement impossible to contain.

Sam frowned at the text message titled *"I'm in love,"* hoping he hadn't received a message meant for someone else. When he clicked on the photo and saw the light-filled condo overlooking the Passage, he grinned. Heather had shown Dana countless properties and had wondered if she would ever find the right fit. Unlike Sam, she had professed this would be her lucky day. He scrolled through the photos and easily envisioned the stylish woman turning the blank slate into a beautiful home. He replied with a happy face and a thumbs up, unsure what words were appropriate for this situation.

He signaled to the waitress, too old to be wearing stockings and a miniskirt, while her thick mid-section bulged over. "What can I get ya, honey?" she asked, parking her gum in her cheek long enough to get the sentence out.

"Coffee with cream, please," he said.

"Want Baileys in that?" she asked. "It's free as long as you're gambling." She eyed the machine, not acknowledging that it was obvious he hadn't put any bills in.

"No thanks." Sam retrieved five dollars from his wallet and placed it on her tray. "I'll take a packet of sugar, though."

"Coming right up, sweetie," she tottered off to retrieve his order.

Sam pulled out another bill from his wallet and fed the machine, figuring he owed the casino a few bucks for the rental of the stool. A familiar voice caught his attention, and he tried to remember where he had heard it recently. The woman was obviously inebriated, leaning into the older man next to her as she pounded on the buttons of the slot machine. "This is rigged," she claimed, not happy it wasn't paying out.

Sam gestured to the waitress and put his whiskey on her tray as he took the coffee, figuring it was better to keep temptation at bay. "Excuse me," he said, touching her arm lightly. "Does that woman come here often?"

"That one?" She pointed a long red fingernail at the copper haired woman with the rounded figure across the aisle. "Most weekends. I would say she comes here for free drinks, but I've seen her load a couple of grand into a machine in one night. It would be cheaper to drink at the bar."

"I'll say," Sam agreed. "I feel like I know her."

"Well, Chief, you've either arrested her for drunk driving, or I'm pretty sure she works in that fancy resort in your town."

"How did you know I'm the chief of police in Blackberry Falls?" Sam glanced down at his chest, wondering if he was wearing his badge.

Her face clouded with torment. "In the past, I was a trauma

nurse. I was there the night they brought your son in." She nodded her head. "I couldn't handle seeing young ones dying and their families being destroyed." She clutched his hand. "I know what today is. Tragedy never leaves our souls intact."

Sam pinched the bridge of his nose. "Are you happier working here rather than in the hospital?"

She leaned closer. "You know what, sweetie? I go home with more money every night, and I don't suffer from nightmares. I have to admit that's a pretty good hustle."

"Thank you for trying to save my son," Sam choked.

"They are always with us." She opened a locket to show him a chubby-cheeked girl. "I lost my little one to cancer. That's when I made the decision to leave. Some nights I almost feel whole again. At my lowest moments, I swear I can hear her laugh, and it gets me through the rough times."

Sam observed her as she made her way to serve another customer and viewed her with a different lens. She was a fighter and deserved his respect. He pulled out his phone and captured a photo of the intoxicated woman and sent it to Shelby with a question mark. Within seconds she responded, "That's Jocelyn from work. Is she drunk?"

"Appears to be." He craned his neck to see the stack of bills in front of her. "And she's gambling up a storm."

"She claimed to be on the wagon. And she complained she doesn't have any money," Shelby said. "Will you investigate?"

"There are no legal consequences for failing at rehab or being inept at finances," he said. "I'm in Everett, which means it's not even my jurisdiction," he paused as Jocelyn jumped up from her stool, knocking it to the ground in a fit of anger. She grabbed her cash and stuffed it into her tangerine leather handbag. He frowned, recalling the unusually large bag swinging elegantly from Casi's tanned arm earlier in the week. He quickly texted. "Is this Casi's bag? I remember seeing her with it. I can't imagine there are duplicates."

He laughed at the expletives she sent before adding, "Yes! She bought it in Italy, and we all drooled over it. Arrest her!" Shelby demanded.

"I can't arrest her for being drunk in a casino, even if I suspect she stole the purse." He glanced over at Jocelyn, reading her angry expression as she stood in the aisle and glared at him. He slipped his phone in his pocket and took a sip from his coffee cup, wishing he hadn't gotten rid of the whiskey. He was not in the mood to talk to the stone-faced woman about clues and purses, especially tonight, when all he wanted to do was drown his sorrows and detach himself from reality. He stood slowly and scanned the area for Jocelyn, wondering how she had disappeared so quickly. With a sigh, he sipped his coffee, deciding whether he should go home to Heather or join the men at Kyle's and lose himself in meaningless conversation at Poker Night.

35

LOOSE ENDS

The house felt too still without Alan working on his laptop, quietly extending his workday without drawing attention to the extra hours he put in on top of being her caregiver. His presence had become a constant staple, a reassuring backdrop she rarely acknowledged until it was gone. Shelby had grown used to having Stella in the house again, cheerfully organizing the living spaces and cooking meals for Alan before running off to the resort for a shift. The routine soothed her mind, the small acts keeping the household humming without complaint, proof that life could still move forward even when hers felt frozen in place.

She glanced at the clock, noting it would be several hours before Alan returned from Poker Night, which she had begged him to attend, and Stella finished her shift. Too many nights had slipped by with him hovering at her side, exhausted but unwilling to step away. Tonight was supposed to be quiet, and uneventful.

She shifted in her recliner, the gentle whir of the feeding pump rising and falling like a mechanical heartbeat beside her. The sound had once unnerved her. Now it grounded her, a reminder that the tube and the machine were keeping her alive. On TV, a detective questioned a suspect under harsh fluorescent lights, his voice calm, methodical, and unyielding. Shelby let the familiar rhythm of the mystery relax her, comforted by its predictable outcome. Justice always arrived neatly packaged by the final commercial break. Real life was never that kind.

Her phone, faced down on the end table, still showed the last text from Sam. She had not turned it over again, as if staring at the words might somehow change them. At first, she worried it might have been a drunken mis-text, typed in grief and lacking the careful restraint he usually showed. Being friends since childhood, he held a special place in her heart, and it troubled her to know how deeply the tragedy had cut him. The weight he carried had been visible lately, pressing into his posture, flattening his smile.

A cautious hope rose that his questions about Jocelyn, even if tied only to theft, meant he had not fully let the case go.

Shelby realized how little she truly knew about her coworkers, regretting not consoling Kristen when she had the chance or offering Jocelyn support with her troubled daughter. She sighed, recognizing that the possible murder highlighted gaps in her relationships, an ache settling heavily in her chest. Sorting through the women from the coffee circle, especially those on the list, she resolved to be more present. If cancer had taught her anything, it was that time was fragile, and the smallest connections often carried the greatest meaning.

Gus lifted his head from his bed and released a low growl as tires squealed to a sudden stop at the curb.

Shelby turned toward the sound but could not pinpoint its source. Alan and Stella always parked in the driveway, and Gus would have been at the door, tail wagging furiously. This was different. Unease crawled along her spine as the silence of the chilly evening pressed in around her. She reached for the remote to mute the television. A sharp knock rattled the front door, hesitant and uneven, as if the person leaned on it for support.

Shelby frowned when Gus growled again. She had not locked the door, customary in Blackberry Falls, but it had become an essential protocol in case of an emergency and another ambulance call, thankfully avoided so far.

"Shelby?" a thin, wavering voice called. "It's... it's Jocelyn."

Her chest tightened as she tried to reconcile Sam's text about Jocelyn at the casino with her sudden appearance here. The timeline blurred in her foggy mind, details slipping as panic spiked and her heart rate surged. Her body betrayed her at the worst possible moment. "What on earth," Shelby muttered, pressing the control pad on the chair as it bumped into several positions she didn't want. Finally locating the proper button to lower the footrest, the chair hummed sluggishly, as though it too was reluctant to move. The feed tube line twisted between the blanket and chair, anchoring her in place. Come in," she called, forcing her voice to remain calm while her anxiety escalated.

The door swung open and Jocelyn stumbled inside, swaying, one hand clutching the doorframe to stay upright. Her eyes were glassy and unfocused. Auburn hair tangled around her face, lipstick smeared as if wiped away in frustration. And in her hand was Casi's oversized tangerine purse.

"Long night?" Shelby asked, keeping her voice steady, even as her pulse thudded painfully in her ears.

Jocelyn shut the door with a shaky hand. "You talked to Chief Adakai." Her words slurred, sharp with accusation. "You involved yourself in things that were none of your business."

Shelby's stomach dropped. "Jocelyn, you should not be driving. Sit and relax while I put the kettle on. I will make you tea and we can catch up."

"Don't play dumb." Jocelyn clutched the purse like a lifeline. "I saw him texting, watching me. I know he was talking to you. You should have left this alone. Kristen was not your friend." She stopped abruptly, breath hitching. Tears filled her eyes, but her jaw twisted with rage. "You complicated everything."

The words hit like a slap. Shelby decided not to mention Casi's purse, instinctively understanding it would escalate the tension. "Why are you blaming me?" she asked. Gus crouched by her side, muscles taut, eyes locked on Jocelyn as she paced the room.

Jocelyn shivered involuntarily, like a spasm as she lost control. "I want things to go back to how they were… you know, before."

Shelby slid her phone into her lap, pressing call back as discreetly as she could, tucking the blanket over it. Her thumb shook as she forced it still. "Tell me more about Kristen," she urged. "I regret not knowing her better. I want to be more supportive of my friends. I was thinking you and I should have lunch next week. I have not asked about Becca and how she is settling into her job."

"Don't do that!" Jocelyn screamed.

"Jocelyn, you're scaring me," Shelby said, her heart racing. "Why are you here? Alan will be home any minute and he does not like to see me upset."

"Alan is at Poker Night and Stella is at the resort. The Chief is at the casino getting hammered. No one is here for you, Shelby." Jocelyn made a sharp turn into the kitchen and yanked open the refrigerator, easily finding the box of insulin pens. "It is time for your medication."

"No, I don't take insulin, Jocelyn. I'm not considered diabetic anymore." Shelby desperately tried to lower the footrest of the recliner, but Jocelyn kicked the power cord from the wall, trapping her in the chair. Shelby tried to slide to the side, but the feed tube tugged painfully on her stomach, awaking a sensation that was previously numb, locking her in place.

Gus barked furiously, sensing Shelby's fear. Jocelyn eyed him, then smirked. "I only came to check on you. I'll let you get some rest now."

"Yes, I'm very tired." Shelby said carefully, watching her dial the settings on the pen. "You can take the insulin with you. I don't need it anymore."

Jocelyn opened the door wide and shoved Gus outside as he lunged at her. She closed the door with a thud and threw the deadbolt. Gus's wiry body slammed against the wood as he barked frantically, desperate to get back to Shelby.

Tears streamed down Shelby's face as Gus howled outside, fear for him eclipsing her own fate at the hands of the woman now standing over her. Jocelyn's breathing grew ragged, her hands trembling.

"You ruined everything!" Jocelyn screamed. "You and Casi couldn't just leave it alone."

"Things like the emails you and your daughter altered?" Shelby said, forcing her voice steady. "The stolen employee information? You can walk away from this, Jocelyn. Stop now before you go too far."

Jocelyn froze. Her eyes went flat. "Too far? That already happened. There is no stopping now." She stormed forward, wild-eyed. "I cannot go to jail, and I need to take care of loose ends."

Shelby shoved at her with her free hand as Jocelyn lunged, the feeding tube wrenching painfully at her abdomen. The recliner trapped her, heavy and unmoving, as Jocelyn fumbled with the pen.

The sting was sharp and immediate. A small click. Ten units.

Shelby gasped. "Stop."

Another jab pierced her skin. And another.

Heat surged through Shelby's body, followed by a terrifying cold. Her heart began to race, then stuttered. She clawed at Jocelyn's face, nails scraping skin, but Jocelyn clung to her like a drowning swimmer. Shelby managed to twist, knocking the pen loose, but Jocelyn recovered it quickly.

"You should have died in the hospital. No one wants you here!" Jocelyn croaked, raising the pen again.

As the needle pierced Shelby's skin once more, the blanket slid from her lap, and the lit-up screen of the phone caught Jocelyn's attention. "Who did you call?"

Sirens cut through the night, piercing and undeniable, louder even than Gus's frantic barking. Heavy footsteps pounded across the porch before a fist slammed against the door. "Shelby? It's Sam. Are you okay?"

Jocelyn froze, terror flashing across her face.

Shelby surged forward as dizziness flooded her vision. Pain exploded through numbness as the feeding tube dislodged, but she managed to shove Jocelyn backward. "Sam, help me!" she screamed.

The shattering of terracotta indicated Sam remembered where the spare key was hidden. Shelby had an abstract thought of her newly planted periwinkles strewn across the dirt and broken pottery.

A frantic twisting of a key scraped against the metal as Sam desperately tried to unbolt the locks that were rarely used. The door frame splintered as he shoved through the passageway before it was open all the way. Gus bolted inside, racing to Shelby, while Chief Adakai barreled in behind him, gun raised.

Disbelief crossed Sam's face as he took in the scene. Shelby slumped on the floor, tangled in tubing, pale and gasping. Jocelyn scrambling to her feet, insulin pen clutched in her hand.

"Don't move!" Sam shouted.

Jocelyn shrieked and charged. Sam took in the distance and

her erratic movement in a heartbeat and knew this was a situation to contain, not escalate. He holstered his gun in one smooth motion, caught her wrist mid-swing, and twisted her arm behind her back with swift, practiced force, the same steady control he had used more times than he could count breaking up drunken scuffles after last call. The pen clattered across the hardwood as Jocelyn collapsed, sobbing, while he snapped the cuffs around her wrists.

"It's over," he said, breathless but steady. "I figured I had you on theft. Sadly, it looks like you are facing a lot more."

Shelby moaned, her strength draining rapidly. Tears streamed down her cheeks as the adrenaline left her shaking and weak. The feeding tube lay dislodged, tangled in wires and pooled nutritional supplement soaking the floor. Gus pressed his body against her legs, whining softly.

Sam knelt beside her. "An ambulance is coming." His gaze flicked to her face, pale and clammy, and recalled Alan's recap of Stella's rapid intervention when Shelby had an episode while the detectives were questioning him. "Sugar?"

Shelby nodded weakly as the room dimmed around the edges. "Hurry."

36

LOYALTY AND LIES

Sam stood in the hallway, observing through the two-way mirror as Jocelyn fidgeted in the plastic chair, clasping and wringing her hands until her knuckles bled. Jagged scratches scarred her cheek; evidence of Shelby's determination to fight back. He hoped her second cup of coffee would help her become lucid enough to answer his questions. He skimmed his text messages, deleting anything Shelby had warned him might compromise the case. Chuckling to himself that he was taking advice from an amateur sleuth. He was pleased Detective Sanchez had agreed to include him in the questioning, hoping he would finally succeed in finding closure for Kristen.

Jocelyn rocked slightly, her knee bouncing beneath the table. Every few seconds she glanced toward the door, as if expecting a hero to burst in and rescue her. Sam had seen the look before. It was the brittle hope of someone who still believed loyalty would shield them from consequences.

The ambulance had arrived minutes before Alan, who panicked when he saw the state Shelby was in. He called when they arrived at the hospital, saying Shelby's blood glucose was stable. She was on her way into surgery to reinsert the feeding tube as she entertained the nurses with her colorful description of the night's events. Sam could picture her now, bruised and shaken, masking fear with humor. The thought tightened his chest.

He turned to the sound of footsteps in the corridor. Detective Sanchez approached with a file tucked under his arm and a paper bag in his hand. His expression was calm, almost unreadable, but there was a weight to his presence that commanded the room before he even spoke.

Sanchez nodded once at Sam, then unlocked the interview room. They entered together, pulling out chairs across from Jocelyn. The scrape of the metal legs on concrete echoed sharply. Jocelyn flinched, her shoulders drawing inward.

"Hello, Jocelyn," Sanchez said evenly. "You know Chief Adakai, and I believe we met at the Blackberry Falls Resort recently."

He set the paper bag on the table, slowly, deliberately, ensuring Jocelyn could see the contents inside. The evidence was not dramatic. It did not need to be. The knowledge of what it represented was enough.

"Maybe. I don't know," Jocelyn muttered, picking at her hands, refusing to make eye contact. "I'm seeking help for my addiction. You can't prosecute me."

"Your employer's policy does not override the law," Sanchez said. His voice was steady, without judgment. "Aside from the drunk driving, let's focus on what else transpired in Blackberry Falls. I see you waived your rights to have an attorney present."

Jocelyn shrugged. "I haven't done anything. This is all a misunderstanding."

Sam leaned forward slightly. "Why did you attack Shelby Kincaid?"

The question landed hard. Jocelyn sucked in a sharp breath, her practiced explanation derailed. "I needed to make her stop snooping. I warned her to leave it alone. I didn't want to hurt her."

Sanchez studied her face. "Yet you injected her with insulin. A drug not prescribed to you. A medication that could have killed her."

"I didn't know how sick she was," Jocelyn cried, panic edging her voice. "I thought it would just scare her."

Sam leaned back, his chair creaking softly. "What didn't you want Shelby to find out? Was it about Kristen?"

Jocelyn's bottom lip trembled. Tears spilled before she could stop them. "I never intended to kill Kristen. I wanted her to miss the event that night to give me time to find the files on the computer and destroy them. She threatened to send them to the Board."

Sanchez flipped open his file but did not look down. "Threatened how?"

"She said she was done covering for everyone," Jocelyn whispered. "She said she was tired of lying. Kristen always had that look, like she thought she was smarter than the rest of us."

"What was in the files that you were desperate to keep hidden from the Board?" Sam asked.

Jocelyn folded in on herself, shoulders shaking. "I gave Becca the password for the office computer. She accessed personal files to sell information online." Her voice cracked as she lifted her head. "I'm the one who was stealing the money. Becca is unemployed, and I needed her to know she could depend on me."

Sanchez raised his eyebrows slightly. "Depend on you," he repeated. "Or control her."

Jocelyn shook her head violently. "She needed me. Her boyfriend was getting into trouble again. He said he could flip the data fast. They promised it was harmless. Just names. Emails. Payroll."

Sam felt a chill crawl up his spine. "Her boyfriend," he prompted. "The one with the fraud charges in Oregon?"

Jocelyn nodded weakly. "He always had a plan. A new scheme. Becca believed him. I trusted her instinct. I thought if I helped them just this once, it would stop."

Sanchez leaned forward, his voice quiet but firm. "It never stops. You know that, Jocelyn. Every line you crossed made the next one easier."

She wiped her nose with the back of her hand, leaving a faint smear she did not bother to clean. "When Kristen found the discrepancies, she said she would take it to the Board. She said she wouldn't cover for me anymore."

Sam folded his arms. "You decided to take care of it yourself."

"I was protecting Becca," Jocelyn insisted, desperation rising. "She has nothing. No savings. No safety net."

Sanchez tapped the folder lightly. "She also has a criminal record now. Courtesy of your misplaced loyalty."

Jocelyn's breathing grew uneven, shallow gasps stacking on top of one another. "I never meant for anyone to die."

"How did you acquire the insulin?" Sam asked.

Jocelyn's gaze went distant, her voice flattening. "I got it from Shelby. We had a girls' night at her house because she couldn't come out with us. I noticed Alan administer the shot, and I seized a vial."

Sam's jaw tightened. "You stole medication from a cancer patient."

"At first, I gave it to Becca," Jocelyn continued, as if reciting facts instead of admitting guilt. "I figured she could sell it. Each pen is worth over two hundred dollars. But she was angry. She said she needed cash, not more drugs."

Sanchez interjected gently. "So, the medication became leverage."

Jocelyn nodded. "When I found out about the cameras, I

panicked. We thought our conversations were recorded. We needed the files to be gone. Everyone could go back to living their lives." Her eyes filled again. "I stopped drinking. I really tried."

Sam believed her. Abstaining from alcohol would have felt monumental to an addict like Jocelyn. That did not make her choices forgivable.

"Is that why you started the fire?" he asked. "To destroy the computer and hide the files forever?"

She stared at the table. "I just wanted it to be over."

"Why didn't you leave?" Sam asked, thinking of Everett. The half plan. The packed bag that never made it out the door.

"I didn't know how," Jocelyn sobbed. "Becca was depending on me. If I disappeared, it would all fall apart."

Sanchez closed the folder slowly. "You did not save her, Jocelyn. You implicated her. You exposed her boyfriend's crimes. And you nearly killed an innocent woman in the process."

Jocelyn's head snapped up. "Shelby is alive?"

"Yes," Sam said, relief softening his tone despite himself. "She survived."

Jocelyn collapsed into sobs, her hands covering her face. "I tried to stop it. I wanted to fix it."

Sanchez stood, his chair scraping loudly as he pushed it back. "Fixing it starts with telling the truth. Every detail."

Jocelyn looked between them, terror fully replacing denial. "I'll confess," she whispered. "I'll tell you everything."

Sam let out a long breath, absorbing the details Jocelyn had shared. For the first time since Kristen's death, he felt the faint pull of resolution. Not justice or closure yet. But the slow, painful unraveling of the truth had finally begun.

37

CRIMES AND CLARITY

Shelby placed the medication beneath her tongue and waited for the bitterness to dissolve and enter her bloodstream. She had voiced her wish to be strong for her friends and to give them hope that the cozy town of Blackberry Falls would return to its idyllic lakeside charm, where nothing bad ever happened.

"You ready, Shelly Bean?" Alan inquired, giving her hand a tender squeeze.

"Right as rain," she falsely claimed, enduring the sensation of acid in her throat. She pressed her hand to her abdomen, which was still tender from the reinsertion of the feeding tube. The crunch of the gravel on the long driveway awakened her senses, bringing her back to the first day she entered the stunning Blackberry Falls Resort. She stopped to admire the stone exterior, scrubbed clean of the ivy that had once overgrown its walls. A breeze caught the curtains in a window on the upper floor, making them dance in the sunlight that filtered through the clouds. Shelby smiled at the expanse of blue sky past the gray, knowing it was moving toward them with the promise of a beautiful day. She smiled at Alan as they waited for Sam to park the patrol car. "Thank you for dropping me off. I'll have Casi bring me back home on her way to Seattle."

"Speaking of Casi," Alan grinned. "She called me last night and asked if it would be alright to offer you your position back. She promised it could be done at your own pace and from home as needed."

"She asked your permission?" Shelby gasped.

"She wasn't seeking approval. She was informing me she would make the offer and wanted me to be aware so I could support you," Alan nodded in agreement.

"That sounds more like the partnership I'm used to in our marriage," she said.

Sam walked toward them as Ben slowly disentangled himself from the vehicle, distracted by the notepad he had been ordered to use. Sam swung an arm over Shelby's shoulders. "Sorry about the planter. I'll come over later and take care of it."

Alan shook his head. "The plant is nothing compared to Shelby's well-being. Besides, when we got home from the hospital it was already cleaned up and replanted. Plus, the addition of several new plants that really cheered Shelby up."

Shelby smiled. "Stella contacted her brothers and they were thrilled to have something constructive to do to help." She glanced at Gus. "I'm more concerned about him. The whole thing was terribly upsetting."

Sam gave the dog a pat on the head. "He's a highly intelligent animal. I'm sure he senses you are okay now."

Alan gave Shelby a kiss on the cheek. "I'll see you this afternoon. Have fun with your crime crew." He smiled as he watched her expression brighten when she heard laughter erupting from the coffee shop.

Sam held the door for Shelby. "Ben will give the busybodies a quick rundown and then we should head back to the station."

"You had better not let them hear you call them that,"

Shelby warned. "Without us, you wouldn't have figured out the case."

"That's painfully true," Sam admitted. "I suspect it may have ignited an urge for you to continue to be a crime solver, but..."

"I know," Shelby raised her hand. "I crossed a few lines and potentially jeopardized the case."

"Yes," Sam grimaced. "Going forward, we'll discuss proper protocol for reporting evidence and clues."

Casi was the first to jump up from the table to embrace Shelby tightly. "What a horrific thing to be attacked in your own home? Are you sure you are up to being here today?"

"I'm fine, just a little bruised and mentally worn down," Shelby assured them. "I'll rest for the next few days, but I wanted to be here with everyone..." Tears filled her eyes. "I'm a bit overwhelmed by Jocelyn's actions. I considered her a friend." Shelby instructed Gus to lie beside her feet and observed Casi's small rose leather purse hanging from the back of her chair. "Did you get your handbag back?"

Casi reached into her bag and produced an envelope with cash. "I did, but I don't want it anymore. This is the tip money you guys should have gotten the other night. I filled in what was missing."

"I can imagine it feels strange to use the handbag after it was stolen. It's unnecessary for you to give us money." Shelby held out the bills.

Casi shook her head. "No, that's yours. I'm not emotionally attached to the handbag. It was never intended to make others envious. I'll sell it online and get more than enough to cover the lost tips."

"Good morning, ladies," Sam interrupted. "Officer Tanner will give you the facts that we have at this time."

"Who's that?" Lia asked, looking behind them. "Oh, you mean Ben?"

Sam rolled his eyes as the table erupted with laughter. "Alright, let's get started."

Ben fidgeted with his notepad, trying to compose himself in front of the group, eagerly awaiting what he had to say. "Um, Jocelyn is being held at the Seattle County Jail."

"For how long?" Casi asked. "Should we be afraid if she gets out on bail and comes back for revenge?"

Ben paled. "I'm not sure."

"Jocelyn was processed and placed in custody last night. She will be held until a hearing is arranged. Because of the nature of the crimes, bail is not an option currently." Sam surveyed the group. "She will also get counseling. It will be months before a trial date is set."

"I wish we could have warned Kristen that Jocelyn was so troubled," Lia lamented.

Gail shuddered. "I have been friends with Jocelyn since our daughters were in preschool together. I never would have suspected she could have done something so horrible. I didn't really know Kristen."

"I was friends with her in high school." Lia blushed deeply. "My algebra teacher was a bit, um, handsy…"

"Yuck, I remember you had such a crush on that creep," Lauren shivered. "What did he have to do with Kristen?"

Lia cringed. "In our senior year, she asked me to report him for improper behavior with students. I was embarrassed that he hadn't only been showing me extra attention, but most of the girls in our class, so I refused to come forward."

"I'm sorry that happened to you, Lia. The guy was a perv, it wasn't your fault," Casi said. "I need his name, and I will track him down and see what he's been up to."

Lia sighed. "Kristen and I reconnected on Facebook a few years ago. She told me how deeply disturbing his advances had been to her, and how the experience had shattered her trust in men. We talked about maybe one day opening a place together, and she even offered to cover the down payment if she could get her mom to part with money."

Lauren shook her head. "But then you had the opportunity to open the coffee shop as part of the resort, and you felt guilty that Kristen wasn't included."

"Yes," Lia nodded. "I tried to make it up to her by referring her for the job. She just kept pressuring me to do more, and I got in over my head."

Shelby wiped her palm across her forehead, and Mary Ann patted her arm. "Are you feeling alright? You look pale."

"And sweaty." Casi looked aghast. "Are you about to barf?"

Shelby laughed. "No, it's not low blood sugar. The recent days have taken a toll, and I'm feeling a bit rough."

"Do you want a peppermint?" Lia asked. "That seems to help me with nausea." She handed her a wrapped candy from her apron pocket.

"Why are you nauseous?" Lauren questioned. "Please don't tell me you're pregnant again."

"No!" Casi spun around to face Lia.

"Why would that be a bad thing?" Lia whined.

"Because you're in your forties. You've just started a business. You have two rambunctious boys and three-step daughters. Do I really need to spell out the health issues like your weight and diabetes?" Lauren snapped. "Let's not forget how well you handled post-partum depression."

As Lia's lower lip quivered and tears streamed down her cheeks, Casi jumped up and pulled her into a hug. "Is that why you've been awfully sensitive lately?"

"And forgetful," Lauren added.

"I found out the week Kristen died. It didn't seem like the right time to announce it," Lia said.

Shelby squeezed her hand. "We are all here for you, Lia. A new baby will be a wonderful addition to Blackberry Falls."

Sam and Ben exchanged glances, unsure how to exit the

coffee shop amidst the pregnancy announcement and personal reflections. "We'll let you know when there are updates." Sam took a step toward the door.

"Wait, what happened to Becca? Jocelyn may have been the one who committed the murder, but she was the reason behind it," Lauren said.

Ben exhaled; glad the subject had returned to questions within his comfort zone. He briefly glanced at his notebook to make sure he had his facts correct. "Actually, Becca was arrested as well. She is being charged on several counts..." he glanced at Sam and realized he shouldn't continue. He snapped his notebook closed. "And her boyfriend was also arrested."

"It just sucks that the cyber-crime guys got away with stealing all that money," Mary Ann commented.

"Unfortunately, that is out of our jurisdiction," Sam winced.

"That sounds like what the potato head detective would say because he's too lazy to do a proper follow up," Shelby said.

Ben covered his mouth to hide a smile at the description of the detective. "Do you have a lead, Casi?" A flush spread across his cheeks when he spoke her name, and Sam shook his head.

"More than a silly little lead," Casi savored a sip of her coffee to drag out the reveal. "They were a bunch of kids who worked out of their parents' basement. When my friend found their VPN, he traced where they were putting their ill-gotten gains. He redirected it to the proper place," Casi winked. "Let's just say the cat sanctuary received a large donation. Ryan has agreed to build it on an acre of his farm. This will serve as an amazing tribute to Kristen."

"Do you think the initial S on the bottom of the list was because Kristen realized she had been scammed?" Lauren asked.

"Maybe it was for sanctuary," Shelby said. "Kristen needed to belong to something bigger, and she was betrayed by people running an amateur scam. She put her heart and money toward a project to rescue pets from awful circumstances. Deep down she was a caring person, and I'm sure that hurt."

Sam nodded. "Kristen's unhappiness and Jocelyn's jealousy led to the murder. You gals should look out for one another, especially in a tight-knit community like this. We need to keep our faith in everything good."

Shelby reached out and grasped Casi's hand on her left, and Lia's on the right. The chain continued until hands were linked. "I'm so thankful for everyone at this table. You have all contributed to making sure Kristen's death was solved and the people who are responsible will be punished. I understand I have a rough journey ahead, but I know I'm not alone, and I appreciate how each one of you has made getting through this illness easier." She smiled at her friends. "We will all be here for each other, no matter what the future holds."

"Here's to the crime solvers of Blackberry Falls," Casi cheered.

"Not a thing," Sam said.

"Oh, it's a thing, and it's amazing!" Shelby concluded.

A TASTE OF BLACKBERRY FALLS

Lia's coffee shop at the resort is always buzzing with gossip while they enjoy a favorite crime-solving treat.

Blackberry Cream Scones
    2 cups (250 g) all-purpose flour
    1/3 cup (65 g) granulated sugar
    1 tablespoon (12 g) baking powder
    1/2 teaspoon (3 g) fine sea salt
    6 tablespoons (85 g) cold unsalted butter, cubed
    3/4 cup (180 ml) heavy cream, plus extra for brushing
    1 large egg
    1 teaspoon (5 ml) vanilla extract
    1 cup (140 g) fresh or frozen blackberries
    1 tablespoon (15 ml) honey
    Raw sugar

1. Preheat oven to **400°F (200°C)**. Line a baking sheet with parchment.
2. Whisk flour, sugar, baking powder, and salt.
3. Cut in the cold butter until the mixture resembles coarse crumbs.
4. Whisk cream, egg, vanilla, and honey; pour into dry ingredients and stir gently.
5. Fold in the blackberries without crushing them.
6. Pat dough into an **8-inch (20 cm)** circle; cut into 8 wedges.
7. Brush with cream, sprinkle with raw sugar, and bake **18–20 minutes** until golden.
8. Serve with butter and jam.

BEFORE BLACKBERRY FALLS MYSTERIES

If the side characters in *Unravel* caught your attention, explore the intertwined stories that shaped their lives before the mystery began.

In the **Catwalk Series: Dream, Hope, Trust, Seek, and Love**, travel through five years of friendships, betrayals, heartbreaks, and second chances; the history that built the Blackberry Falls Resort and the bonds that still hold the town together.

Discover how Casi and Kyle fought for a love that nearly fell apart before it began, and why this is not the first time Casi has found herself accused of murder or tangled in a dangerous drug ring. Uncover the truth behind Jake's three wives and five children, Anna's complicated past, and Lia's determination to raise her boys, and how Shane entered the picture. Learn why Mary Ann and Gail spend their days at the coffee shop. Explore why Lauren's husband went to jail and the resentment that lingers between her and Lia.

The story continues through the **Catwalk Cookbook Companions: Taste, Tipsy, Twist, Tempt, and Toast.** Each collection features recipes inspired by the characters themselves, celebrating the meals, treats, and traditions that knit this small town together. In Blackberry Falls, cooking is not just nourishment; it is how people comfort one another, show love, and stay connected.

For even more flavors of small-town life, the **Blackberry Falls Cookbook Collection** expands the world further, capturing the seasonal dishes, cozy traditions, and everyday rituals that define the resort, the town, and the people who call it home.

THANK YOU FOR READING

Thank you for spending time in Blackberry Falls and for joining me on this journey through *Unravel*. Every reader who steps into this world, the trails, kitchens, and tangled secrets, helps bring these characters to life in the most meaningful way.

If you enjoyed the story, I would truly appreciate a short review. Even a sentence or two about your experience helps other readers discover the book, and it means more to an author than you can imagine.

For behind-the-scenes updates, bonus content, book news, or early access to upcoming releases, you are warmly invited to join my newsletter:

sqorpin.com

Thank you for supporting my work, for turning the pages, and for caring about these characters as much as I do. I hope to see you again soon in Blackberry Falls.

S. Q. Orpin

ABOUT THE AUTHOR

S. Q. Orpin is a Canadian-born author known for emotionally resonant women's fiction and small-town mystery. Her novels explore themes of love, loss, resilience, and perseverance, blending compelling plots with deeply layered emotional journeys.

She is best known for the **Catwalk Series**, set in the fictional town of Blackberry Falls, Washington, and the **Blackberry Falls Mysteries**, inspired in part by her personal journey as a survivor of esophageal cancer. Her stories are often described as emotional mysteries, not just whodunits, but whydunits, driven by personal stakes, intricate relationships, and the quiet secrets of close-knit communities.

When she isn't writing, Suzy teaches culinary career skills to adults, develops recipes, and finds inspiration in tangled family ties, small-town lives, and the resilience people summon in life's hardest moments.

Visit sqorpin.com to learn more about Blackberry Falls and upcoming releases

9 781954 349018